MIDNIGHT WITH THE HEXED

CELESTIAL HAVEN
BOOK TWO

L.R. FRIEDMAN

Midnight with the Hexed

Copyright © 2023 by L.R. Friedman

This book is a work of fiction. Names, characters, places, brands, and incidents are the products of the author's imagination or used fictitiously. Any resemblance to actual events, locales or persons, living or dead, is entirely coincidental.

ISBN 979-8-9891984-0-5

Edited by The Editor & The Quill

Cover by A.T. Cover Designs

AUTHOR'S NOTE

Midnight with the Hexed is the second part of a supernatural MMF why choose paranormal romance duet. It contains some explicit content best suited for readers over the age of 18.

While Wicked in the Pines was more of a slow-med burn... the sequel has dialed up the spice. This is your not-so-subtle warning.

For a comprehensive list of content and possible triggers for the duet, it can be found by turning to the very last page of this book.

INTRODUCTION

There's a long and winding road that leads *nowhere*.

That is, if you don't know where you're heading.

Many have traveled its unmapped black path. The one flanked by bushy pines that cradle the moon above, as if spelled to hold it in place.

For minutes, they'll follow its glittering beacon, drawn toward something they don't understand. That is, until they're deterred by the thick fog that blots away their visibility. Or until they pull on the emergency brake before they slam into the wayward tree trunk left discarded on the pavement.

Yes, the average person sees these obstructions, shifts gears, and finds themselves heading wherever they came from.

Never looking back.

Never finding themselves on that road again.

As if it disappeared from existence. Or was merely a figment of their imagination...

Then there are the others.

The ones who smirk at the first sign of fog; at its smoky claws beckoning their cars in the moonlight. The ones who press down on the pedal, speed kicking up with a violent pulse, spearing straight toward the brittle trunk strewn across their path.

Yes, those are the blessed few that shriek in giddy fits of laughter as they vault through its sacred bark, pulled where the oblivious never land.

Car humming down the blissful path, past the illusions set for the world they've left behind, they edge toward one of the few places forged into existence for their kind. A utopia, hidden away from prying and persecuting eyes, tucked within the heart of Washington's Artemis District.

A partially rotted sign floats on the side of the road, crystals hanging from the thick cords nailed across its top.

Welcome to Celestial Haven.

The crisp October breeze tousled Hunter Astro's hair as he stepped out onto the creaky porch of number 6 Starry Night Lane. He rubbed his eyes and descended the steps, waving to the few neighbors who passed. Barefoot, in a pair of flannel pajama pants and a matching robe that hung open, he went to say good morning to his beloved.

His mint-condition 2042 Ferrocious 666 with midnight-black paint and blood-red leather interior.

Despite its ability to go from 0 to 150 miles per hour in less than six seconds and its one thousand nightmarepower engine, its aerodynamic design kept it silent as a ghost on the road.

A classic car collector, Hunter visited it first thing each day, casting protective enchantments and wards to ensure no harm came to his prized convertible. He'd refused to park it in the garage, earning a few emails from the HOA.

It would be disrespectful to hide such a hauntingly beautiful car away where no one could see, he'd replied.

If any neighbors happened to walk by, he always called them over to admire it. He'd even offered to take Sage Harlow for a ride around Celestial Haven, but she'd declined.

Seven times.

This particular morning, though, Hunter cast an additional spell over his love, gaze darting around the neighborhood. When witches strode by on the sidewalk, he remained quiet, even when Sage smiled up at him.

How unusual.

With a final glance over his shoulder, he headed up the stairs. The door was a muted shade of basil and had circular glass cutouts. The moment his foot tapped the Ferrocious emblem decorating his doormat, it swung open. Swallowed back into number 6's shelter, he drank his coffee and watched from the window. Waiting. For what, he wasn't sure.

Hours ticked on.

Days slipped by.

It would take a week for Sage to notice Hunter hadn't emerged for his daily engine enchantment, bringing it to the attention of the new Starry Night coveness, Ruby Cove.

As the investigation went underway, security footage and firsthand accounts concluded it was the last time anyone had seen or heard from the hot-wheeling witch.

CHAPTER 1

OAKLEY

The perky jack-o'-lantern smiled with one tooth jutting up from its carved grin, matching the giggling witchling seated next to it in his highchair. Drool spilled over Aspen's lips, and my sister tickled his chubby cheek before scooping up more squash purée onto her spoon.

"Open wide for the ghosty," Hazel teased, making exaggerated ghastly moans. The spoon swooped in circles and landed in his mouth.

About two-thirds dribbled down his chin, then plopped onto his bib. He continued to laugh along with her, reminding me how grateful I was to have her back. It'd been a month since she'd returned after being kidnapped by the neighborhood's deranged hermit, Acacia Mirabel.

"Are you almost done?" she asked, nodding to the silly pumpkin seated on the counter in front of me.

"Just about." I sprayed it with an anti-aging potion, waiting a few minutes for it to set. "There we go. Perfect."

I stared a moment at my handiwork before picking the gourd up and carrying it outside to join its bobbing brethren.

Casting the flotation spell, I watched the happy little pumpkin ascend into the bare branches of the maple tree out front. Next to it wobbled an angry cat forever posed mid-hiss, a warty crone, and a bat that was all fangs.

"Wow," Hazel said, carting Aspen on her hip down the front stairs. His face was wiped clean and his messy bib removed, showing off his navy playsuit sprinkled with golden rib cages, pale-pink hearts in their centers. "There's got to be at least thirty of them."

"Thirty-one to be exact." I puffed with pride. "One for every day of October."

She shook her head, chuckling to Aspen like they had some inside joke between them.

"What?"

"You're really outdoing yourself." She pointed over to the stuffed striped stockings hanging out from the side of the house, a broom propped next to them, representing the original Wicked Witch of the West.

"Just because we don't live in Arbor Sanctum anymore doesn't mean I can't decorate like Dad did for us when we were kids."

"Yeah, I mean, if you don't mind sticking out like a sore thumb, then go for it."

"Oh, I am."

Growing up so close to the mortal portion of Salem, Oregon, we'd always found Halloween funny, learning about how their kind viewed us; what they believed we looked like, what we could do, and how we talked. We'd spend hours watching movie marathons of classics depicting witches and our lives. Our parents always poked fun at what people believed to be the truth. In fact, our whole neighborhood did.

If we wanted more traditional décor, we could always go into the capital. Here in Celestial Haven, the decorations around the neighborhood fell right in the middle of those two aesthetics. Our house would definitely stand out, not that I cared.

"Just remember, those decorations need to come down by the next new moon," Hazel said, tossing Aspen into the air. He squealed, a line of drool falling from his lips and landing on her cheek. She laughed and hugged him to her, using her sleeve to wipe up the dribble.

"Seriously?" I groaned. "We used to leave them up *at least* a month after."

For the amount of work I'd put into the display—one that would surely give the neighborhood something to talk about that didn't involve Hazel's disappearance, the Wellses' arrest, or Acacia's murder—they could make an exception. It'd been a busy few weeks of ghoulish gossip on Starry Night Lane. I wouldn't have been surprised if the rest of Celestial Haven heard all about the scandal by now. "Look at all this beautiful handiwork. The kids on the street are going to love it."

"You're right about that," she agreed, scanning over the airborne gourds in shades of fiery orange, mustard, and black. "It's the HOA you have to worry about."

I frowned. "Who's on the HOA here? Because I will happily invite them over to test drive the caramel apple dipping station or the flying broomstick photo booth."

She shrugged, booping Aspen on the nose with her own and making silly faces at him until he shrieked with glee. "I don't know."

"You don't know?" In Arbor Sanctum, they would meet quarterly and then report to the respective streets they oversaw within the community. "But you're the exclusive realtor. I'm sure you've dealt with them?"

"Well, yes, I have, but I don't ever *meet* with them."

"They don't have regular meetings?"

"They do—" A *buzz* sounded from her back pocket, and she danced back and forth while pulling her phone out, then typed a response. "But we just get emails with updates afterward."

She'd returned to work a week ago, wanting things to get back to *normal,* according to her. We'd had a few talks about what happened while she'd been held captive, but not much. She didn't seem ready, and I wasn't going to push her. Luckily, she'd decided on her own to start seeing a therapist. If she couldn't talk to me yet, at least she could talk to a professional.

Though I had to admit, I hoped she would eventually confide in me.

"Interesting." I reached out for Aspen, taking him so it would be easier for her to type with both hands. "Well, I guess they're doing a great job since the neighborhood is ranked so highly. The houses are only going to increase in value."

"Oh yes, exponentially." She nodded, attention glued to her phone. "I expect the houses I'm about to list will have intense bidding wars."

"I wish you'd been able to start a bidding war over number 5, maybe then—"

"Oakley—"

"What? I still can't believe he was able to get the Wellses' house."

Just my luck.

"It's not like they're using it." Hazel sighed, brushing some brunette strands behind her ear and adjusting the lapels of her black crushed velvet blazer. "Besides, we both know how persuasive Atlas can be."

"As soon as he moves in this week, so will the rest of the neighborhood," I countered.

No doubt he would happily take on throwing coven soirées in the half glass-encased mansion in his capacity as the new Archon of the Artemis District.

"I'm sure you aren't too unhappy since he still paid you commission even though you didn't do much at all." I tried not to let it sting that they were still so chummy.

"That didn't hurt." She slipped the phone into her pocket, putting an arm around Aspen and me. "I adore Atlas. He's still family even if you aren't together."

"I suppose you're right." *And at least our house is somewhat hidden from view of his, thank Goddess.* "I know I shouldn't grumble. It's great he wants to be here for Aspen."

She nudged me in the side with her elbow. "We both know he's not just here for him."

"Haze—"

"That's all I'm saying about it," she said, throwing her arms up in mock surrender. "Besides, I'm sure you have your hands full already with two other—"

"Shh!" My attention darted around the street. The few witches outside weren't looking in our direction, but I felt no less seen.

"*What if the neighbors hear?*" Hazel mocked. "I know the drill, Oakley. Any word on when they'll be back?"

"They had no idea when I was able to talk to them last week. Hopefully soon."

We hadn't really seen each other since our night in the pines—a full moon I couldn't help but replay in my mind each night when I tried to fall asleep. I wondered if they were thinking about it as well. It hadn't come up on our call. They'd just checked in, asking how Aspen, Hazel, and I were doing. Things felt a bit up in the air between us with Atlas's transfer and recent takeover for their undercover operation.

"Going to get some use out of that long-distance talisman

I've seen you trying to conjure up?" Hazel asked with a waggle of her brows.

I shot her a glare.

She wasn't supposed to know about that.

I'd been toying with an idea for a long-distance romance package for clients: a small ring light, a toy, flavored lube, one lingerie outfit from the upcoming line, and a talisman that would allow the other person to channel your pleasure. An idea that Lynx's Empathy had inspired.

Of course, it still needed a few tweaks. Without his innate abilities, I imbued general lust into the talisman, but it didn't mimic the personalized pleasure being simultaneously felt by your partner, or partners.

I had two of the talismans delivered to them last week to see if he could help me figure it out...

...And maybe secretly because I wanted to give it a test run.

"You're so nosey."

She looked down at my chest that was heating, probably splotched red.

It was time to turn the tables. "What about *you*?"

"What about me?"

"You still haven't told me who you were on a date with when you were—"

"Because it's unimportant," she said, waving me off. "There won't be another date."

"It was that bad?" I grimaced, wondering what had her so snippy.

She gave a nonchalant shrug. "It was fine, just no future there. And remember, I would know."

One of the perks of Precognition, I guess.

I followed her into the living room and sat on the floor with Aspen, propping him up in my lap while she continued talking. "Not that I'm looking for that with anyone. I'm perfectly happy playing the single-witch card for a while. Especially with all the festivities coming up."

Aspen shot off like a dart, crawling toward the coffee table and staring at the mug situated atop it. I jolted after him, knowing he couldn't pull himself up to stand yet but still wanting to make sure he didn't hurt himself. I was finding new spots to babyproof each day and quickly understood why people hired companies to do it for them. There were so many things at his eye level that I'd never realized would be interesting to a tiny witchling.

When I collected him in my arms, he reached for my shirt, tugging right as my chest began to tingle. Feeding time.

Hazel leaned against the countertop, continuing to sip her water. "I'm just glad Ruby didn't cancel everything."

"Same, though the coven might have revolted if she had," I agreed, getting Aspen situated and lifting up my shirt. I unclasped my bra and lowered the fabric. He eagerly maneuvered for my breast, clamping down. I hissed as his tooth jabbed into my nipple. The blunt shape was deceiving—more like a tiny fang missing its vampy mate.

Hazel chuckled. "You're not wrong. And if I were her I wouldn't want to be on the other side of the neighborhood's wrath."

As quickly as they had all admired the Wellses, they just as swiftly didn't come to their defense when they'd been accused of Acacia's murder. "How do you think it's going with Chrysanthemum and Atticus staying with Ruby?"

"I'm sure she's keeping them in line."

"It's got to be so hard on them." The two teens were in the middle of the school year at Nyx High School, where their mom had been heavily involved as head of the PTA. It was hard enough being a teenager without dealing with fellow teenage assholes. "I can't imagine having both your parents in prison."

"I still can't believe they killed Acacia." Hazel's voice was low, nearly a whisper, like if she said it any louder someone would hear and that would make it true.

"No offense but I never really got warm fuzzies from Aurora, so I'm not too shocked."

While I didn't love that Atlas was moving into their old home, I didn't miss her one bit.

"There's nothing warm or fuzzy about her, but that doesn't make someone a killer," Hazel replied, almost defensively.

"Well, she confessed." I unlatched Aspen, internally blessing my other boob before he latched and nipped that one too. Having your body used in place of a teether was no fun. "Now they just need to uncover a motive."

"Yeah," she said, back turned to me while she grabbed some food from the fridge and began heating a pan on the stove. "Any news on Hunter yet?"

"I don't know. I doubt that's something Lynx or Saros would text or discuss over the phone."

"They will be back soon with some more answers."

"Yeah, hopeful—" A melodic tune trilled from my phone. I groaned. "Ugh."

"That time already?"

Aspen popped off my nipple to look at what was making the noise, and I arranged myself within my bra before clasping it shut. "Yep."

She grinned at me as I finished burping Aspen. "Better get going. Wouldn't want to show up late to your family date at the pumpkin patch."

"It's not a date."

"Uh-huh," Hazel halfheartedly agreed, a smirk playing on her mauve-painted lips.

"It's not." I didn't want to get into this with her. "We are just taking our son to the pumpkin patch at a mutually agreed upon time."

"Glad you clarified that for me." Her tone was dripping in sarcasm and amusement. At least someone found this whole thing entertaining. "And you're sure there's nothing more there?"

"There isn't." I stood up, handing Aspen to her while I packed up the diaper bag. Once I'd gotten everything in it, I looped it over my shoulders and took him back. "There can't be."

"Who are you trying to convince?" she asked, not letting go of him until I met her dark-brown gaze.

"You, obviously," I scoffed, dismissing her. "We both know why nothing can ever happen there." I swallowed thickly before I asked the next question. "Why? Has something changed?"

"It doesn't work like that." She shook her head, and that sinking feeling I'd had since she'd first told me her vision started up all over again. "Even if it did, I told you I learned my lesson about sharing what I saw last time." She spun me around toward the garage door and gave me a light shove.

"Sure I can't convince you to come with us?" I called out over my shoulder.

"I really need to get some contracts drawn up." She pulled out her phone, typing up a text and sending it off. Then she shifted her attention, giving me a slight smile. "Otherwise, I'd be there in a heartbeat."

"Fine," I grumbled, watching the door open in front of me and loving the fact that I didn't have to free my hands of Aspen or my diaper bag to do it.

You can do this, Oakley.

As I buckled Aspen into the car seat, I reminded myself to keep the conversation civil and focused on our son, or pumpkins, or the windy weather, and to steer clear of any walks down memory lane.

And if Atlas asked about how I replenished my magic, I'd lie through my teeth.

CHAPTER 2
LYNX

"I refuse to speak without a lawyer present," Aurora said, hands clasped in front of her, chin held high. If it weren't for the puke-green jumpsuit, you wouldn't think anything had changed for the forty-five-year-old socialite turned suburban queen bee.

"We've contacted your lawyer, Ms. Brooks. They're on the way." My gaze dropped to the VIS stamped over where her heart would be—if she had one.

Very Influential Supernatural.

AKA fuck your rules.

"In the meantime, we figured we'd keep you company." I nodded to Saros who sat next to me at the steel-bolted table.

"I know what you're doing, and I also know my rights."

The fact that they had a special facility for VIS-level felons pissed me off to no end. A criminal was a criminal. Who gave a shit what their position was on the outside, they'd confessed. Soon, once everything was processed, they would be heading to prison. "You murdered someone."

"And I'm guilty." She arched a brow. "There's no reason to

keep holding me here. Just send us off to jail and be done with it."

Believe me, we would if we could.

The Wellses were taken into custody for Acacia Mirabel's murder and soon after we were called in to handle their case. I still didn't understand the connection to our missing suburbanites, but a job was a job.

To everyone in the neighborhood we were off celebrating our wedding anniversary touring supernatural pockets of Scotland and Ireland.

I fucking wish.

Instead, we were holed up at headquarters, wandering musty yellow hallways between interviews, meetings, and looking through case files. While most of the government buildings in the capital boasted modern architecture and grandiose designs, many of its departments, including ours, operated underground where the dankness somehow permeated the walls.

No one realized we were down here keeping their world safe, and it was supposed to be that way. The shiny offices with spacious window views were left to the politicians, the overseers—the higher-ups. People like Archon Thorne.

Of course, *he* wasn't here right now. He was still in Artemis, settling into his new leadership position.

Unease washed over me in an acidic wave at the thought of him being there with *our* witch. I conjured some of the emotion, swishing it toward Aurora. Her face fell almost imperceptibly. Lucky for me, I never missed even the tiniest cracks in someone's emotional armor. Hopefully, it would help move this little interrogation along so we could return to our crappy lodging.

Goddess above, I missed Wicked.

"So eager to be imprisoned?" Saros's smooth baritone cut

in, slicing through my thoughts like the steely barrier he always drew up for these interrogations. "You see why that might raise some alarms, Mrs. Wells?"

He was so good at this. Much better than I was. While I wanted to get this over with and get the fuck out of dodge, he was still maintaining the professionalism I'd been ready to ditch a week and a half ago when we arrived.

I was born to be in the field, interacting with people, wading through their emotions for clues. Saros, however, was a natural whenever we got called in for these interviews. He'd done thousands of them after earning his stripes deep under-cover within the Vivaldi Syndicate—basically the vampire equivalent of the mortal mafia. Apparently, they kept a small number of witches in their crew to feed on, among *other things*.

He never talked about his time undercover with them, but that was the point wasn't it? Saros was the best at his job. He hated undercover life, but he excelled at it. The fact that he'd told me he wanted out after this assignment shocked me at first, but the more I thought about it, the timing couldn't have been more perfect. We could finally build a future together.

"The facts are, Mrs. Wells, we have both you and your husband in our custody. If one of you won't speak, the other will. It's just a matter of time."

Aurora snorted. "Good luck with that."

Saros's lips fell into a straight line, bitter annoyance scenting the air. "What can you tell us about the various disappearances on Starry Night Lane?"

She leaned back in her chair, the heels of her sneakers smacking onto the table. "Does my lawyer look like they are here yet?"

Her ankle sported a tracking rune drawn with special ink

—the same one integrated into our false vow marks. Usually there would also be one to smother out any abilities the person in custody might possess, but she didn't have one of those. Either they knew what her gift was and didn't believe it to be a threat or they were still trying to learn about it, waiting for her to slip up and show it off.

Saros's brows lifted a moment before his evergreen attention turned to me.

He'd noticed too.

Time for me to play the good empath to his broody asshole. "Look, Aurora, I know how much you and Fitz care about our community. How much work you've put into building the best supernatural street in Celestial Haven. You even helped them earn those six Stellar Street trophies posted up in the Coven Community Center, didn't you?"

"Seven," she cut in, gaze darting in my direction. Pride in the achievement outlined her in a rainbow of colors.

"Seven," I repeated, playing along like I didn't already know that dumb statistic that was waved in our faces by the HOA in their monthly newsletter. "See? I know you care about the street and want to see it thrive. Don't you want to help us prevent more disappearances?"

Aurora uncrossed her arms, sliding her hands into the pockets of her jumpsuit. Feet coming down off the table, her lips began to part just as the door swung open.

"That will be enough," demanded the redheaded lawyer barging in wearing an expensive suit. A young man, probably an associate at whatever firm she worked for, straggled behind her in a much cheaper ensemble. It was always a mix of who we got from their well-paid legal team. "Don't say another word, Aurora."

Her lawyer cut us a glare before grabbing the door behind

her associate and holding it open. "Now if you'll excuse me, I would like to speak to my client alone."

She raised her brows as we walked out the door.

"Ugh," I groaned once we were a few paces away. "I almost had her right where we wanted her."

Saros merely shrugged. "Should have amped up her anxiety."

"Oh, I have been," *for days now*, "but either she is so used to hiding it that it isn't showing or she's got some work-around to my magic that I don't know about."

"Think she's another empath?"

I couldn't contain my laughter. "She might have some kind of emotion-related magic, but she sure as hell doesn't seem concerned with other people's feelings."

We continued down the hallway, making a swift left and running smack-dab into our handler, Agent Aleander. Antici-pation popped off him in citrusy bursts as he nodded for us to walk with him, heading toward his office.

The room was small, stuffy, and full of boxes packed with files that reached the corkboard ceiling.

Aleander gestured toward the two seats across from him. "Get anything before the suit barged in?"

"I'm not sure," I said, dropping into the chair. Saros sat in the one next to me. "It's strange that she has admitted to plotting Acacia's murder, and I still can't put my finger on how they are tied to the disappearances."

"Dr. Mirabel was researching the strange timing of people suddenly moving away within the neighborhood. There are lunar charts, street maps, and detailed daily notes that go back well over a year. We are still working through the wards on some of the evidence, but we have our best teams on it." He opened one of the files stacked on his desk, flipping through the pages. Some of them looked familiar, but a handful were ones we hadn't been sent.

Saros frowned.

"Are we sure Hazel Brooks is purely a victim in all this?" Agent Aleander asked.

My partner bristled. "I took a *detailed* account from her. Nothing from her memories indicated she was more than a victim, and to be frank, I'd prefer not to traumatize her further without cause."

The scent of steel cleaved the air. Saros's hackles were raised.

"Fair enough," Aleander conceded, lifting a hand. "Maybe it's time to break out your Recollection and do a little in-depth prodding into the Wellses' last year?"

"No," Saros snipped, before clamping his mouth shut.

Aleander shut the file quickly, pushing it off to the side and leaning forward, elbows perched on the desk with his hands clasped. The temperature in the room dialed up a few notches, frustration radiating off our handler in orange fumes that wafted in Saros's direction.

I cleared my throat, trying to rid myself of the thickness swirling in the tiny room. "They are aware of Saros's gift and have made it clear they will get legal involved if any action is taken."

"They are convicted felons at this point. Who would believe them?" Aleander nodded to Saros. "If they aren't willing to tell us the truth and we need it, it's simple enough. You've done it hundreds of times before."

"Absolutely not."

I swear my jaw dropped straight to the floor. Saros never took a tone like that with Aleander, at least not in front of me. But I'd seen the pale-blue shame that trailed behind him every time he'd used his Recollection like this.

He never talked about it, and he sure as fuck never openly defied our handler.

"Are we certain Aurora's connected to the disappearances?" I offered, trying to dissipate the red curls of angry smoke beginning to cloud the air between us.

Aleander's attention narrowed on me. "She killed Acacia Mirabel. Acacia was looking into the disappearances. Those dots are already connected, we just need the how and why."

"What was a geologist doing looking into people going missing from a suburban neighborhood?" Saros asked, brow buckling in concentration as he probably flitted through files and files of information in his head.

Must be nice to have a photographic memory.

"I'd love to know that as well," Aleander continued, the red coils of smoke starting to thin. "Unfortunately, we can't interview the dead."

"Shouldn't we exhaust the other avenues first, sir, before moving to something so *extreme*?" I asked, ready to get out of there and into some fresh air, even if it was just to walk the five minutes across the courtyard to our room.

"It'll only be *extreme* if they have something to hide. We've given them multiple opportunities to talk. Every time we have to sweep these cases out of the public eye, it threatens to come out and make us look bad. No one wants to feel unsafe in a supernatural neighborhood. They had enough of that in the mortal world." Aleander's hands clenched into tight fists, pinned onto the open case file in front of him. "Now, Agent Holt, which one should I have brought downstairs first for you to work on?"

Saros was nearly enveloped in a crimson cloud, but I cut in before he could respond. "Get us back into the field. We can do more interviews, check out Hunter Astro's house, see if there's anything from when he went missing that we overlooked."

"Let me remind you, Agent Holt," Aleander gritted out at Saros, ignoring me, "I put myself on the line to get you out in the field. The higher-ups were content to keep you here, doing what was needed."

Saros swallowed hard, the ball in his throat turning.

"Think about it." Aleander lifted the file in front of him. "We have a lot of pressure on us to make this go away quickly. If it continues or gets worse, more supernaturals will feel the need to live among the mortals again. That puts us *all* at risk."

Saros's chair scraped the floor, giving me a tight nod before leaving the room.

Shaking his head, Aleander turned his attention to me. "Agent Carver, I hope you can get your partner in line."

"Get us back into the field." I knew how bad Saros wanted to return to Celestial Haven. To see this case through and see Oakley again—even if he wouldn't admit the latter. "I'm banking there's more intel we can grab there. Maybe something to get the Wellses talking."

"I'll consider it. But if I do send you, I need assurances there will be results. Otherwise, we do things my way. It's been over a year and we have nothing to show for it other than a dead body and the scandal of a highly respected couple being arrested." Then Aleander waved toward the door, effectively dismissing me. "Thank Goddess Archon Thorne will be there. You're lucky he's personally overseeing this case."

I nodded at him, before rushing after Saros, our handler's final words replaying in my ear with each step.

Lucky wasn't the first word that came to mind.

CHAPTER 3

OAKLEY

When we pulled up, Atlas was already standing outside the pumpkin patch. He walked over donning a pair of dark denim pants and a maroon-and-black flannel shirt, two cardboard cups in his hands.

Goddess above.

Atlas was handsome in a power suit, but in casual attire, he was on a whole nother level.

I set the car in park and popped the trunk with a snap of my fingers. As he got out the stroller, I opened my car door, tugging down my mustard chunky-knit sweater over my high-waisted jeans. I'd thrown on a nursing tank beneath it, figuring it would make things easier if Aspen got hungry.

"I went ahead and grabbed tickets and some caramel apple ciders," he said, opening the side door where Aspen slept soundly.

Of course he passed out on the drive over here.

Atlas unbuckled the car seat, pulling him out of it to nestle Aspen against his shoulder. My heart ached at the sight, thudding all-too-loudly in my chest. Then he grabbed one of the cardboard cups off the stroller tray and handed it to me. "Figured we'd start off with the wagon ride and take Aspen through the little hay maze, then grab a few pumpkins that he can decorate at the station over there."

He pointed to a covered section where children were sitting at long benches, painting their pumpkins with fat brushes and tiny fingers.

"Wow." I got the stroller ready, then Atlas situated Aspen in it so he could still sleep while we walked around. "You have it all planned out, don't you?"

"You know me," he said with a shrug before sipping his cider.

I sighed. "Always a planner."

His eyes shot down to our son, whose head was slumped to the side as his leg and hand jerked a moment. "Of course, I didn't take into account someone's sleep schedule."

"He should be up soon. He won't want to miss out on all the fun." I brought the cup up to my nose, inhaling the rich scent of cinnamon, caramel, and nutmeg. It was divine. If I just kept my focus on this delicious fall staple, maybe my heart rate would come down to a manageable level.

"Also, I already put in a pickup order for apple pies so we can grab them on the way out. Didn't want them to run out before we left. I know how much you love them," Atlas added, beaming at me.

My mouth watered. Apple pie was my all-time favorite fall treat. My chest pinched with a tinge of bittersweet nostalgia, but I returned the smile. "Thank you."

Wrapping his hands around the stroller bar, he guided it toward the entrance of the pumpkin patch. "Thanks again for agreeing to do this."

"Aspen should enjoy his first Hallowed season with both of us." We passed beneath the pumpkin arch towering on either side of us, bales of hay lining the path toward the open area where a bunch of long picnic tables sat and trails jutted out in different directions toward the various stations and activities.

I sensed Atlas drinking me in while I looked around, Desire stirring deep in my belly.

"As co-parents, of course," I reiterated for the both of us.

Why did this witch have to be so Goddess-damned perfect?

He cleared his throat and nodded, smile faltering. "Of course."

I sipped my cider, trying to break up the silence billowing between us like a thick cloud of smoke. "*Mmm.* This apple cider is great. Not as good as Phil's, though."

"Never as good as Phil's," Atlas agreed, grin returning to his face. As we strolled, a few people seemed to notice him, a telltale way to spot who was from the magical community. Not many supernaturals went to the pumpkin patch—they were more of a mortal tradition—but I always loved going to the ones outside of Salem. Phil's Pumpkin Patch was where I had met Atlas.

Had that been the driving force of him suggesting we come here together? I'd planned to bring Aspen before I knew his father would be moving to Celestial Haven, but it only made sense to take him together now. Besides, it felt wrong to deprive Atlas of these festive memories with his son, even if I had to constantly remind myself not to let my guard down when he was around.

"Remember the time it started pouring, so we hid in the refreshment booth and drank cider for hours while everyone else went back home?"

I looked over at the hay wagon trotting down the path toward the hay and corn mazes in the distance, a smile playing at my lips. "How could I forget?"

We'd jumped onto the wagon that afternoon, the rain pelting down on us in frigid streaks, but we didn't care. Atlas illusioned us some privacy from the driver he'd tipped handsomely ahead of time, before hiking up my dress so I could ride him, the ground vibrating beneath us. When we'd made the full loop much too quickly, he'd fished out some extra money from his partially pulled down jeans and handed it up to the driver before flipping me over and taking me from behind.

We had been so wild. Carefree.

I clenched my thighs, Desire threading my veins until it burned at my fingertips, ready for a reenactment.

Nope, nope, nope. Don't even go there, Oakley. Bad witch.

Could I hire someone to spray me with a water bottle every time my ex got my Desire unnecessarily riled up?

"What about the time I snuck bourbon in my purse to add to the apple cider?" I added, trying to change the direction of memory lane.

"That was a fun time." Atlas chuckled. "Nothing like thirty-year-olds riding the rope swings into a foam pit with a bunch of kids gawking."

We laughed at the memory as we came up to the wagon, parking the stroller off to the side. I stuck my cider into one of the cupholders and took Aspen out, watching his sleepy lids drift open. Facing him away from me, I savored his tiny chestnut eyes taking in everything around us. I loved this stage he was entering: less spit-up and more curiosity. Atlas helped me up the steps and onto the platform, climbing in after us. Sitting side by side, I situated Aspen in my lap, Atlas tickling under his chin until he giggled, showing off his single-toothed grin.

"How's everything going with relaunching Full Moon Emporium?" he asked, the wagon jostling toward the mazes jutting up in the distance, large hand-painted signs hanging over them. "Hazel said you've been prepping the boudoir shoot for the Moonlit Masquerade display."

Ugh. Of course she did. Just another reminder that the two of them stayed in touch, which I didn't really love but also couldn't hold against them. She'd been right, we were family, even if it wasn't in the way Atlas desired. Even if it wasn't in the way part of me did—a part I very much needed to ignore.

"Yeah." I kept my gaze on our surroundings and Aspen, avoiding eye contact with Atlas. "There's going to be a little kickoff a few days after the Moonlit Masquerade."

"That's amazing. I'm so happy for you, Oaks." His hand came to my shoulder. "I can't wait to see what you've been working on."

"Thanks."

A few new designs were releasing, each in different colors to kick off, along with some old stock I was restructuring. Everything was nursing friendly, meant to help women feel sexy in every season of life. I got out my phone and quickly texted Hazel to remind her to pick up the masks, then sent off a note to the manufacturer about the samples I'd recently gotten in. "I'm excited for it."

"Have you thought anymore about my offer with the Mystic Square space? It would be great for you not to have to work out of the garage, and I'm more than happy to do it," Atlas asked, keeping his gaze trained forward.

He'd found a vacant storefront in Celestial Haven's shopping center and contacted Hazel about the logistics of leasing it for Full Moon Emporium. Since he hadn't brought it up himself, having her ask me on his behalf, I was hoping to avoid talking about it just yet. "I don't know, Atlas. It's a big thing to do, considering..."

"We aren't together?" he finished. A dull ghost of pain streaked through his eyes.

If only he knew how much it took for me not to reach out and touch him. If only things could have been different for us.

Maybe in another life...

"I appreciate the offer, but I need to think about it." Taking a deep breath, I ran my hands along Aspen's chunky thighs. "Can we just focus on this little witchling? I'm excited for his first Hallowed season."

I withheld the tears threatening to streak down my cheeks and forced a halfhearted smirk. It was the best I could do.

Why did this have to be so fucking hard?

"Oh yes, looking forward to some family time. I'm glad I'll be in town for all the festivities," Atlas said, smiling at his mini-me. Then his attention darted back to me, tone dropping to a more serious octave. "At least promise me you'll do a walkthrough of the Mystic Square space before deciding?"

I nodded, glad he was willing to end the conversation there.

The wagon came to a halt, and all of us got off in a single-file line. Peeling away from the rest of the group heading for the large corn maze, we strolled toward the hay one that stood only a few feet high. Not that Aspen couldn't go through the taller one, but the prospect of getting stuck in a maze with a crying witchling sounded like the furthest thing from fun.

I stepped into something squishy, my boot lodging in the mud with a wet *squelch*. "Shit!"

"May I?" Atlas asked.

After I nodded, he knelt and gripped around my calf and ankle, sending electricity zinging through me. I held my breath and tried not to focus on my body and Desire's response.

With a few quick jerks and a tug, my boot finally wiggled free, dark-brown muck flinging in all directions. I grimaced before hiding myself from view to wave my hands in front of my legs, casting a cleansing enchantment. My magic stretched its replenished wings and trickled through my palms, the spicy scent of it peppering the air.

I inhaled deeply, savoring its return.

When my gaze dropped to my body, the dirt merged together, slithering down my jeans like a tiny snake and slipping into the puddle it'd come from.

Goddess, it's good to have my magic back.

By the time I made it over to Atlas, he'd already cleaned himself off. It was much easier for him to disguise his magic with Illusion, hiding it in plain sight. His brows lifted in surprise. "Someone was busy this last full moon, it seems."

"I beg your pardon?" I asked defensively.

"You've got magic."

Fuck.

There was no use lying about it. "Oh, yeah."

"I was wondering how you'd get all the charms and tonics ready for reopening Full Moon Emporium." His eyes were downcast, as if deep in thought. "Makes sense."

The last thing I wanted to do was hurt him, but I had no regrets about getting my magic back or how I'd done it. "Atlas, I'm s—"

He held up a hand, stopping me.

"No need to apologize." He gave me a small smile. "I'm not hurt."

"You're not?" Now I was the surprised one.

"I know what I offered when I was here a few full moons ago, but you were right, it would complicate things." He ran his thumb along Aspen's cheek before meeting my gaze, his aqua eyes swimming with an emotion I couldn't place. "So, thank you."

"Of course," I managed to rasp out.

He wasn't mad but somehow it still stung.

Did I expect him to be? Or *want* him to be?

"I know if we went there, I'd want more." Intensity flared to life in his gaze. "Hell, I will probably always want more."

The air disappeared from my lungs. Heat bubbled in my chest, but I couldn't bring myself to tear my gaze from his. "Atlas…"

"Don't say anything. I'm glad you took things into your own hands."

Own hands.

He assumed I'd been alone. I didn't know if that made me feel guilty or glad that I didn't have to come up with a lie right now to protect Lynx and Saros.

"Honestly, I'm just grateful to be close by so I can be here for you both," he added, reaching out to take Aspen. He sat him in his arms, bobbing along as we continued walking through the maze. With each step, the tension began to uncoil, but an even clearer concern boiled beneath the surface.

What would happen if he ever learned the truth?

CHAPTER 4

LYNX

"I forgot how much I hate this place," Saros grumbled the moment we got back to our hotel room and shut the door. We'd been silent the entire way here. The tension in our handler's tiny office was smothering, coiling around me from every direction. But as much as it took a toll on me, I knew the stress and emotional cost that came with his Recollection had to exhaust Saros even more.

"I know," I said, squeezing his shoulder. "Hopefully we can get back home within a week or two."

He walked straight into the bathroom and washed his hands, twice, as if questioning Aurora and dealing with Aleander had soiled them. "Let's face it, Lynx, we don't have a real home. Never have, and probably never will."

I knew when he got in moods like this that it wasn't worth pushing. "What are you going to do about Aleander's request?"

I'd seen what Saros's old job at headquarters had done to him. Despite the emotions he attempted to hold inside, I had a front-row seat to how much effort he put into repressing them.

"I don't know," he shrugged, wiping his hands on the towel before coming out into the room. "It doesn't really seem like a request, does it?"

"You always have a choice, and I'll back you up, whatever the consequences." I removed my SNO-OPS vest, draping it over the chair. Saros threw his into a heap in the corner.

"I'm just tired of having this choice to make, Lynx. It's why I left headquarters in the first place."

"Let's focus on getting through the next few days, interviewing Fitzge—"

"That's if he doesn't try to lawyer his way around everything, like he's been doing," Saros cut in, rolling his eyes. He wasn't wrong, Fitzgerald Wells would use everything in the book to wriggle his way out of this. The real question was, why did they admit to killing Acacia in the first place? Surely, they had enough money and legal knowledge to skirt around that.

I suspected whatever they were hiding was much bigger than a murder. We needed to figure out what that was and soon, before there was another disappearance.

Either way, we weren't getting answers tonight, and the tension at work and in this room was suffocating me.

"Look, why don't we have a night off?" I offered, opening the nightstand drawer and pulling out a handful of takeout menus before sorting through them. "Order some food, finally open the care package Oakley sent us, maybe watch some reruns of *Which Witch?*"

"That show is garbage," Saros groaned.

I grinned. "Maybe so, but you secretly love it."

"Fine." His shoulders dropped, the tension already loosening its coiled grip on the room's oxygen.

I grabbed the remote, flipping on the reality show about a single witch stranded on a deserted island. They would have their pick of eight witches to survive a week with. If they both did, they left the show with a set of marital vow marks and one hundred thousand dollars.

It was probably all staged, but I was still here for the drama.

Reaching out a hand, Saros took the menus from me, hunting through the pile before picking out two of them and handing the rest back. "Gyros or Chinese?"

"Chinese," I said, definitively. Then I sidled up beside him and tucked myself into the crook of his arm, feeling him relax against me as I tapped on the UndeadEats app on my phone to place our order.

(((●)))

"That was so good," I said, slurping down the last bit of beef lo mein.

Saros nodded in agreement, stuffing the paper container into the trash. His eyes flitted across the room to the desk for the twelfth time since we'd started eating. "Let's open the package."

"Someone's eager."

He shrugged. "I feel bad it's been sitting there for days. She's probably wondering if it arrived."

Uh-huh. Sure. I didn't know whether to be annoyed or entertained that he still thought he could keep his feelings hidden from me.

"So it has nothing to do with the fact that you miss her?" I asked with a smirk, making his brows furrow. "You don't have to pretend you aren't checking your phone for messages ten times a day. I am too."

"I just want to make sure she's okay. I'm sure the neighborhood has been full of talk since the arrest, not to mention Hazel's return."

Because you care about her, idiot.

"Plus, Atlas is there now," he added quietly, green prickles of insecurity rippling around him.

"They aren't together anymore." I'd been reminding myself of this daily since he'd returned to Washington and left us here. Sure, they had a history, but *we* had a future with Oakley. Hopefully Saros wouldn't self-sabotage his way out of it.

"Maybe not." He inhaled deeply, pinching the bridge of his nose before sighing. "But you haven't touched her the way I have."

I arched a brow at him. "Oh, really?"

"You know what I mean." Saros glared, shaking his head at me. "Get your mind out of the gutter."

I cast a wide grin in his direction. "But you love when it's there."

"I've seen them together, Lynx. What it was like between them." His throat bobbed, hands held firmly at his sides. "They were very much in love."

"Were, Saros," I reminded him. "*Were.*"

"Has she even said why they aren't together now?" he asked, genuine curiosity lacing his words. "I doubt he's going to just accept us being with the mother of his witchling. He's our boss, for fuck's sake."

In reality, I still hadn't been able to get a read on their relationship. While I knew I needed to talk to her about it, especially with Atlas in town permanently, I didn't want to overwhelm her or push her away.

"She says they aren't together. She sent us this package. Meaning she misses *us*," I reiterated. "What her deal is with the Archon is between them."

"Until it isn't," he muttered.

Fuck.

"You're welcome to walk away, Saros, but I'm not." I refused to smother out a flame that'd barely kindled. "If I have to steal time in the dead of night to have a chance with her, I will."

"I'm not walking away."

"Then it's settled." *Thank Goddess.* "Now, do you want to open the package or not? I know the suspense is killing you."

"Yes. Open it."

I moved to the desk, grabbing my keys and swiping them down the tape, before I pulled the sides of the box apart. Peeling back the layers of black shimmering tissue paper inside, I found two long chains with chunky rose quartzes hanging from them. Picking up the note and reading it to myself, my heart rate kicked up with each word. "Damn, Wicked."

"What is it?" Saros asked, sitting upright on the bed. He lifted his chin, probably in hopes of sneaking a peek.

I reached into my back pocket to retrieve my phone, but it wasn't there. "What time is it?"

"9:02 p.m."

Finally, I spotted my phone on the nightstand but decided to grab my laptop instead. I propped it up in front of the TV screen and dialed Oakley, pressing the small video icon. Praying under my breath that she'd answer, I listened to it ring over and over.

Saros sat there, bewildered.

"Hey, Wicked," I breathed out, my voice an octave higher than usual.

"Hey there." Her auburn hair was pulled up in a messy bun, and she was in her fuzzy black robe, the neckline slightly askew, giving a peek of cleavage at the bottom of the screen.

The bed rustled, Saros scooting to the edge before planting his heels firmly on the floor next to me to get a better look at our beautiful witch.

"How are you?" This was exactly what I needed after today.

She grinned back at us, dissolving any tension I still carried with me after leaving Aleander's office. "Good, just been sketching out ideas for a new line now that Aspen's down."

"How is the wildling?" I asked. The thought of that little pumpkin had me smiling wider than a jack-o'-lantern.

"Great." She sighed, gaze drifting in the direction of the nursery. "Just started crawling, so he's keeping me on my toes."

"I bet," I chuckled.

"How's everything going out there?" She yawned, obviously exhausted but still just as stunning. My heart ached, wishing we were there with her. With them both.

"It's...going," I replied, then scooted a bit to the side so she could see Saros better. He gave her a single awkward wave, which she returned. *These two.* "Looking forward to getting back there."

"Can't wait." She smiled, then bit her bottom lip and damn if it didn't make my zipper suddenly much too tight. It had been way too fucking long since our night in the pines.

"Well, we don't want to bother you if you're busy getting stuff done but...we finally got a chance to open your care package," I said, nodding down to the box in front of me.

"You did?" Her chest flushed pink, along with her cheeks, a coy smirk arching the corners of her lips.

"It's cute that you're blushing about something *you* set in motion, Wicked."

"I can take a break." Her eyes darted around, and she

started moving quickly through the house until she made it into her bedroom and shut the door behind her. "Umm...Do you think you can get it to work?"

"I make no promises, but I'm eager to try." I grabbed the quartzes and pushed some of my gift into the talismans, following the instructions Oakley had sent along with them. "So is Saros."

"What—"

Before he said anything else, I threw one of the talismans to him before looping the other around my neck. The instant it was set in place, my dick went from six to midnight. "Damn, Wicked. What'd you put in this?"

"Just a little magic," she replied, bowing her head and looking up through her lashes.

Goddess above, if this was a *little* magic for her, then I would probably combust if she ever used more on me.

"Well, fuck." I summoned every ounce of control so I wouldn't just rip down my zipper. The discomfort was unreal. My pulse and erection both throbbed with anticipation. From the grumbled curses coming from Saros, I was certain it was doing the same to him. "Once we get this *up and running*—pun totally intended—couples are going to go feral over these talismans."

Oakley smiled, pride blooming like a vibrant flower surrounding her.

"What do we do now?" Saros asked, his tone a bit breathless.

"You'll see." If we couldn't be with our witch in the pines, we would give her everything we could from two hundred fifty miles away. "We need a guinea pig to test it out and I've nominated you. Saros, why don't you lose the shirt and pants?"

He glared, hesitating a moment before I nodded toward the screen that gave a clear shot of the bed.

"Go ahead and get yourself ready, Wicked," I told her, turning my attention to Saros.

"What the hell is happening?" he asked, gaze snapping down to his lap.

I flashed a devilish smirk, then tugged my zipper down and nodded to him. "You in?"

Eyeing me curiously, he followed, stripping off his pants. "Obviously, I just wish I knew what I was in for."

"What would be the fun in that?"

Now, I wasn't lacking by any means. But Saros? He had a thick-ass python tucked in his trousers. The moment he unleashed it, I was salivating.

"Holy shit," Saros groaned, staring in equal parts impressive awe and terror at himself. The veins on his shaft were aggravated, clear lust already beading at the tip. His eyes drifted up to Oakley, who slowly removed her robe and dropped it to the floor. She made her way to the bed, positioning her phone on her nightstand. "What kind of magic is this?"

"Tell Saros how it works, Wicked."

"So the crystals are imbued with an aphrodisiac charm I performed," Oakley explained, finally moving her hand away from the camera. She was naked, her soft curves begging to be touched.

Fucking perfection.

"It's strong," Saros gritted out, watching her trail her hand down her thigh. His fist stayed clenched at his side, as if waiting for instruction, not wanting to break any rules. Sweet, mouthwatering lust filled the air, the decadent aroma sending a bolt of need through my body.

"Our witch is strong with all her power replenished,

aren't you, Wicked?" Saros might have the self-control of a priest, but I was eager to worship her in the most sinful ways. My fingers itched, tension spinning down my spine. I palmed my cock, giving it a few long strokes. Oakley bit her lip. Her knees were still tucked together, but I'd have her glistening and spread for us soon enough. "Just wait until we recharge with you on the next full moon."

"Will you be here?" Her voice was cautious. Nervous.

"We don't—"

"We're gonna do everything in our powers not to miss it," I said, cutting Saros off. "Aren't we?"

He nodded in silent agreement, keeping his mouth screwed shut. His clenched fists now clutched his thighs, that prior restraint waning.

"Why don't you finish telling him about the talismans, Wicked?"

"Right. So, they are connected, carved from the same crystal and then enchanted by the same spell. Lynx is testing the final aspect of my design. I needed his gift to make it possible for the wearer to be able to experience everything their partner, or partners, are feeling. It won't work on mine since I don't have Lynx's magic embedded in this quartz, but it should work on yours if he got it right."

"Oh, I have a good feeling about this," I said, continuing to stroke myself slowly. "Did you grab anything out from your treasure box?"

"I did." Her eyes dropped to something next to her, pink brightening her freckled checks.

"Show us," I encouraged.

She lifted a long, partially translucent navy dildo with gold glitter flecked through its veins. It was thick, complete with a small, bulbous nub strategically placed near the base.

It looked about my size, so in my mind, I'd be the one fucking her tonight.

Hell yeah.

"Don't be shy." I nodded to her, licking my lips as she spread her thighs wide for us. The camera was at the perfect height to see every inch of her wet, pink pussy. Saros sucked in a breath next to me, watching. She rubbed some lube up and down her slit before sliding two fingers in and her gaze drifted from between us.

Saros stroked his cock from root to tip, precum leaking from it more than usual.

Goddess, the power the two of them had over me. "You like that don't you, Wicked? Work that pretty pussy for us and we'll give you a private show."

She brought the tip of the toy down, easing it in one inch at a time until the small nub hit her clit, then she pulled it out a few inches before pushing it back in again.

Out and in.

Out and in.

My eyes were glued to the movement, turning me on so much I could no longer resist the lust rushing through me from the quartz around our necks. He might have been quieter about it, but Saros's desire could overpower mine in a heartbeat. It was almost as if repressing his emotions made them all the stronger. He groaned, attention flitting between me and our sexy witch on the laptop screen.

I leaned forward and wrapped my lips around his cock, sucking down the salty precum spilling eagerly from his tip.

"*Fuck, Lynx,*" he gritted out.

From my peripheral vision, Oakley was working the toy in time with my mouth sucking down every inch of Saros. Her strokes became shorter, thighs shaking. She only paused for a second, an audible *click* filtering through the speaker before a steady *buzz* took its place and her head tilted upward.

"Eyes on us, Midnight," Saros demanded. I loved when he got like this, and from the way Oakley's gaze snapped to us, lips parting, a soft whimper escaping them, she did too. He gripped my hair, my scalp zinging at the intensity, and thrust up into my mouth, hitting the back of my throat. "Goddess, this talisman. Is. Fucking. Amazing."

Saros guided me down his thick shaft, and Oakley's lust pulsed from the talisman, radiating through my body. I released him from my lips, stroking him a few times. "I think she wants more, Saros, and so do I."

He looked over at Oakley, who was rubbing the tip of her dildo against her clit, breaths shallow. She nodded in answer, and I sat up, reaching into the nightstand to pull out the travel-sized lube, tossing it to Saros and getting onto my knees.

Squirting some into his hand, he kissed and bit along my hip and ass before prepping me with languid circles. Then, a moment later, his thick tip pressed against my tight hole. I relaxed into the sensation, letting it burn as I pushed back onto him. My cock was ramrod straight, cum leaking onto the bed. Not that I cared. The messier the better when it came to them.

Saros eased in slowly, pulsing in and out until he finally filled me to the hilt.

As Oakley fucked herself with the dildo, she poured into us with her ecstasy through the crystal. Saros growled, plunging into me in time with her. It was like he'd gone feral, pounding harder with each drive of his hips.

"What would you do to our witch if she were here right now?" I teased him, wrapping my fist around my cock and working myself eagerly. The scent of powdered sugar and sweet syrup blended together, fueling me to arch into Saros's thrusts. Her eyes jolted, attention piqued, but she kept fucking herself like the Goddess-damned queen she was.

His baritone came out in short, breathy rasps, and he pulsed in small strokes, staying deep inside me. "I want to taste you. Bury my cock so deep that when you shatter, you're clenched around it. So all you can feel is my hot cum as I fill up every inch of you. Then I want to watch Lynx fuck it back into you until you overflow and we're spilling down your thighs."

"Goddess," she cried, throwing her chest out, her breasts full and heavy. If she were ever comfortable enough to let me, I would caress every inch of them with my tongue.

So fucking beautiful.

"You ready for us, Wicked?" I rasped.

Saros replaced my hand, gripping my shaft tightly and jerking me with each powerful thrust of his hips. My stomach clenched, electricity rioting through my bloodstream. It was overwhelming, the room feeling much too small for all the pleasure bolting between the three of us.

She nodded wildly, incoherent sounds spilling from her lips. The waves of her ecstasy crashed into me through the talisman hanging around my neck, drenching me with her decadent Desire.

"Just like that, Midnight," Saros whispered over me, his delicious tugs making my balls tighten, ready to unleash.

"So fucking soaked and perfect. I can't wait to be inside you again," I heaved, my release closing in.

"Give us one more," Saros ground out toward the screen, body slapping into me. He was getting close. His hand shook around my cock while he continued stroking it in long, steady measures.

Oakley pushed the toy deep into her, its nub buzzing against her clit.

"It's—too—intense," she whimpered, shaking her head, her body trembling.

"Let go for me, Midnight," Saros demanded, voice low. "I *need* to see you."

Her eyes glinted with renewed purpose, the pleasure building between the three of us connected by the talismans.

When a guttural cry split her lips, Saros emptied himself, warmth flooding into me. My tentative restraint unleashed, thick ropes of cum spraying onto the comforter until my body was drained.

"That's our Goddess," I said to Oakley, her breasts heaving as she caught her breath. Her eyes began to flutter, exhaustion returning to her face, now mixed with post-sex haze.

Saros removed the talisman from around his neck. "Get some sleep, Midnight."

She yawned, grabbing her robe and pulling it over her shoulders. Moving from the bed, I savored one last look at her beautiful face, unsure when we'd see her in person again. "Amazing as always, Wicked."

When she smiled in response, my chest ached, longing to be closer to her despite her brilliant and creative work-around.

"Goodnight, you two," she said before I waved at her to hang up. For some reason, I hated the prospect of being the one to do it. Her chestnut irises shimmered, lips parting as if to say something, but then she pressed them shut and the video chat ended.

Never had I thought I'd find someone who could make both Saros and I feel this way. Sure, we'd shared men and women before, but as a one-off thing. This was different.

This was a future. A *life*.

One I would give anything for.

We padded into the bathroom, Saros turning on the water before coming up behind me and pressing a tender kiss to my shoulder. "I hate being here, but at least I've got you."

I spun to face him and clasped my hands at the nape of his neck. "Always."

Pale-green prickles outlined his body, a silent warning that he was more anxious about dealing with the Wellses again than he'd ever let on.

"Let's kick ass at tomorrow's interrogation," I encouraged, before I nipped his bottom lip. He nodded in agreement, the green paling to a soft haze. The steam around us thickened with sweet syrup, pink puffs swirling through it. I kissed him, savoring each stroke of his tongue as he guided me backward until my shoulder blades jolted on the cold tile.

I arched a devious brow, attention drawn to his deliciously hard length nestled against mine, settled perfectly between us. "Somebody's ready for more."

He chuckled, gripping my chin. "When it comes to you? Always."

CHAPTER 5

OAKLEY

A gossip-filled wave of whispers crashed into us the moment Hazel opened the Coven Community Center doors. A handful of witches' eyes darted in our direction before returning to their huddled neighbors, deep in conversation. Ruby, our interim coveness, was up at the front looking through some papers at the podium, coppery stars smattering its onyx metal.

My sister greeted everyone with a big, bold smile, radiating pure confidence that I hadn't seen from her since she'd been taken. Her mask was on, something I envied her for. I was much more the heart-on-my-sleeve kind of witch.

One of the many reasons it was so hard for me to have Atlas in such close proximity now that he'd moved in.

Aspen sat nestled on my hip, head perched on my shoulder, his padded carrier strapped around my waist. I pressed a kiss to his temple, continuing through the crowd until I spotted Ivy and Jade with their families. At least they felt like a safe place to land among the nosey throng of Starry Night Lane residents.

"Hey, Hazel," Jade said, waving from the ground while she

wrestled an empty chip bag from her toddler. "So glad to see you here."

Ivy smiled, and my sister returned it tenfold. "You've been missed."

"Just been busy catching up on work," Hazel replied, that brilliant crimson grin never leaving her face.

Anytime she was in public, she was *on*.

I knew better, though. I saw the moments she wasn't exuding lively energy on the phone. The hours tucked away in her room.

The things she didn't say.

As wrong as it sounded, I wished Lynx would return so he could help me get a clearer read on her. I needed to know things were going to get better for my sister.

"How are the designs coming along?" Jade asked, pulling me from my thoughts.

"Good!" A smile streaked across my lips, thrilled to show them what I'd been working on. "You two still available tomorrow for the boudoir shoot?"

"Sure thing!" Ivy seemed genuinely excited.

Jade stood up, waggling her eyebrows. "Can't wait."

I was so pumped for the shoot, for these women to see how amazing they looked in Full Moon Emporium's line. Pulling out my phone, I jotted down a few notes for my next grocery order, making sure I had some snacks and drinks for when they came over. Then I scrolled through my photos of the collection, imagining which looks to try on the two witches in front of me. The idea of my shop opening again had giddy bubbles floating up and popping in my belly. As nervous as I was, sharing this new chapter of my business with the world excited me more.

A loud set of claps silenced the room.

"Good afternoon everyone, I know there's been a lot of

upheaval and rumors going around the last few weeks." Ruby's voice wavered a bit, but she cleared her throat and straightened her spine. "I'm here to reassure everyone that coven leadership is doing everything we can and cooperating with Archon Thorne and the team at SNO-OPS to keep our community safe." Her gaze shifted to Atlas walking up from below the raised platform. "The Archon will say a few words and give an update."

Of course. This was his new jurisdiction after all. Something I was trying to avoid stewing over, especially after our family outing. It was easier to think of him being around off and on. Temporarily. The reality that he'd be here for at least three years, likely more if Aspen and I stayed, terrified me. Having to keep him at arm's length for a few hours was doable, but on a consistent basis?

It was too damn much.

He strolled up to the podium, confidence and power wafting off of him, almost sending everyone into a trance. He was enigmatic, and watching him speak in public, in his element, filled me with so much pride.

Unfortunately, it also had my Desire surging through my veins.

Goddess, I am truly fucked.

Shaking out my tingling fingertips, stray bolts streaked into a few witches standing around. They all exhaled ill-timed groans.

Oops.

"Thank you so much, coveness," Atlas said, clearing his throat before addressing the room with his smooth tone. "While the Wellses have been taken into custody and confessed to the murder of Acacia Mirabel, we still do not have a motive or connection to the..." he paused for a moment, as if weighing how to finish the statement, "other disappearances."

"Disappearances?" Forest Delta asked. "Have there been more than just Hazel and Hunter's?"

The crowd began to murmur, but Atlas lifted his hand, silencing them.

"SNO-OPS received an anonymous tip regarding a series of odd disappearances within Celestial Haven. At first, we didn't think much of it, but when we began to observe trends of people moving in and out of the neighborhood, Starry Night Lane stood out with its abnormally high residential turnover rate, considering it'd only been built eight years ago. The few leads we have are currently being investigated."

"Are you saying that Hunter Astro is one of these disappearances?"

"We suspect so," Atlas replied to the young witch at the back of the room. She looked familiar but lived farther down the lane, near Celestial Haven's main drag. Her name was on the tip of my tongue...something that started with an *S*, maybe?

Laurel Pierce raised her hand. When Atlas called on her, she smiled, twirling some of her brunette strands while she spoke. "Will this cut into any of our Hallowed celebrations?"

All the rest of the Blessed Crescent families nodded, looking concerned. They'd probably been planning the events for months, already making new accommodations with Aurora gone.

Ruby walked over, nudging Atlas back from the mic. "No. All events and activities are still taking place as planned."

He leaned over her into the mic, quickly adding, "Thank you for your understanding while we focus on keeping our neighborhood safe."

Our neighborhood.

Because this was his home now too.

"Are the other streets experiencing similar disturbances?" someone shouted from the other side of the room. The voice was feminine, but I couldn't make out who had asked.

Ruby moved out of the way, granting Atlas full control of the mic. "We don't believe so, but we're looking into all possibilities."

Orion Archer called out among the crowd. "Are we allowed to know who is currently on the list of suspects?"

"No," Atlas said, taking a pause for the murmurs to quiet down again. "As this is an ongoing investigation, we will not be sharing any further details at this time. All we ask is that you work with our team and give them minimal push back as they try to locate Mr. Astro and solve this case."

The gossip returned, whispers spreading like wildfire. Atlas cleared his throat, lifting a hand to command the room's attention again. "If you have any information that could help with the case, please let me know so that I can relay it to those at headquarters. It would be much appreciated. Thank you for your time."

Atlas walked away from the podium, coming down to pick up Aspen and nuzzle him nose to nose. The coven watched him in awe. Always the politician. He walked through the crowd, stopping to talk to various witches as he passed, waving to others with Aspen's tiny fist, Hazel and I trailing behind him.

Once we were heading up the driveway, Atlas handed Aspen to me. Then he pulled Hazel and I close to whisper, "Agents Carver and Holt get back tomorrow and should be checking in to see about any other information on the case." My heart caught in my throat, butterflies bursting to life in my belly. "Obviously, keeping their identities intact is of the utmost importance."

So keep pretending we didn't have a full moon ménage? Got it.

"Did you know they were coming back?" my sister asked once we were in the house and the door shut behind us.

"No," I replied, confusion washing away the anticipation building in my mind. "And from our conversation last night, I don't think they did either."

CHAPTER 6

OAKLEY

"Maybe they were trying to surprise you?" Hazel offered, scooping up some puréed sweet potato and making it soar into Aspen's mouth. "Some grand romantic gesture?"

"Maybe..." It made enough sense and things had been ridiculously hot between us all during our long-distance rendezvous, but my insecurities were creeping in, making me question everything. Circumstances had shifted so quickly between our night in the pines, case developments, the Wellses' arrest, and then them leaving for Salem.

Considering their new boss was my ex and would be around a lot between the case and co-parenting, everything was about to get pretty complicated.

A buzz sounded from the counter, and Hazel got up from her chair to check her phone. She frowned down at the screen, then swiped, bringing her cell to her ear. "Hey. Now's not really a good time."

Her voice was low. Serious. As whoever on the other end continued talking, her gaze moved up toward the ceiling, as if biding her time to hang up.

"I know," she replied, sighing deeply. "Are you doing okay?"

Aspen gripped the small bowl of purée and knocked it to the floor, creamy orange gunk splattering in all directions.

"Fuck!" Hazel's eyes went wide, and she moved to begin cleaning up, but I held up a hand, scurrying over to the high-chair. She tossed me a towel, and I clutched it in my hand, reciting an incantation to dampen it before swiping it over the mess on the counter until it disappeared.

There definitely were some major perks to having access to my magic again.

"What do you need?" she asked, pulling the phone away from her ear to swipe and type into it. Then she brought it back up, rushing through her words. "Okay, okay. I'll see what I can do."

A moment later, she hung up, exhaling like she couldn't be more grateful for the call to be over.

"Who was that?" I asked, wiping down the highchair before taking Aspen out of it. His onesie was splattered with orange, so I lay him on the floor, waving a hand over his sullied outfit to clean it off.

"Just a client." Her tone was short. When she went to put the phone on the counter, she hesitated a moment, slipping it into the pocket of her jeans instead. "Why are you looking at me like that?"

I tickled Aspen's belly and gave it a raspberry, relishing the fit of giggles that burst from his tiny body. The material was still damp, even with the cleansing spell, so I headed into the nursery to grab a new outfit.

"You said it wasn't really a good time, but it's not like you couldn't handle a call," I said loud enough for her to hear from the other room while I picked out a set of pajamas with inky pumpkins scattered across the white. When I brought it into the living room, Hazel was on the floor playing with Aspen's toes. I handed her his jammies. "I'd understand if you needed to work."

"I know that, but I'm trying to set some better boundaries." She fed Aspen's arm through the sleeves, then zipped it up before pulling him into her lap and nodding to the pile of fabric and sewing supplies spread across the coffee table. "Besides, I'm more excited to help you get things set up for the relaunch."

"Well, thank you." My attention dropped to the floor. I didn't know why I sometimes was embarrassed to be pursuing this dream again despite all my excitement. "It means a lot."

I went over to the clothes, picking up the needle. Waving my other hand, the nursing pad pocket scuttled onto the lacy bodysuit, lying flush as I twisted my palm to move it into the correct position. Then I pricked the pad of my finger with the needle before casting the sewing enchantment to the pattern I'd laid out in front of me. Magic filtered through my palms, spicing the air, and the needle began steadily stitching the pocket onto the piece I'd retrieved from storage, following the directions on the parchment.

"Given any more thought to Atlas's proposal?" Hazel asked, interrupting my concentration.

A strangled sound escaped my lips, and the needle wobbled with my loss of focus. "No. We aren't getting married, Hazel."

"Not *that* proposal." She rolled her eyes. "I meant the one for leasing that space in Mystic Square."

"Oh yeah. Duh." My face heated. I inhaled deeply, gaze pinned to the needle threading the bodysuit in front of me. "Still thinking about it. It feels weird for him to do something so big for me. It's a large investment."

After our pumpkin patch outing, I'd promised Atlas I'd go see the space. Hazel had scheduled a visit for a few days from now. Luckily, she'd be there as a buffer. It was hard to keep him at arm's length, even with Aspen third-wheeling.

He was certainly attractive when we were dating, but that paled in comparison to watching him care for our child. I recalled the memory of the two of them together at the pumpkin patch, Aspen seated in Atlas's lap as he slid down the hay bale slide. My heart squeezed in my chest, tears building in my eyes, but I blinked them away before any fell.

You chose this, Oakley. And with good reason.

"Wanna talk about it?" Hazel asked. Aspen rested his cheek on her shoulder, eyelids fluttering while she stroked his back. He'd be out in a few minutes.

I shook my head. "Not really."

Noticing her nephew dozing off, Hazel brought him over to me to kiss him goodnight before she started for the nursery. I pressed the tops of my breasts, making sure they wouldn't be too uncomfortable if he went to bed straight away. There was enough give that I'd probably be fine until his middle-of-the-night feed.

"The future isn't set in stone, Oaks," she reminded me for the dozenth time, bouncing Aspen toward his crib. While she got him down, I picked up another piece of parchment, adjusting the previous pattern before spelling another needle to begin working on a mesh corset.

Walking out of the nursery, Hazel went over to the fridge, picked out the pint of rocky road ice cream, and grabbed a spoon. Popping off the top, she scooped some up. "You still love him."

I swallowed that truth instead of choking on it. There was no use trying to lie to Hazel. She'd been there through our relationship, all the way up until its end. "Maybe I do, but I wouldn't be able to live with myself if that somehow led to his death."

She kept enjoying her dessert, eyeing me.

"I already tried to change things by getting away from him and look how well that turned out for me," I added with a shrug.

She sighed. "Maybe that's a sign to stop fighting it. You may have already changed fate. I tried to tell you, there are always things that can shift to alter it."

I brought my attention down to the lace in my hands, flicking my wrist for the needle to knot the end of the thread. "Plus, there's Lynx and Saros to think about."

"What's there to think about?" Hazel asked between shoveled spoonfuls into her mouth. "If you can handle two, you can handle three."

My eyes snapped up at her boldness, and she waggled her brows and gave a few little thrusts with her pelvis.

"Oh my Goddess, Hazel." I chuckled, stuffing the nursing pad into the pocket and holding it up to my chest, wanting to make sure the padding wouldn't make the women's breasts appear lumpy in the design. She gave me a thumbs up, and I went to work on the opposite side.

"Don't act like you haven't thought about it."

"Never gonna happen." There was no way that would be possible, even if my imagination got carried away sometimes...

When Atlas was out of sight, it was much simpler to not recall the times we had together, or be reminded of what an amazing father and partner he was. Sometimes I didn't know which was a greater punishment: watching him die having had more time with him or forcing myself to stay away so that he would live for our son.

Lynx understood my emotions—the inner battles I faced

—and Saros never judged me for wanting to be rid of my gift. He knew the cost of having an ability that could potentially do more harm than good.

They both made me feel seen. Cherished.

As much as I wanted to know, I knew better than to ask Hazel about the future when it came to them. She'd already shot me down multiple times. And part of me wondered if she was team Atlas, despite her premonition. She'd never say it, though. She knew all I'd given up to keep him safe.

"Atlas is overseeing their case, which means he's their boss," I reminded her. And myself.

"Only until the case is over, right?"

"I mean, I guess?" Being with Lynx and Saros was messy with their job. My current dealings with Atlas were messy because of my fear for him. The dynamics between the three of them? That would be pure chaos.

The mischievous devil on my shoulder, my Desire, was giddy at the prospect.

Naughty bitch.

"Sounds like a pretty good incentive to solve the case," Hazel said, enjoying another spoonful of rocky road.

"Yeah, only then they will have to return to Salem." My shoulders hunched forward, and I tried to smother the disappointment crowding my rib cage.

"No use worrying about things you can't control, Oakley."

"You're right." A lovely platitude, but easier said than done.

"Oh, I know I am." She puffed out her chest and smirked. "Question is, are you actually going to listen to me?"

Worry was etched into my bones, anxiety taking shelter in me ever since I'd learned of Atlas's fate—our fate.

"Are you going to tell me who was really on the phone?" I asked her, deciding redirection would be a better tactic than trying to rid myself of my jumbled nerves—a task that no amount of magic could tackle.

"Point made," she conceded, jabbing her spoon at me before setting it on the counter. "When you're ready to really talk about things, I'm here."

I arched a brow at her. "Likewise."

CHAPTER 7
OAKLEY

"What do you think?"

Pulling the black lace so it sat flush against her hip, I stared up at Jade, her eyes narrowing on herself in the mirror propped up against our living room wall.

The house was bustling, witches from the street all in various states of dress. Hazel was out in the garage, thumbing through the designs in my makeshift studio, coming in periodically with different outfits for them to try on for today's photoshoot.

These pictures would be featured at the Moonlit Masquerade, and while I was so excited to be back in business again, I was equally terrified. This wasn't the same Full Moon Emporium people had known. It had evolved.

And so had I.

Would the supernatural public be receptive to it, though?

"I think I'm in love." Jade twisted her hips to see the bra and panty set with crisscross embellishments from different angles.

A smile ripped through my previous fears, the nerves

within me simmering until they disappeared completely. She loved it. And from the way she was staring at herself in the mirror, it was like she'd put on a new layer of confidence.

Exactly what I wanted.

"You look incredible," Ivy said, coming over to check out her friend. She was wearing a deep-blue nightie with a plunging neckline that stopped just above her belly button. "If Jacob saw you right now, he'd be whisking you away."

"If he doesn't, I volunteer." Hazel threw us a wink. Pink smeared Jade's cheeks, but she didn't seem too opposed to the idea.

I cleared my throat, sending her off the platform before pulling Ivy onto it.

"Let me loosen the strap here," I said, adjusting the material so the neckline fell at the perfect spot, caressing her curves beautifully. "Now the girls are really on display."

Ivy chuckled. "They need all the showcasing they can get."

"Everyone," I called out, waiting a few moments for the witches to gather. "Thank you so much for being so amazing and doing this."

Whoops and cheers echoed around the room, a few even clapping. Looking out among the crowd, it was the first time I truly felt like a part of this community here in Celestial Haven. I'd been so focused on moving and caring for Aspen and then Hazel's disappearance, making friends, setting down roots, it all felt unimportant.

But these witches were my friends. My community.

My coven.

"And we may have left some favors for you on your way out," Hazel added with a wink.

She pointed to the ten bags sitting on the counter, stuffed with goodies like pumpkin spice–flavored lube, carnelian crystals imbued with increased libido, and vials of my own homebrewed full moon elixir. I'd almost skipped out on making those since it reminded me of Aurora and what she'd done to Acacia, but if she hadn't killed the mysterious witch, I honestly didn't know if my sister would have ever been found.

The Goddess worked in mysterious ways.

Around the room, everyone's eyes lit with excitement, shouting a ripple of thanks.

"You are so welcome. Thank *you* for being my guinea pigs." They were all dressed in my designs, ready to go for the photoshoot, and they looked incredible.

I summoned the last few witches to me, making small adjustments to their lingerie.

"Let's head out back," I called to everyone once I'd finished the final tweaks. "Hazel set up some fun spots to shoot."

Leading them onto the porch, I pointed toward the tree line.

"Wow," Heather said, awestruck. Murmurs of a similar sentiment echoed all around.

Hazel had gone all out, curating four separate scenes. There was a cream tufted chaise nestled against the pines; a pile of autumn leaves in vibrant crimsons, mustards, and orange; a hexagon-shaped wedding arch with crystals dangling from its top at varying lengths; and a flannel blanket with a beautiful spread of white candles and fall treats.

Ivy came up next to me, running her hands over the deep-blue material hugging her hips. "This is stunning."

"Who wants to go first?" Hazel called out. About five different hands shot toward the sky.

My sister swung her gaze over to me, eyebrows raised as if waiting for me to make the final call. Scanning the group, I knew instantly who I wanted to shine first. One who hadn't raised her hand. "Heather, why don't you kick us off?"

"Me?" Her eyes went wide as her arms crossed over the pleated black babydoll with large crescents embellishing the otherwise sheer bra cups. "Really?"

"Yes. Look, you didn't have six kids in eight years from being shy, so get on out there and have fun."

There were some hoots in agreement from the rest of the group, and she smiled, a slight tinge of crimson staining her cheeks. Of the Blessed Crescent group, she didn't seem to really be into the gossip or pomp. She was probably too busy for it.

"We are all gonna cheer you on." Jade ushered her forward.

"Hazel is an amazing photographer." I waved the rest of the group over to the outdoor seating area. "You're in great hands."

Heather hesitated a moment before heading toward Hazel, whispering with her a few moments as my sister looked at the camera, making some adjustments to the settings and taking some test shots. Photography had become a hobby of hers over the years, and she'd helped me so many times with Full Moon Emporium by taking pictures for the shop.

"Come right over here. I want you to lie on these leaves," Hazel said, pointing to the autumnal pile. Then she floated the camera above, using its twin enchanted lens that was clasped in her hand to change its positioning. Heather followed her instructions, lying back onto the lush maple leaves and brushing off a few stray ones that had clung to the bottom of the babydoll's skirt. "Good girl. Now bring this arm up and let it rest above your head; the other one I want you to trace along the lace near your hips."

She seemed to have everything handled. I shuffled inside the house to grab some waters and snacks for the group while they waited, listening to them whisper.

"Hazel really should watch how she says *good girl* or she'll end up invited to join every couple and singleton the next full moon," Jade teased.

"I call dibs."

"Better beware, I heard the last person that crossed Aurora ended up dead."

"True," Cordelia's voice filtered to me. "But she's not here. That means full moon invites are fair game."

"Alright, Ivy, you're next," my sister's voice called out as I hurried into the kitchen. I didn't know how I felt about them talking about Hazel that way. And how would inviting her to the pines be crossing Aurora?

The sinking feeling in my gut was trying to tell me something, but I refused to acknowledge it. If Hazel had something to say about Aurora, she would have told me.

Wouldn't she?

Though she was very adamant that Aurora couldn't have killed Acacia... Could she have been defending her because they were somehow involved? Did the guys know this? And if they didn't...was it important to the case somehow? Should I tell them?

No. This was all just neighborhood gossip I'd ask Hazel about later. We'd probably laugh about it.

Dropping the waters and snacks off at the table, I went to watch Hazel in action when Jade called me over. "Will we see them before they're put on display?"

"Yes. We will send out the best of the bunch in a few days and let you each pick which photo you want displayed at the masquerade."

"I'm so excited to see the finished product." Cordelia's

words filtered out, her gaze locked on Ivy who was owning her shoot in front of the hexagon and its hanging crystals. A small flame was ignited in her palms, held near her breasts. Hazel was capturing the witches up close and far away through the camera lens.

"I can't wait for my husband to see these," Jade said. Then she scanned me over, her lips downturned. "Are you going to model?"

"I am." I chuckled, gesturing at my oversized sweater and leggings. I definitely was overdressed in comparison to everyone around me clad in next to nothing. At least the outdoor heating pods were turned on, the home system sensing the lowering body temperatures. The last thing that felt sexy was the cold wind whipping at your sensitive witchy bits. "Later tonight, once everyone else has gone and Aspen is down."

"I have to ask..." Laurel started, eyeing me curiously. "What's going on with you and Archon Thorne now that he's moving here?"

My whole body froze. But as soon as I realized, I shook it off, replacing the reaction with a pleasant smile, repeating the line I'd rehearsed to myself only a thousand times since he'd told me he was coming to Celestial Haven. "He moved here to be closer to his son. That's really all there is to it."

"So you're saying he's single?" she asked, head cocking to the side. Everyone else looked up at me expectantly. Curious.

"Yep," I managed to croak out, despite the tension roiling through me.

He wasn't mine. And I loved him enough to want him to be happy.

Did I really expect he'd be alone forever? Not with his charm and confidence or his obvious good looks and powerful position. He was a catch, and I'd somehow lured him in...only to let him go.

Not mine anymore.

"Oh, that's good to know," she replied cheerfully. "I was thinking about trying to fix him up with Sage Harlow, but I didn't want to overstep."

I tried to remember who Sage was. She had been at the blackout bash, as I recalled, but lived all the way at the end of the lane closest to the main road, so I didn't see much of her around the cul-de-sac.

"Not at all." I shrugged, feigning nonchalance despite the envious heat spreading through my chest. "Go for it."

"You're sure?"

"Of course. Sage seems really nice."

"You're much cooler about this than I would be," Jade whispered, giving me a once-over, like she didn't believe me. But I wouldn't admit she was onto something in front of the rest of the witches here.

"Excuse me," I said, flashing an overdone smile. "I need to go inside and grab some bubbly for everyone."

My heart raced, and I reminded myself to slow my steps as I nearly sprinted into the house. First Hazel and Aurora. Now Laurel wanted to fix up my ex with someone new. This was turning out to be a night of unexpected surprises, and I didn't think I could handle another one. I should have been celebrating, but all I felt was dread.

"Hey there, Wicked."

I halted in place, my heart ramping up its pace. All the anxious worries clouding my head sifted away in a puff of smoke.

"Lynx, you scared me," I rasped, catching my breath.

He was standing in the living room, smiling at me with

his usual mischievous smirk as he ran a hand through his sandy-blond waves.

Goddess, he was beautiful.

Desire slammed into my fingertips thinking of the last time I'd seen him, stroking his length, kneeling, Saros pistoning into him. My thighs clenched at the image, heart racing with Lynx's sinful words replaying in my mind.

Ready for us, Wicked?

So fucking soaked and perfect.

I can't wait to be inside you again.

I couldn't wait for that either. My body heated, the space between us much too large, and I was certain the only thing that could bring me relief would be to run into his arms, pull him into my bedroom, and press my skin directly against his.

"I didn't realize you'd be having company." Lynx slipped his hands into his pockets, gaze darting to the window. "Happy to see me, Wicked?"

He took a step closer, as if daring to see what I'd do. And Goddess, *all the things* I wanted to do to this witch. The murmur of my gossiping guests filtered into the room, and I leaned against the counter, praying it would tether me in place. I shouldn't go near him. There were too many people here and the way gossip spread around this town, Atlas would find out immediately, possibly shattering their newly-wed-couple-moves-to-the-suburbs ruse.

"Of course I am." I tried to keep my tone cool, casual, not wanting to draw any attention from the witches outside. "But you already know that, don't you?"

After all, he could sense every emotion coming from me.

"Maybe I do." His hair had gotten a bit shaggier, falling into his face as he looked at me with that panty-melting smolder that had swept me away the first time we'd met.

"But you have no idea just how happy I am to see you. If only we were alone..."

He trailed off, arching a brow at me in challenge.

My Desire was ready to kick everyone out. Immediately.

I clawed at the marble countertop, resisting the urge to tear off his fitted brown Henley and kiss that knowing smirk right off his face. "Well if I had known you were coming, I would have adjusted my plans."

"We didn't want to get your hopes up in case things changed and we got stuck in Salem longer."

I nodded, swallowing thickly. "When do you head back?"

"Not until after the Hallowed celebrations have concluded."

The weight on my chest lifted a bit, giving me enough room to take in his words. They'd be here for all the events and festivities. That meant not returning to Salem for at least a week or so.

"I missed you so damn much." His eyes darted behind me to the window. "And that little witchling. Where is he?"

"Ruby took him on a stroll and then was bringing him back here."

His neck craned over my shoulder toward the windows. And if my stomach wasn't fluttering before, it now was.

"I don't want to interrupt, and I still need to unpack, but can I come by later?" His sienna irises twinkled in question, making me giddy to rekindle whatever had stoked between us before he'd left town. But I couldn't help the twinge of disappointment that he'd only said *I*.

"Saros is back at home. He wanted to unpack right away."

My chest flushed with heat. I was still getting used to Lynx being able to read me like this. No one ever had before. And realistically, no one ever would. "Any time after eight should work."

"We can talk more tonight," he offered with a halfhearted smile that didn't quite fill the span of his lips.

Goddess, I just wanted to kiss him. To follow him home and ask Saros for myself what was going on between us. "Okay."

"Wicked, I can sense you spinning out and there's no need for that," he tutted.

I swallowed my unease, taking a deep breath.

His gaze roved over me, then he arched a brow. "When are you modeling your designs?"

"Once I get Aspen to bed."

"Well, I don't want to miss out on that." He dragged me in for a friendly-looking hug, but when he whispered into my ear, his gravelly tone was anything but. "Text me so I can say goodnight to Aspen and then I'll stick around for the *private* show."

Full-body tingles erupted beneath my skin at the implication of his words, and when he pulled away, I was buzzing. Giving him a devilish smirk, I discreetly waved my fingers, unleashing some Desire. He shifted uncomfortably, the bulge growing in his jeans.

"*Fuck.*" He glared at me. "Leaving me hot and bothered for the next few hours while I try to unpack? You truly are wicked."

"It's only fair." I shrugged, pleased with myself, knowing I'd be counting down the minutes until we were alone.

"In that case…" A flood of want rushed between my thighs. *Shit.* I zipped them together, and Lynx smirked at me victoriously before striding toward the door and adjusting the waist of his jeans in one fluid movement. "I'll see you later, Wicked."

CHAPTER 8

LYNX

Saros lay on the bed, his e-reader blocking half of his face from view. When I walked into the bedroom, he hadn't even acknowledged me, pretending to be glued to whatever he was reading.

I knew better.

He was trying to avoid something, and I was pretty sure it had to do with our beautiful autumn-haired neighbor. If I asked him about it, though, he would snap at me. I could tell from the steely scent cleaving the air between us.

I unpacked in silence, shoving my clothes haphazardly into drawers. If there was anything that would draw commentary from my partner, it was my lack of rigid cleanliness.

But there was nothing. Only silence and the occasional grunt in response to whatever he was reading.

Once I finished, I climbed across the bed, clamped my fingers around his e-reader, and pulled it away from his face. He had his glasses on, glaring at me from behind their rectangular lenses.

"What?" he huffed out before pursing his lips together.

"I'm heading back to Oakley's in a few." My knee was notched between his legs, and I cocked my head at him. "Are you sure you don't want to come with?"

"Yes. I want to take another look over the notes from Aurora's interrogation. Something isn't adding up." His words were calm but his breath came out unsteady, the steely air around us bubbling into pale-green anxiety. He'd been on edge ever since we left Salem.

"We can do that together when we get back?" I offered. Oakley had been so rattled when he hadn't been with me earlier.

Sometimes having a front-row seat to everyone's emotions felt like a curse. There wasn't a simple way to manage a multitude of feelings at once. And worse yet, it truly wasn't my job to manage them. Even if I wanted to.

Right now, though, I wanted to shake the witch in front of me. Since we'd been paired up on our first undercover assignment, it'd been Saros and I against the world. We hadn't had anyone else. Not really. Not until now.

I knew he cared about Oakley and I'd be damned if I let him screw this up for himself.

For *us*.

Hadn't he wanted a future after this assignment? A real life, as he'd said. She could be a part of that. No more secrets. A real, loving family.

Not to mention mind-blowing sex.

"If I go over there, I won't be focused. I'd just ruin the mood for you two." He snatched up the e-reader again and raised it like the wall he pretended he could construct between us.

"You know, moods are kind of my specialty," I teased, earning a flicker of his attention. I set his fictional friends to the side, and curled my pelvis against his, hoping to coax him out of his brooding. He hardened beneath my rolling hips. "I'd be happy to help shift yours."

He arched a brow. "Is that so?"

I ran my palm up his chest, resting it on his neck. He wasn't able to hide his true feelings from me anymore than I could hide my entire past from him.

I thought about last night: Saros pressing me against the cold tiling, sending ripples of pleasure streaking down my spine. We'd moved together, picking up speed, urgently seeking release. Saros reached between us, gripping firmly and owning us in smooth, powerful strokes. It was a frantic and beautifully desperate dance we'd done a million times, the movements choreographed over a decade of familiarity and love. Our eyes locked, foreheads notched together, chests heaving. We came nearly in unison, grinding out curses, bodies slick and sticky with sweat—

Saros wrapped his hand around my wrist and pulled me off of him. Then he cupped my chin and kissed me. "I appreciate the effort, but it's not going to work. Not tonight."

I groaned out my disappointment. "Are you sure you're not allowing your fear about her ability to borrow your power get in the way of seeing her? You clearly missed her."

"I did miss her, but no." His evergreen gaze narrowed on me as he released my chin.

I'd tried climbing through that slightly open window into his emotions while we were away, but just like he was doing now, he'd shut me out so quickly I had to check that my fingers were still attached.

"What is this about, then? Finally admitting you're jealous?" I teased.

"Of course I'm fucking jealous." He picked up the e-reader again, his knuckles drained of color, clenching it so tight I thought it would crack from the sheer force.

"It's insanely hot seeing you two together," he said, sweet lust scenting the air around us. "But it also reminds me of what I can't have with her. Regardless, that's not why I'm staying here. I just need to be done with this case—with headquarters and their bullshit."

So that's what this was. Either way, Oakley was going to be hurt by it. Even if I tried to explain it to her myself, which it wasn't my place to.

"She was disappointed you didn't come with me earlier and that you weren't coming tonight."

"Look, I'm disappointed enough in myself right now. For that and a whole slew of reasons." He swallowed hard, the ball in his throat rolling. "I need a night to get my head on straight. She deserves to have a nice reunion with one of us. I'd be shitty company if I went."

"And how is that different from your usual?" I chuckled, then sat on my heels, accepting I'd lost this battle.

He waved me off. "Just get going."

"Want me to bring you a *doggie bag*?" I teased, knowing he'd be too curious to resist. That earned a pillow smack to the face.

"I hate you so much for asking that," he gritted out, rightfully pissed. Sometimes pushing him was the only way to elicit a reaction, though, and I was tired of watching him hide. Not when we were so close to having everything we both wanted with her.

Before I said another word, his e-reader was back to blocking me from view. Maybe one day he'd stop being his own worst enemy.

But that wouldn't be today.

In the meantime, I had a witch to spend the evening with —and I refused to waste another minute.

))(((●)))((

"Yes, sis," Hazel whooped as I walked out back after saying goodnight to Aspen who'd managed to fall asleep just before I arrived. Oakley was already posed within the carved hexagon perched in the yard. She held each diagonal, legs settled in the corners beneath her, rocking strappy nude heels and looking like a Goddess-damned queen. "Really sink into that hip."

Oakley shifted her curves, gripping the wood, crystals swaying in the autumn breeze. Her body looked incredible, but her eyes were anxious, shoulders slightly too tense. Insecurity casting a pale-green highlight around her.

"Didn't realize we were getting a special audience tonight," Hazel called out over her shoulder. "But while you're here, think you could help my sister remember how stinking hot she is?"

"Happy to." Taking a few steps closer, I brought my hand across my chest, reminding my heart not to beat right out of it. My attention roved over the lace bodysuit that clung to every beautiful inch, mesh covering most of it, aside from a few strategically placed stars—a constellation I couldn't wait to trace with my fingers. My tongue. "You're absolutely spellbinding, Wicked."

I sprinkled some sweet seduction her way, savoring how her cheeks flushed and her chestnut gaze became hooded when it locked with mine.

That's my witch.

The switch had been flipped, and for a moment, I forgot anyone else was there. She was eye-fucking the shit out of me, and I was tempted to drop to my knees and crawl to her altar for some proper worship.

Hazel's voice cut into my thoughts. "Got it. Thanks for helping her out, Lynx."

I blinked rapidly, watching Oakley move out of position and stride toward me. She looped a finger around my belt and dragged me to her by my hip. "You think you're the only one who can play that game? Think again."

Fuck. Me.

I placed a hand on the small of her back, leading her inside. You never knew when someone could be out in the pines or snooping from their windows around here. "Saros will be sad he missed this."

At the mention of Saros, her face fell, and I instantly regretted my words, fumbling for some way to comfort her. "He had a pretty rough time at headquarters. Being there just brings up...things he'd rather forget."

When she didn't respond, disappointment clawing along her sides in dull charcoal grays, I added, "He needed a night to unplug and be solo."

The garage door was hanging open, several outfits hanging on the rack set against the opposite wall. "Are those your other designs?"

"They are," she replied, pride brightening her words in a beautiful rainbow.

"You keep them in the garage?"

"Yeah." She shrugged, heading in that direction, gesturing with a nod for me to follow her. "It's my studio for now."

"For now?"

I joined her, sifting through the designs on the rack, each one more delectable than the last. I wanted to see her in them all, lace and satin caressing my skin while I fucked her senseless. To clutch them in my fingers as I peeled them away and took her again with nothing between us.

"Yeah, there's a space that's available in Mystic Square that I'm thinking about renting."

"That's an amazing location. You should snag it." Rocking on my heels, I retreated a few steps and slipped my hands in my pockets, trying to stoke out my half-mast erection.

I scanned over the seemingly hundreds of designs papering the walls, swatches of fabric tacked around them. It was like a window into her creative mind, and it had me in awe.

"I don't have the funds to invest in it just yet. Atlas offered to handle it for the first year while I get on my feet, but—"

"You should take him up on it."

Confusion spread across her face. "Really?"

"Yeah. It would be an amazing opportunity for you."

"But wouldn't it be weird for me to accept that help from him?"

I shrugged. "You're the mother of his child. You paused your dreams in order to raise your son. This seems like more than a fair offer."

Her lips pressed together, an expression I was all too used to from Saros. The thought of him grumbling at home, looking over our case files flitted through my mind, but I brushed it away. He'd made his choice. I'd help him later. Right now, I needed this.

Her.

It'd been too freaking long since we'd been together, but I'd thought about it every single day. Yes, playing with her from a distance was incredible, but to be a few feet away, within reach of the feel of her... Nothing beat it.

Other than if Saros hadn't been such a shit and had joined us like I knew he was desperate to. Oh well. I'd just have to make her come for the both of us.

"How are things going with the Archon, by the way?" I

asked, hands still gripped tight in my pockets, digging crescents into my hips. There were a few other emotions flaring through her, but they were conflicting and moving so quickly I couldn't piece them together.

"Is that really just a *by the way*?"

"I have to admit, I'm curious where we stand now that he's back in the picture."

It would be easy enough to expect things were the same as where we'd left them, but the truth was he was here now. And I knew better than to think that didn't change things at all between the three of us—and him.

"We aren't together. There's nothing going on," Oakley assured me, closing the distance between us. Her hand traced along my belt, and she bit her bottom lip. "He will always be Aspen's father. I'll always care for him, but that's where it ends."

I inhaled deeply, trying to keep my mind focused on the topic at hand in case this was her way of deflecting. Not that I'd resist wherever it was headed. I'd follow her into Hell if she beckoned me there. "If that changes, Wicked—"

"It won't," she said, tone honed like a knife, cutting me off.

That's what I get for trying to manage emotions.

Her chest rose and fell, pale-orange frustration billowing between us like smoke. I stepped the fuck through it. I'd spent the last two weeks waiting to see her. I wouldn't let anything ruin this moment.

"If it does," I gripped her chin, willing her chestnut eyes to meet mine, "you deserve everything you want, Wicked. Whatever *you* decide is best for you and Aspen, I want to be a part of it." Her gaze softened, the pale-orange smoke curling in, disappearing into a pink warmth, flecks of sweet white powder cascading down on us, a blizzard of lust and an emotion I refused to name until she spoke the words. "I'm in this, Oakley. Are you?"

"I am," she whispered with a nod.

I covered her lips with my own, tasting her tongue with a swirl of my own. My hands ran along the lace of her bodysuit, thumbing over the constellation set across her ribs that zigzagged down in eight stars, the final one landing between her thighs.

"Wicked, if I didn't know any better, I'd think this design was constructed with me in mind," I said, kissing along her jaw and sliding a hand over that last star.

She moaned, sweet sugar flavoring the air as she gripped my shirt. "Perhaps."

My lips brushed along her neck, lowering to her collarbone, her sternum, before I lowered to my knees.

There it was, staring back at me. A collection of stars I'd gazed at too many nights to count growing up in the mortal world.

The Lynx constellation.

I arched a brow at her. "Well, it's only fair I get to test drive this new design, don't you think?"

She nodded.

"Hands on the hood, Wicked," I instructed, guiding her near the SUV. She pressed her palms against the metal, then leaned forward, arching her back, that final star nearly in sight, settled above a series of three small snaps.

"Wider." I ran my hand from just above her heel and up her thigh, nudging one foot out until she was spread before me like my own astral buffet. "Just like that."

Her breath hitched as I palmed her over the mesh, hooking my fingers around it and slowly undoing each snap. "I want to taste that Desire of yours straight from the source."

I groaned, feeling her soaked between my fingers. "Is this all for me?"

"Yes." She nodded eagerly. Then she whimpered, pushing into my palm.

"Yeah it is, Wicked." Removing my shirt, I threw it to the side. Then I stared at that perfectly pink, lickable treat made for me. "And I'm going to have you gushing soon enough."

Lust sweetened the air around us, making me salivate. My cock strained against my zipper, begging to drive into her glistening pussy.

She yelped in surprise when my lips kissed the top of her thigh, trailing over every perfect inch of her before nipping her ass.

"Oh!"

Clear nectar flowed out from her, every delicious drop lapped by my tongue. It'd been so long since I'd gotten to taste her, and tonight, she was all mine.

Mine to cherish.

Mine to devour.

Her legs stuttered on either side of my face, and I reached up, grabbing her ass, kneading it as I continued to lap at her pussy. She shook, arching and searching for friction.

"I-I need you inside me," she heaved, fingernails scraping the metal of the hood.

"Soon." I moved one hand from her perfectly round ass, and slid two fingers into the warmth of her center, curling them in earnest against the spot I knew would drive her wild. Pink smoke billowed around her skin like a brilliant stage light, encouraging me to push her, to give her everything she deserved. To wring out every ounce of pleasure from her.

"You trust me, don't you?" I whispered against her, peppering kisses along the tops of her thighs.

She groaned but nodded, hips dancing around as she rode my hand as best she could.

"Relax for me, Wicked."

I strummed her insides with my fingers, increasing the pressure, lips wrapping around her clit. She quaked beneath my touch, spurring me on with her whimpers. But I wasn't stopping there.

I wanted every last drop from my witch. And she was about to give it to me.

She just didn't know it yet.

"*Oh my Goddess,*" she slurred, her lust whipping into something thick and decadent.

"That's my good witch," I whispered. Her ass lifted higher, exposing more of her beautiful pussy to me, and I dove even deeper, continuing to make her shake in my grasp.

"*Oh, oh, oh,*" she chanted with a final guttural cry that probably could be heard from the street, but I didn't fucking care. Not when a gorgeous gush of fluid streamed down my lips. I beamed, pleased with how well I'd satisfied my witch.

"*Mmm.*" I slowly removed my fingers, lapping up every drop of her.

Her shaking ceased and she took a step forward, leaning against the hood, chest heaving.

My cock was bursting at the seams to be inside her, to be drenched in her warmth.

"Someone's happy with themselves," she said, pink painting her cheeks. "I don't think I've ever—"

"Oh, Wicked, why do you think I'm so pleased?" I helped her stand, turning her around and lifting her onto the hood before settling between her thighs. "I knew you had it in you. And, Goddess, you taste fucking incredible. I will be requesting an encore."

"You better," she heaved, voice sultry with satisfaction and need.

She unsnapped the button of my jeans and unzipped them, assisting me as I wriggled them and my boxer briefs down my hips. Then she wrapped her hand around me, sliding my tip against her glistening center. I lowered her onto the hood before pressing into her an inch, taking in her breathtaking beauty. Her hair lay in loose curls framing her face, eyes half drunk in her post-pleasure haze.

"Lock those legs around me," I gritted out, sinking into her. "So. Fucking. Perfect."

I looked down at the constellation adorning her, missing one star that would have been right where my cock was now driving. Gripping one hand under her ass, I lifted her hips a bit, burying myself as far as I could within her.

"*Lynx*," she whimpered, head thrown back, breasts bouncing in time with my thrusts. Her legs wrapped around my waist, pussy clenching like she wanted to grip every damn inch. My balls tightened, electricity shooting down my spine.

Locking my eyes with hers, I sucked in a breath, trying to hold on for her. "Come for me, Wicked."

She cried out, squeezing my body between her thighs like a boa constrictor until my cock was so deep I no longer knew where she ended and I began. I rocked my hips, spilling into her in dizzying spurts that lasted what felt like an eternity.

Pink swirled around us. I leaned down, scooping under her torso to drag her to me, kissing her over and over, my tongue and lips and shared Empathy telling her everything I'd never be able to articulate. How much I needed her —*needed* us. I pulled out an inch before plunging my cock back into her, making her groan against my lips. When I lifted my head, she brushed the strands of my hair away from my eyes.

"I think all the designs will need to be officially tested—for quality assurance purposes, of course. Don't you agree?" I exhaled with a smile.

"Yes." She nodded, attention flitting to the rack full of clothes behind us.

"Grab something else and get right back here," I said, slowly easing out of her. Then I helped her off of the hood before giving her ass a gentle smack. Oakley strode over to the lingerie, the sight of me streaking her inner thighs making me groan and palm my cock, growing hard again.

She quickly slipped on a sheer black corset with a matching G-string, not once moving to wipe between her legs. When she returned, I drew a constellation of kisses along her neck.

"That's my witch."

I hopped onto the hood and then lifted her on top of me. When she sank onto my cock, my earlier release coated her as she slid up and down my shaft. Her eyes were soft, never leaving mine, a cloud of pink enveloping us both.

"What does the pink mean?" she asked, gaze drifting above my head.

"It means I'm yours, Wicked." I clasped her hands, bringing them to my chest and holding them there. "And I'm never letting you go."

After pushing the crib against the jet-black wall, I stepped back, ensuring it was centered within the nursery. Silhouetted treetops poked up from the carpet with dragons hovering above them, flying among the clouds. Then I nudged the crib a few inches to the right and reappraised the room.

Toadstool seats peppered the reading nook, an open hollow tree installed into the corner with books flitting within its bark. It'd taken me three tries to get the enchantment to work.

Worth it.

Some of the books were new ones I'd picked up at the local shop, others were yellowed, crumpled around the edges from the years—books from my own childhood. An old set of intricately patterned fairy wings hung from the wall, a family heirloom.

I was used to growing up with busy parents, busy grandparents, but I had so many fond memories of story times nestled up in my bedroom, staring up at those wings.

Now I'd be able to do the same thing with my son. Something I'd dreamed about since even before learning of Oakley's pregnancy. Of course, in my visions she was here with me, Aspen tucked between us as we regaled him with our favorite stories like "Goodnight Moon Goddess" or "The Little Hearse that Could."

Even though she'd made it clear that we couldn't be together romantically, I'd hold out hope until my dying day that she'd come around. In the meantime, I was grateful to be closer to her and our son, to make memories together, even if those memories were all G-rated and revolved around giving Aspen everything he deserved.

A flash of gray passed the door. I'd nearly forgotten the servicemen were still here. It'd been two hours of them getting the house adjusted per my very specific instructions.

I stole another glance of the room before following their project head, a greed demon named Walt, down the hallway, spotting a few other supernaturals working around the house. When Walt noticed the sound of my footsteps, he turned around, clipboard held tightly in his blueish-tinged hand.

It made sense his kind would want to work for Pierce Protections. There was good money in it, and he would be making a fair share of house calls with how rapidly the company was doing installations.

"Are you almost done?"

"Yes." Walt scanned over the checklist on his clipboard. "We've babyproofed the lower level and most of this one. Just have a few more spots to do, like the cabinets and staircase."

"And you checked on the system as well? Made sure it's up to date?"

"We did. This was one of the first systems we installed. It's got all the bells and whistles and now the additions you've requested." He flipped through the screen on his phone until he came to one with bars lit up at different levels, but I couldn't make out the labels from where I stood. "However, since the house monitors itself for any issues so it can self-repair and learn your preferences, it does take some time for that to take effect."

"Learn?" Just when you thought you understood magic, it'd find a way to surprise you.

"Yes. You may have to cast it to your specifications manually, but within a few days it should be able to predict the temperature you want, when to light areas, turn the privacy glass off and on, etc."

"How is that possible?" I walked over to the rectangular panel boasting about twenty buttons on the wall by the kitchen.

"Pierce Protections secret," Walt replied with a slight lift of his brows.

He probably had no fucking clue. But Wade Pierce next door would——whenever he returned from his business trip. It made sense he traveled a lot, Pierce Protections had nearly serviced our entire street and had begun work on some of the others, including many in other supernatural districts.

I sent off a message to my assistant to set up a meeting for whenever he was in town.

"What about 13?" I asked Walt.

"What about it?" He moved toward the kitchen, but I held up a hand, catching his attention. I knew I probably shouldn't ask—it really wasn't my business—but... "Is their house up to date with all its security measures?"

His gaze darted toward the house situated on Starry Night Lane's main road, the last one before it curved into its cul-de-sac.

"Should be." Walt gave me the side-eye, probably wondering why I was asking. But I narrowed my gaze, waiting for him to tell me more. "Granted, they didn't opt for as elaborate of a set up as this house. It was installed only a few months ago, so it should be settling in."

"Settling in?" I'd heard of foundations settling, but not home systems.

"They take a bit to reach full functionality, drawing on the power of the home's tenants."

Interesting.

"So you're saying there wasn't enough magic to fully power it before? But now there is?"

"Yes, sir." Walt pulled out his phone, flipping through some app I didn't recognize.

"And their house? It's at full functionality?"

"Yeah." He shrugged. "I'm guessing the delay was caused by the owner needing a full moon juice-up. Looks like there haven't been any issues since the last one."

I'd been so distracted between getting the house set up and the case I'd been overseeing, I hadn't put two and two together. Of course, I'd seen her use her magic at the pumpkin patch, but that was a small enchantment—not enough to power a self-regulating home system. To channel that much magic, she'd need to have come over and over under the full moon.

Not that it was my business.

I swallowed down the heat radiating through my chest, reminding myself she did have Hazel there with her now. Maybe that's why there'd been a power surge.

"Fascinating." My phone vibrated, **Clio Meeting**.

"I'm so sorry, but I forgot I have a meeting. If you can let me know when you're on the way out, that would be wonderful."

"Of course, sir." Walt nodded curtly, heading toward the kitchen.

I headed toward the office and then dialed her number the minute I'd shut the door. With the Moonlit Masquerade just around the corner, I didn't want to miss finalizing the details. "Hey, Clio."

"Archon Thorne," she replied in her sweet, overly attentive voice. "Hope you're doing well."

"I am." I pulled my charming politician tone to the forefront, but my mind wandered to Oakley. The thought of her under the moonlight, skyclad, its buttery glow spread over her skin while she came—no doubt thinking of how good we were together, hand between her thighs.

"I got it," Clio said, giddiness bubbling through her tone.

Focus, Atlas.

"You were able to secure the amp?" I shifted in my seat, willing down my body's response to my overeager imagination.

Clio huffed through the line. "Did you have any doubts?"

"As always, you continue to amaze me." I brought up my email, scrolling to the most recent one from her, looking through what we'd need for it to work. "This party is going to be unforgettable."

"Of course it will be, Archon," she replied. "It'll arrive tomorrow morning, and I'll be there to help get everything situated."

"Thank you, Clio. Talk soon."

Clicking off my phone, my thoughts went to the jack-o'-lanterns floating within the branches of the trees in front of Oakley's house and all the elaborate decorations she'd spelled this year, along with the relaunch of her shop.

I waved my hand in front of me, watching her auburn waves, sin-inducing curves, and large chestnut irises come to life. Since she'd left, I'd done this—conjured her mirage. Even though I knew this was all in my head, that she wasn't really here, it somehow felt less lonely.

My witch had reclaimed her magic.

What had changed her mind?

Whatever it was, maybe there was a chance she'd be open to reclaiming *us*...

CHAPTER 10

OAKLEY

The next morning was a blur of motherhood and preparations for the relaunch, and before I knew it, Aspen had gone down for his long midday nap.

Lynx said Saros would be by in the morning. He'd even reminded me of that fact before he left.

Now it was 1:00 p.m. and Saros had never come by.

Picking up my phone, I swiped through for any missed messages, but there were none. Then I looked out the window, spotting a dark shadow moving within Luna's lit truck.

Anger flared through me. I still had a trace of Lynx's Empathy. If I wanted to know how Saros felt, there wasn't much more time until the effects ran out. The longest I'd ever had access to someone's gift was twelve hours, and I doubted I'd somehow now have more than that.

Hazel's bedroom door creaked open, and she slipped her phone into her back pocket.

"Do you have any showings this afternoon?" I asked, still fixated on the truck and the faux-brewista within.

"Nope. Just some contracts to draw up, but I can do that

later." Her attention shifted to where I was looking. "Need me to keep an ear out for my bestie?"

"Do you mind?" I needed to see Saros, to understand what the hell was going on between us—or not going on, at this point. He kept his emotions so tucked into his chest, I couldn't miss this opportunity to peel back what truly lay beneath that gruff exterior. "I hate to put you out."

"It's not a big deal," Hazel said, pointing at the door. "Go see him. Just don't forget we are visiting Mystic Square in a few hours with Atlas so you can walk through the space and make a decision."

Ugh. "Don't remind me."

I was just grateful she'd be there. The pumpkin patch family outing was hard enough.

"Thanks, Haze," I said, darting into my room. Looking into the mirror, I lifted my T-shirt, making sure I had on one of my new bras, the nursing pads discreetly slipped into the added pockets. When I dropped the hem back down, I noticed a few splattered food stains, so I quickly changed and put on a plain black dress with plunging neckline and a long slit up one of the legs.

Yes, it was completely impractical mom attire, but I needed every confidence weapon in my arsenal to do this.

I threw on my booties, then waved quickly at Hazel before I stomped out the door. No one was out in the cul-de-sac, the morning rush far over. Rarely anyone went by Luna's in the afternoon. It was usually when the guys prepped things for the coming day and got ready to close up. In fact, it should be closing within the hour, so I didn't feel bad catching Saros there before he had a chance to duck out and hide at home.

Pale-blue rippled from him when he noticed me. That was, until I skipped the window and walked right around to the door, twisting the knob and pulling it open. I stepped up one stair, poking my head in. "You have a minute?"

"I have more than a minute for you, Midnight." He finished drying off the coffeepot with the towel half hanging from his shoulder before returning it to the machine. Despite his calm exterior, a popping sensation fizzled out from him. It felt...anxious. I was still trying to figure out how the emotions appeared to me; I'm sure it would take some practice.

"What's going on?" he asked.

Be brave, Oakley.

"Is there a reason you didn't come by yesterday?" I took a deep breath to get out the bigger question that had hung over me like a thick storm cloud. "Are you ghosting me?"

"Why would you even think that?" His brows furrowed, evergreen eyes glaring at me and making me feel naked. Vulnerable.

"I don't know. I just thought that before you left—while you were gone—I thought there was something growing between us. Then you come into town and *nothing*," I muttered, quickly averting my eyes from his. "Plus, Lynx said you'd be by this morning, and you never showed or texted."

"It was a busy morning, and I was trying to catch up on things since we just got back." He cocked his head to the side, crossing his arms. "Lynx not satisfactory enough on his own last night?"

The previous heaviness that'd settled around him seemed to lift into something brighter, like amusement.

He thought this was funny.

My chest and cheeks heated. "I'm plenty satisfied with Lynx. It's *you* I'm struggling with."

That managed to suck that emotion straight out of the small truck, Saros's lips pressing into their usual firm line. "Look, I didn't come by last night because I needed to decompress and rid myself of the reek of headquarters. I hate that fucking place. I hate what they want me to be for them there."

That was the most candid he'd ever been with me, red wisps of smoke slipping from his skin. My heart stuttered in my chest. "And what's that?"

"A monster." His hands were balled into fists at his sides, the air tinged with something metallic. "My *gift* makes everyone's jobs a lot easier. But memories aren't always full. They are subjective, and they should be fucking private. I have an ability that has no business existing."

I stepped toward him and reached out a hand, wanting to brush my fingers over the tension coiled in his palms. "I get it—"

"No, you don't, Oakley." He retreated out of my grasp, looking at his shoes. "You don't have people threatening your livelihood if you don't use your gifts the way they want. You don't have to look people in the eye knowing things you wish you never did about them. Things you can't forget." He released a heavy exhale. "I witness the worst moments of people's lives. I live through them when they relive them for me."

"What do they want you to do?" My hands itched for something to hold onto, so I gripped the counter, resisting the urge to touch him.

"They want me to rifle through Aurora's memories, even though she and her lawyer have already said no. They want me to hunt for evidence of how Acacia is tied to the disappearances and possibly the Wellses. And they don't care that it's illegal or unethical. They just like that it's easy."

"Easy for them," I huffed, anger boiling in my bones.

"I'm sorry I didn't come by earlier today. I honestly didn't know where we stood." He stepped closer, placing his hand on the counter a foot away from mine. "You and Lynx were together first, then we shared that incredible full moon and then shit hit the fan. Now Thorne is here, and—"

"And what?"

His fingers began tapping nervously against the countertop. "I've touched you enough to know there's more between you two than you let on." His lips turned downward, and he cast his gaze to the floor. "I've seen it."

"Seen what, exactly?"

He avoided making eye contact with me. "Glimpses. Some things more romantic, others more...intimate." Something acidic and green bubbled from him before disappearing. "I'm sorry. I'm sure that's embarrassing to know, but I just can't get it out of my head."

"So you didn't want to come over because you have seen my ex and I *in the past*?"

His fingers stopped their tapping before he slipped them into his pocket. "First of all, I really was in a horrible mood and didn't want to ruin your reunion with Lynx. You deserved better than that. But I'll admit, part of me didn't want to see you yet because seeing you with Atlas—seeing you with Lynx —it makes me want... Never mind."

"Want what, Saros?" I closed the distance by about half, leaving a handful of inches between us for his own comfort. Did the idea of being with me now disgust him? I needed to understand. "Tell me now or I'm walking away and not coming back."

"It makes me want that for myself." He towered over me like a beautiful dark pine bending in the fall breeze. "Want you for myself."

He lifted his hand, ghosting it along my neck and shoulder without touching me, but I felt its effect no less. "I don't care if you want them, but it infuriates me that I can't give you *that*." His breath was a caress, filtering down my body and drilling deep into my core. "I'm stuck stroking myself to the scraps that Lynx shares with me afterward, like some starved junkyard dog." His voice rose in anger, a few smoky red tendrils drifting away from him as he stepped away, like he needed the distance. "The pleasure he gets to have with you... He gets to *give* you..."

Oh.

"I want it to be *my* tongue on your clit, making you shake beneath my lips; *my* cock notched deep inside you as you scream my name; *my* cum painting your insides."

Well damn.

"I want that too." My mind flitted to last night and the hours I'd spent in blissful rapture with Lynx. The idea that he'd gone and shown it to Saros... My thighs clenched, underwear becoming damp at the thought. "But why can't we—"

Something metallic settled at the back of my throat, like the air had filled with iron. "I won't risk burdening you with my curse, even if it's temporary. And Goddess only knows what would happen if anyone found out you could borrow my gift—or any other rare ability for that matter. That would put you in danger."

Huh?

"What do you mean?" My heart began to race, the idea of any more threats to my family sending me into self-preservation mode.

"There are powers out there that are extremely rare. Yes, your Desire is rare, but being able to borrow other people's gifts... If your ability's existence were to be known by the wrong people, who knows what they'd try to do with it."

I'd never thought about it that way. Atlas worked for the government, and he'd never presented it with so much fear behind it, but we had also been diligent about keeping that part of my moon-blessed gift a secret. Besides, there wasn't much I could do with borrowing his gift other than creating some illusions.

"But couldn't we still...you know, work around the transference if you're that worried about it? Like what we did the night of the full moon?" I offered. That night had been incredible. I'd felt no less connected to him, even if he wasn't the one plunging into me. The pleasure we shared, the intimacy of it all, it was just as strong. "I don't understand why we can't be together in that way... Don't you want that?"

"More than anything, Midnight." He stared at me with an intensity that had me feeling more bared than I had been beneath the moonlight that night in the pines. "But if I'm going to be inside you, I don't want either of us holding back from the other. I want you to crave me as much as I crave you."

"Saros—"

"Do you understand now?" Rich magenta pulsed from him, fading in and out. "It's not that I don't want you. I want you so much it's physically painful to resist being near you. Because I know when I touch or kiss you I will see glimpses, whether you want me to or not. And worst of all, I can't give you those things you want—things you deserve."

Goddess, this witch.

"I won't give up a future with you because of my past. I'll take whatever you're willing to give." Maybe we were two mutts scrounging for scraps from each other, but I'd rather be a junkyard dog with him than without.

I wouldn't touch him until he said it was okay. No matter how much I knew we both wanted it, I needed his words.

His choice.

The ball of his Adam's apple bobbed, and in two strides, he gripped my neck, surging onto my lips.

"What if someone sees?" I heaved between kisses, starting to twist my head toward the window.

"No one comes by this late in the day." He walked me backward until his hips pinned me against the side of the truck, lifting me until my legs were wrapped about him. He continued to stroke my tongue with his own, groaning into my mouth, the hard bulge straining in his jeans grinding against me.

Goddess, I wanted this. I wanted *more*.

But I wouldn't push him.

Hooking his hands under my ass, he carried me to the counter and pushed the coffee machine off to the side to perch me there. Hiking up my dress by its slit, he spread my thighs wide, settling between them. Magenta pulsed faintly from him, warming my body, his gaze trailing over every inch and landing on my panties. He supported me while I lifted my hips, wriggling them down until they dropped from my feet onto the floor.

Then he knelt down, focus glued to my sex.

"Goddess above, Midnight." He licked his lips. "You're soaked."

My instinct was to squirm, feeling so exposed, light beaming in from the midday sun through the window. But here Saros was, showing me what he wanted.

Us.

I wouldn't allow my insecurity or nerves to stop this.

"Warn me when you're close?"

I nodded. "I will."

Maybe it wasn't everything we wanted, but it was *something*. I could warn him, then use my Desire to get us both—

He dove tongue first into my folds, the magenta continuing to pulse from him hitting me in waves, his desire blanketing my body with the scent of freshly baked brownies. I leaned against the truck's wall as his large, callused hands gripped my thighs, pushing them even wider.

He shoved his tongue deep into me, twisting it in divine circles, bringing one hand to cover my womb, pinning me in place.

Oh Goddess.

Saros devoured me with singular purpose. My gift flowed to the surface, wanting an escape.

"Midnight," he growled.

Desire spilled from my fingertips in response, slamming into him.

His tongue kept working, but he released my thigh, the sound of his zipper the only indication of what he was doing. I brought my chin down, overcome with the need to see. He stroked himself in earnest, eyes on me as he ate me greedily, a glistening bead brimming from his tip.

Using one hand to steady myself, I twisted my other, floating the translucent drop of precum and sticking out my tongue to catch it. I hummed, loving the taste of his craving flitting across my taste buds.

It spurred him on. Growling, he speared me with his tongue, then moved up to nip at my clit. I jerked against his face, gripping his scalp.

"I'm getting close," I warned, beginning to wriggle my hips away, trying to tamp down the delicious pressure building deep in my belly.

"Stay with me, Midnight." His eyes pleaded from between my thighs. "I haven't had my fill."

I nodded, taking a deep breath, not wanting this to end. I sent more magic toward his cock, and he jerked it wildly, chasing his release.

"Saros, I need you to come," I whimpered, desperate to watch him fall apart with me on his tongue. *"Please."*

Puffs of magenta filled the truck, fading in and out. Tendrils of red smoke mixed into the vibrant hue, drawing my eyebrows together. Saros roared against me, sucking my clit between his lips in pulsing waves while he unleashed.

He groaned, shoving his glistening fingers deep inside me, curling them until my body was shaking while he twisted his tongue around my sensitive bud.

The crimson smoke tainted the magenta further, its trail leading outside the window.

My breath hitched, and I craned my neck toward the thin wisps, finally spotting their source. Atlas stood out in the cul-de-sac, glaring at us with white-knuckled fists balled at his sides, his chest rising and falling rapidly.

Then he broke his stare, his gaze drifting down Saros's head buried between my thighs.

I couldn't breathe, my body in complete shock as his red smoke twisted into magenta tendrils of desire.

"Oh my Goddess," I choked out.

His fists were still clenched, but his attention didn't move, his rage and lust pulsing over us as Saros continued to devour me.

Ecstasy coiled deep in my belly.

"You're so worked up. Did Lynx get you this wet last night?" Saros whispered, his wicked words licking up my center. "I saw you gush for him, Midnight. One day I'll have you gushing for me."

Atlas's focus narrowed. I moved to wriggle from Saros's grasp, but he curled his fingers faster, chasing my pleasure with his tongue.

My attention was pinned to Atlas, the aqua of his irises glinting with something akin to possessive want, magenta and red fading in and out around him. The edges of his eyes softened despite his glare, and a glimpse of the bulge in his slacks caught my notice, untethering that coiled knot in my belly.

I parted my lips to warn Saros just as he nipped my clit. Stars burst in my vision, and I clamped a hand over my mouth to stifle my scream in release.

Oh shit, oh shit, oh shit.

Saros didn't have the chance to get out of reach fast enough. The space between my quivering legs that once held him was now replaced with cold emptiness as the rush of his Recollection flooded my veins.

He grabbed a few towels, spelling them to clean us both up without saying a word. Then he knelt down to wipe up the floor, very intentionally making sure to keep away from me.

When I glanced back out the window, Atlas was gone.

I jumped off the counter, pulling my dress down around myself, wishing I could crawl into a hole somewhere and never come out.

How the fuck did I let this happen?

"I-I'm so sorry," I said, body still shaking from the after-shocks of my release. "I got distracted. Atlas—"

"You were thinking about Atlas?" Saros accused.

"No," I shot back, anger flaring through me. But how could I admit that Atlas watching us together had lit the match, despite promising to warn Saros? There was no good way to say this, and I was still so confused by the entire exchange. "Atlas saw us." I pointed to the open window. "He knows."

I'd managed to make Atlas and Saros hate me in one fell swoop.

"You're sure?" Saros rubbed the back of his neck, and I wished more than ever that I saw his emotions in this moment, to know we would be okay, but Lynx's borrowed magic had vanished.

A buzzing came from the counter, and Saros lunged for it, frowning when he tapped the message.

"What is it?"

He held the screen up to show me.

ATLAS:

Went by Luna's. Obviously wasn't a good time. Need to meet to discuss next steps. 3 p.m.

"Fuck. I need to go," Saros said. "And so do you."

I nodded, refusing to meet his gaze, and descended the stairs. A moment later, my own phone buzzed. I grabbed it, awaiting the onset of an all-caps message from Atlas. But instead it was Hazel.

HAZEL:

Rain check on visiting Mystic Square. Atlas got called to a last-minute meeting.

He hadn't even texted me himself. My hands shook the entire walk home, wondering who was more screwed in this scenario: me or Saros.

Oakley was off somewhere with my power right now and no clue how to use it. Not that telling her everything it could do would be much safer for her. It was probably better for her to accidentally touch someone and witness their worst moments.

Goddess, how did I get so carried away?

And what the hell was about to happen in this meeting?

The front door had opened on its own when we arrived, a note left on the entryway panel to head to Atlas's office and wait for him there. Lynx leaned back into one of the chairs, hands clasped behind his neck, fully relaxed. Meanwhile, I sat with my feet pressed to the floor, elbows perched on my knees. His attention narrowed on me, doing his inconvenient empath thing.

The sound of footsteps echoed down the hall.

We both stood up quickly.

The door swung open smoothly, perfectly in tune to his pace, which was eerie enough, but the calm expression trained on his face was what was truly terrifying.

He was a politician, though. Maybe the face he used for

hiding political scandal was the same he used for coping with seeing his ex spread eagle for another witch.

"Agent Carver. Agent Holt," he said with a quick nod to each of us before striding around his desk and gesturing for us to sit down.

"Archon," we replied in unison with a bow of our heads, taking a seat.

He pulled out some small files from the tiny lockbox in the corner, swishing them in the air so they'd become full size before handing two to us and keeping one for himself. "I received word that the meeting we requested has been accepted. Everyone is in except for the aquatic folks, not that they were likely anyway."

"But everyone else has?" Lynx asked, thumbing through the file with his brows lifted. "Even the Vivaldi Syndicate?"

"Yes, even them."

I scanned over the contents. It seemed like shifters, vamps, and demons alike were concerned about the strange exodus of supernaturals from Celestial Haven.

"That going to be a problem for you, Agent Holt?" My name on his mouth sounded like an insult this time, whatever façade he'd come in with slowly crumbling.

Lynx looked like he'd just choked on something.

I brought my gaze back to the file, making sure I memorized the different players who would be at the meeting. Some I'd met during previous jobs; some I'd rather never see again. "No, Archon."

"Good." Smugness rolled over his tone. "The point of this meeting is to find out if any of the other areas in and around Celestial Haven have been affected with these odd disappearances. No one has been willing to do a face-to-face until now, which tells me something's changed to make them agree to speak with us."

My eyes snapped up. That definitely had my attention. Some of these groups were rivals... The idea that they were willing to meet over a seemingly witches-only issue definitely piqued my interest. "Any idea what?"

"No." He pursed his lips, browsing through the file. "But if other communities are being hit, then we need to know."

When he looked up, he shifted his attention to Lynx like I wasn't even there. "Agent Aleander is also coming. The four of us are the only ones they are allowing into the meeting." *Could this day get any better?* "Dante Vivaldi personally requested you, Agent Holt. Must have made *some impression* on the mafioso."

His inflection over the words had me shifting uncomfortably in my seat. What was he even implying? Was this about Vivaldi or what had happened at Luna's with Oakley?

"Outside of the vamps, we've got shifters and the Nephilim?" Lynx asked, as if trying to draw us from whatever silent standoff was happening.

"That's right," Atlas said to him. Very clearly *him*—not me. "Look over their files again, see if there's anything we should know before going into the meeting."

"Where's it being held?" I asked, not surprised when his attention stayed pinned distinctly to the left of me.

"Magical speakeasy tucked off Market Street." Atlas shut the folder and put it back on the desk. "I'll send the coordinates once the exact timing is nailed down."

"Sounds good." Lynx waved his file, and it shrank before he tucked it into the hidden compartment in his phone case. "Is there anything else, Archon?"

"No, Agent Carver. You may go. I'd like your partner to stay just a moment."

Fuck.

Lynx's eyes darted to me, but when I didn't give him any

indication what this could be about, he nodded at Atlas, scratching his head and looking between us before leaving the room.

Taking a deep breath, I got to the point. "I'm not sure exactly what you saw—"

"Well, you were very distracted by my—Oakley at the time," he seethed.

He stood and came around to sit where Lynx had been. His hands were clenched at his sides, knuckles devoid of color. Gone was the smooth politician I'd come to know, replaced by a vengeful witch who most likely wanted to hex me so I'd disappear like our case victims.

"I guess that answers that," I replied, then cleared my throat. There really wasn't a professional or graceful way around this one.

Atlas reached over and placed a hand on my shoulder like we were old pals. "Whatever is going on, it needs to stop." He pinched the bridge of his nose, face contorting before he sighed. "You are here for a case. Nothing more."

In a swirl of color, I was dangling over the side of a rocky cliff, the moon standing out among the darkness, lighting the water that rippled much too far below me. A quick glance over my shoulder confirmed who my assailant was, gripping the back of my collared shirt. I stared down at the pointed rocks jutting up from the water that sprayed and splashed with its violent current. I closed my eyes, inhaling the salty sea air, not allowing the fear to get to me.

This wasn't real.

Maybe this tactic worked on other witches, but Atlas should've known better than to think he could scare off or trick someone who often traversed into other people's memories. The visions always felt real, but I'd trained myself to stay grounded in these moments, flicking my finger a few times.

"Maybe we came here for a case but, respectfully, what Oakley wants is her call. Not yours."

He thought he could intimidate me with his hands, but I was as susceptible to his gift as he now was to mine. On the surface of his memories I was standing next to him, watching me devour Oakley.

"You should be focused on keeping up appearances with your *husband*," he gritted out. "I could have you sent back to headquarters over this."

"You could," I agreed, matching his arrogant tone with my own. The Archon may have had the power and prestige that came with his position, but I'd been through Hell and back at least twice while he enjoyed his silver-spoon upbringing. "But we both know she'd hate you for interfering. And that'd kill you more than what you saw this afternoon."

I continued to watch the memory, savoring it for my own. This was one of Atlas's worst moments of his life...and I didn't feel bad about it right now. Not in the least.

Goddess, she looked amazing. Her head falling back, auburn tresses wild as she quivered and whimpered from my touch. It was nice to know he had this visual engrained to memory. A literal mind fuck for Archon Atlas Thorne.

"I hope you don't miss the part when she came. Because her eyes were locked with *mine*." He chuckled in amusement. Then he released me as Oakley stared into his eyes. At first, she was shocked but then those chestnut pools glinted with lust, coming with my face buried between her legs. "I'd be careful thinking you know what Oakley wants. I made that mistake before and look where it got me."

And with that, he walked me toward the door of the office before it slammed shut—as if on its own—behind me.

Atlas's words trailed my every step down the long driveway heading toward Starry Night Lane.

I'd be careful thinking you know what she wants. I made that mistake before and look where it got me.

I came to a halt, staring across the cul-de-sac at the evergreen door.

Her door.

I needed to check on her, make sure she was okay after how we'd left things at Luna's. She probably thought I was angry at her for not warning me and borrowing my gift after I'd told her why it scared me so damn much.

And maybe I should have been.

But I wasn't.

Savoring her taste, her legs wrapped around my shoulders, her quaking against my tongue—it felt so right to give in with her, even if it wasn't as far as either of us wanted things to progress. She'd tried to warn me, but I'd pushed her, selfishly satisfied to own her pleasure in that moment.

When I was with her, I wanted to drown in her lust.

I'd gotten what I deserved.

Sure, I'd been forced to flit through the catalog of sexual escapades she'd had with other men. It filled me with momentary envy, I couldn't control that, but it was something I'd gotten used to over the decades. No one wanted to think about their lovers with someone else when they were intimate, but I could tether myself in reality after the initial flickers.

I'd pushed away the images, focusing on my grip around her thighs, the slick heat coating my fingers plunging in and out of her. For that brief moment, I knew that *I* was the one creating that memory, carving myself into her story. That next time I was with her, she'd recall how good I made her feel when we'd finally given in to the tension that pulled taut between us.

I hope you don't miss the part when she came. Because her eyes were locked with mine.

Atlas had every right to be pissed, to unleash the pain of catching us together in my direction.

And like a lightning bolt striking my very soul, it'd worked.

Fuck.

No matter how much I wanted to thieve that memory for myself, he'd managed to whittle himself into it, chipping away my claim of the moment.

So instead of carrying my feet forward toward her porch —I pivoted, heading into Luna's and locking the doors and windows up behind me.

CHAPTER 12

OAKLEY

"I'm so fucked."

I rocked frantically in the nursery, Aspen curled up eating happily. Hazel carried in the laundry and plopped onto the ground, picking out a sleeper with maple leaves falling toward its toes.

"Well you can't expect to be involved with three dicks and not be, sis," she teased, flicking her fingers so the fabric folded before drifting to start a pile on the floor.

My cheeks heated. "I'm only involved with two. The third involved himself."

"So he just stood there, watching Saros?"

"Yes." Goddess, the moment didn't stop replaying in my mind. It was so wrong. So, so wrong. "He was so angry, Haze."

"Until he wasn't." She smirked, eyes still on Aspen's clothes, folding them with her magic, the stack of sleepers growing by the minute.

"It was so strange." I still didn't fully understand what had happened. He could have stormed off. Could have told me off. Either would have been understandable. Deserved.

But he stayed.

Watched.

Hazel looked up at me, gaze narrowing. "Do you think you liked that he was watching? Or that he was pissed?"

"I'm not sure." I grimaced. "Is it horrible to say both?"

She chuckled, shaking her head. "Well, one of those probably has more to unpack than the other..."

It was no secret that my sister's sexual experience *far* surpassed mine, and even she seemed surprised by what had happened. That felt ominous for my sex life.

Being moon-blessed with Desire with a unique side-effect of gift-borrowing made me very picky about who I shared that part of myself with. Sometimes I'd even tried holding myself back so the transfer wouldn't happen, and with some lovers that wasn't too hard...but that quickly lost its appeal. It wasn't until Atlas had come along that it'd really changed for me. My gift didn't intimidate him. He'd loved seeing how I wielded it. For the first time in my life, I could be myself completely, without worry or judgment.

"I don't know... I think I was into *him* being into it. Maybe I'm going crazy."

"Look, sis," Hazel said, putting down another folded outfit and clasping her hands together, as if about to give me another sisterly lecture. I'd seen *the look* many times over the years. "Sexuality comes in all different flavors. Sounds like you both were into it."

"I'm not surprised that I am..." I mean I had been with Saros and Lynx together and there had been plenty of watching and participating happening. "But Atlas? He isn't the sharing type."

He'd always been extremely possessive. We never even went out into a public forest in our time together—always staying in his property's private woods for our moon rituals.

"Yeah." She pursed her lips a moment, as if to stop herself

from saying something. "And just because he was turned on doesn't mean he'd ever be willing to act on it. Maybe he was really into seeing your body all hot and bothered after it being a no-fly zone for him the last year."

She waggled her brows, trying to lighten the situation. Then they lifted, something mischievous glinting in her chocolate irises. "But if he was somehow willing to share—"

I held up a hand in protest. "Atlas and I can't be together, and I don't know if anything is possible with Lynx and Saros past this investigation. It's not worth going there, even hypothetically."

A tiny fist smacked my drained breast, and I looked down, finding Aspen's chestnut gaze and single-tooth smirk. Then he chomped down on my nipple.

"Fuck!" I screeched as piercing pain shot through my entire chest. I pulled him off immediately, checking for blood, sure a chunk was missing at a minimum. There was none but, Goddess, that fucker was sharp.

Aspen eyed my other swollen boob, reaching out and leaning his face forward. I inhaled some courage, holding my breath, then switched him to the other side. He wrapped his arms around my breast, latching tooth-free instantly.

Thank Goddess. Teething was a monsterfucker. I exhaled loudly.

My sister just stared in horror at the entire exchange.

"I love that little witchling, but he's a great reminder of why I'm good with being gremlin-free for life." She returned to her folding while I leaned back, enjoying the comfort of the tightness leaving my chest while Aspen fed.

"Anyway, maybe this whole thing happening at Luna's is a sign that you need to talk. To Atlas. To them. You can only avoid this for so long." Hazel's tone was calm but firm—the one she took on when she really wanted me to listen. "Especially Atlas."

"Yeah," I agreed. "We are supposed to take Aspen around the neighborhood trunk-or-treat tomorrow."

"That sounds like a perfectly fun time to talk," she joked.

I wasn't laughing. The fact that he'd canceled our walk-through of Mystic Square tonight was a small blessing, though. I had no idea what I would say. How would I face him and not think back to the fierce way his stare penetrated my soul and twisted from wild rage to intense pleasure?

"Any chance you want to come with?" I asked with a silent plea.

"I'll pass." Hazel chuckled. "But I'll totally snap some cute pics of that family costume before you head out."

Aspen finished his feed, and I laid him down in his crib before going over to help her put away the small stacks of his clothes. The side of my hand brushed hers, and she sucked in a breath. In an instant, I wasn't in the nursery, I was in a large black bedroom.

A mop of wild brown tresses spilled over a pillow, a hairy leg half hanging out from beneath the comforter.

Oh Goddess, please bring me out of this. If I was about to watch my sister get railed, I wanted to tap out. Immediately. Knowing about her superfluous sex life was one thing, witnessing it was another. Some things were better left to the imagination.

Everything felt warm. Comforting. Hazel turned away from the man that lay next to her, hand running over the other lump in the bed. The comforter moved and twisted around it.

"I love you," a feminine voice purred, eerily familiar—not Hazel's, though. The words came out genuine, sincere, and I could somehow feel the realness of them.

"You don't love me, you just love how I fuck," Hazel replied coolly.

I cringed, though I also had to give her props, my sister had the alpha-female thing down.

The comforter jostled, and the woman straddled Hazel, writhing against her.

My mouth went slack. The reality of this memory crashed into me like a tsunami, knocking my foundation off its axis.

Aurora Wells.

My hands shook at my sides, my gut twisting. I clamped my eyes shut—not that it did any good. The rumors had been true. Was that who she'd gone to meet the night she disappeared? Had she lied to me this entire time?

A phone on the nightstand began to buzz, and Fitzgerald's hairy arm reached over to pick it up and hand it to my sister. "Hello? ... Are you sure you don't want to reschedule?... Just some harmless fun... I see... Well, hopefully we'll find you something else soon."

She frowned and hung up the phone.

"Another one?" Aurora asked, looking at my sister with something akin to genuine concern.

"Yeah."

"Do you want me to talk to Sandra?" Fitz offered, sitting upright and putting his watch on, his wife still straddling my sister.

It was all so casual, like this was a normal occurrence.

My gut churned, acid boiling up my throat.

"If anyone is going to talk to her, it should be me. I'm her coveness."

"That won't be necessary." Hazel heaved a sigh. "They haven't even cared that the HOA has emailed them multiple times. I'll figure something out."

The nursery slammed back into view, but the vision of my sister and our former coveness was etched into my mind.

"You okay?" Hazel asked, careful not to touch me again.

"No," I said, still shaking from the vision. "Was something going on between you and the Wellses?"

My sister's face drained of all its color, then she turned on her heels, her footsteps echoing off the walls until her bedroom door *snicked* shut.

CHAPTER 13

LYNX

After three hours of looking over case files solo, the door swung open. Saros passed me on the bed and went straight into the bathroom.

"What happened back there?" I called to him, focused on the river of blue and red mixing into purple following each of his steps. "Where have you been?"

He washed his hands twice, then walked over to the board, staring at the orbs hovering there, brows furrowed. Pulling the case file out of his pocket, he shook it a few times until it was full size. Then he climbed into the bed and propped his feet up, reaching over to the nightstand for his glasses. Always a favorite look of mine.

If he thought I was just going to let it go, he knew better than that. There was only so much breathing room in Atlas's office with all the suffocating red smoke blanketing it. I was grateful to get out of there—until I had a moment to wonder what would have them both at odds.

I pivoted my body, sitting cross-legged and making it very apparent I was staring at him. He lifted the paper higher, as if to block me from view. Placing my fingertips on the edge, I lowered the sheet until his eyes met mine. His lips drew into a frown. "You going to tell me what happened or make me play the guessing game?"

A frustrated groan later, he'd put the paper down and turned to face me. "Oakley came by Luna's today as I was closing up. She was pissed I hadn't visited her since I'd gotten back, and we argued."

"Okay..." I said, not sure where this was going. "What does that have to do with Atlas?"

Saros's hands scraped his jeans, gaze lowered, anxiety bubbling up around him in pale-green pops. "He caught us...making up."

I couldn't stifle my smirk. "Making up how?"

His green eyes snapped to mine and he swallowed hard. "With my tongue twisted around her clit."

"So basically, you're lucky not to be a dead man?" I chuckled, not having to imagine too hard how horrible that must have been. Even Saros managed a huffed laugh at his own survival. "What did Oakley do?"

His lips flatlined. "She came."

"I feel like I'm missing pieces of the story here," I said, tilting my head, waiting for more of an explanation before I tried to talk him off whatever ledge he'd found himself on. The temptation to touch him, to calm him with my Empathy, was near irresistible, but I knew how much he hated that. So instead, I twiddled my fingers in my lap.

"We'd agreed she would warn me. It happened so quickly. One second she was coming on my tongue and the next she said he'd seen us." He shrugged, as if it would make the story less shocking if he pretended it was an everyday occurrence to get caught with your tongue in someone's cauldron. "Then I got the text about the meeting and... Well, you were there for that."

"How did you leave things with Oakley?" The silence and charcoal clouds of disappointment told me all I needed. "Shit. Saros—"

"Don't," he stopped me, holding up a hand.

"So now she has your powers? Did she see something?"

"I don't know." He inhaled deeply, pinching the bridge of his nose. "I may have bolted away from her like she was rabid."

Fuck. I bet she was a mess.

My instinct was to grab my phone and text her, or just show up and make sure she was okay. But I left my phone on the nightstand and pulled him into my arms.

Saros was actually talking to me, more vulnerable than I'd ever seen him before. I couldn't abandon him. I loved Oakley so fiercely that it painted us in a pink haze, but I still didn't fully understand what this new dynamic with Atlas meant for us—both with our jobs and with her.

Besides, Oakley had Hazel to vent to. Saros needed me.

"Should you go talk to her?" I asked, hoping to kill two birds.

"And risk her touching me?" His tone sounded like I'd said the most offensive thing possible. "Seeing my past and the fucked-up things I've done? The worst of me? I'd rather spend another awkward afternoon with Atlas."

I squeezed his shoulder. "But what if—"

"No," Saros said, cutting me off. "Besides, Aleander is already up my ass about my *gift*. He doesn't need to somehow learn that I accidentally lent it out."

He shifted on the pillow to grab the file and began scanning over its contents.

"Do you want me to go talk to her for you?" I offered quietly.

"I'm a grown-ass witch," he huffed, sounding more like a

teenage witch than the *grown-ass* one he claimed to be. "I can handle my own shit, Lynx. Don't interfere."

It was a warning—one I knew better than to fuck with.

"Fine," I conceded, pressing a kiss to his forehead. "I'll leave it alone. *For now.* But you're going to have to face her eventually. If we're going to make this thing between all of us work, you'll have to accept that she's bound to have your powers temporarily sometimes." I playfully punched his shoulder, then sidled next to him. "You have two options: either tone down your sexual prowess and suck in bed or let go of the fact that she's going to peek into your past at some point. If you decide to choose the first route, I'll gladly shoulder the responsibility for us both."

"You're already basically doing that," he growled. The sound of it and the thought of sharing Oakley between us again had my dick jolting against my zipper.

"Look, I wasn't the one who got to taste her today." I shrugged, then arched a brow. "At least I share afterward."

"Ass." He cut me a glare sharp enough to slice glass. "Even if I could, that memory doesn't feel like it's *mine* to share anymore." Letting out a frustrated sigh, his eyes softened, dark-gray disappointment wafting off of him. "It feels like it's *his.*"

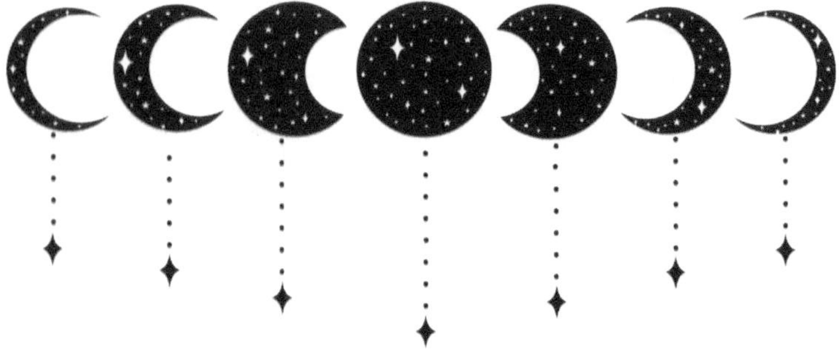

The young witches, home from school, huddled at the bottom of number 11 with their apple cider stand. Ivy Hendrix came down to refill their cauldron a few times when she'd seen it running low.

Ivy looked out at the street, watching the other families back their cars down the driveways, popping their trunks and setting up decorations. Orion Archer had been out since 5 a.m. constructing an elaborate obstacle course that would disappear tomorrow, as if it never existed in the first place. Her kids watched him, whispering to each other and pointing at the different traps and hurdles set along the path.

After dropping off another cauldron's worth of cider, she loaded her daughter, Parker, into her stroller, pushing it toward Café au Luna. Ivy hadn't gotten her daily dose of coffee, skipping the morning workout in lieu of wrangling her small ghouls at home. Halting at the end of the line of about five other witches who'd had the same idea, she scanned over the menu.

Fog crept around the truck's exterior, hugging a floating sign with specialty drinks and baked goods listed for today's trunk-or-treat festivities. The brewista, Saros Colt, was more dour than usual, sticking to the back where he prepped the fall beverages. His husband, Lynx Caven, had taken over the storefront duties, chatting eagerly with each witch that came up. When Ivy and Parker made it to the front, he nodded over his shoulder to Saros, who whipped up her regular.

Walking away, drink in hand, she used the other to steer the stroller, bringing the cup to her lips. As she rounded the cul-de-sac, her attention briefly darted to the blocked-off Blessed Crescent paved loop. Number 1 sat there, still empty, caution tape wrapped around its exterior, blending in with the Halloween decorations peppering the neighborhood.

Her gaze didn't linger, though. Instead, she pivoted and strolled up the sidewalk toward her house. Her neck craned over to number 6 and its now-empty front yard. But just as quickly, she turned her focus to Jade Fischer, eager to chat and let the moment pass.

No one wanted to feel unsafe.

And it was easier for the residents to pretend everything was fine on Starry Night Lane, especially when they'd rather enjoy All Hallows Eve.

CHAPTER 14

OAKLEY

Hazel tucked the last few errant strands of auburn into my bob, scraping against my scalp to secure the wig in place. "Ouch!"

She winced. "Sorry, but you're going to look amazing. I love that this year's theme for trunk-or-treating is witchy starlets."

We hadn't talked about what'd happened yesterday, the vision I'd seen, and I refused to bring it up again. I couldn't risk her running off. I needed her too much.

"Same," I said, heading toward the mirror to fluff my ash-blonde locks before adjusting the sleeves of my black shirt. Holding up my phone, I glanced at it once more before fussing with the last few tweaks to my makeup. "How do I look?"

"Like you'd give Kim Novak a run for her money." Hazel smirked, heading into the nursery. "Now let's get your little Pyewacket ready to go."

When the theme had been announced for this year's neighborhood trunk-or-treat, which always took place on All Hallows Eve, I jumped at the chance to step into the shoes of my favorite movie witch, Gillian Holroyd from *Bell, Book and*

Candle played by the glamorous Kim Novak. Too bad magic didn't exist here back then because she would have made a supreme witch in real life.

I knew instantly that I wanted to go as her, making Aspen my perfect little Siamese cat familiar, Pyewacket.

A moment later Hazel came out with my little witchling, his velvet bodysuit and set of cat ears making me giggle. Luckily, it hadn't been too complicated of a pattern to wrangle together.

When Atlas told me he'd be around for the holiday and asked what we were going as, he chuckled, knowing how many times I'd forced him to watch the movie about a Greenwich Village witch who puts a love spell on a charming and unsuspecting mortal publisher, played by classic heartthrob James Stewart.

"I'll be your Shep," he'd suggested, without missing a beat. "But don't worry, I won't get you to fall in love with me."

Too late for that.

He'd laughed, and I'd tittered along too, my heart threatening to combust with all the emotions I'd overstuffed it with when it came to Atlas. But that was before I mucked everything up. Now, the thought of him showing up here after everything that happened yesterday had my nerves jolting in my belly. I needed to talk to him, but how would I even broach the subject?

Hey, I know you watched Saros eat me like a starved witch at a moonluck and you overheard I'm with Lynx as well. That whole being-in-love-with-me thing really isn't going to work out too well. And by the way, you really can't be with me because I'm certain it ends in your death.

Yeah, that didn't seem like a good conversation starter.

I'd stick with the alternative of silence.

The *ding* of our home system alerted us that someone was coming up the drive.

"It's him," Hazel notified me, not that I'd thought it would be someone else. Trunk-or-treating didn't start officially for another thirty minutes.

I inhaled deeply, fussing with my outfit one last time and mentally preparing to spend the next few hours with my ex.

Here goes nothing.

((❰●❱))

"Smile for Auntie Haze!" My sister cooed at her nephew, making silly faces and floating a stuffed bat into the air to get Aspen's attention. "There's my little witchling."

His eyes followed the toy, chestnut irises twinkling in wonder as he reached up, pawing for it. He looked adorable in his costume, cat ears pricked up from his tiny head.

Meanwhile, Atlas was dressed in a black suit, very usual for him. The only thing standing out was the black bow tie nestled at his neck, when he normally opted for a dark textured tie. His hair was combed over and sprayed light brown to mimic James Stewart's character.

Goddess, he is handsome. Seeing him dressed like my childhood classic movie crush wasn't helping matters much.

Luckily, the perpetual frown on his face lowered his attractiveness level, reminding me of what had occurred yesterday and the conversation I'd need to broach at some point today. Maybe once we'd gotten back home.

"You snap some good ones?" I asked, turning my attention away from my ex and fluffing my bob a few more times.

"Oh yes, definitely." She lifted her hand a moment, snapping a handful of shots. "Now, Atlas, get in for a few with him."

She waved him over, pointing to Aspen. Atlas strolled toward us, a smile plastered on his face for his son. Obviously we were both on the same page about doing whatever was necessary to make this magical for his sake.

He picked up Aspen, sitting him on his shoulder and holding on to his tiny fists, looking up. "How cute are they? Like twins!"

They truly were, with the same lips, nose, tan complexion, and almond-shaped eyes. The only thing that differentiated them was that Aspen had somehow gotten my chestnut irises. Otherwise, he was all Dad.

"Alright, Oaks. Get in there." I shuffled over, standing on the other side of Aspen so he was situated between us like an adorable feline buffer. "Perfect. Now get closer so we can recreate the movie poster."

"That's not necessary," I said quickly. On the cover of the movie, Kim Novak is kissing right next to James Stewart's lips, him holding Pyewacket between them. She looks sultry and seductive over her shoulder, showing off her backless top, and his eyes are wide, in shock.

Maybe this pose hit a little too close to home at the moment: me the seductive witch and him, the one feeling duped. *Betrayed.*

"Hazel's right." He was much too calm. "Have to commemorate the full effect."

I took a deep breath, hovering my lips over his cheek. He was so close... The only thing that felt like it was truly holding me back from actually kissing him was the knowledge he probably hated me. That and the fact I could never actually be with him.

"You know, on the poster she's more at the corner of his mouth," Hazel corrected, showing us the picture pulled up on her phone. She was right, of course, but I still shot her a glare. She knew what she was doing.

She knew.

My body heated, and I slid my lips farther down his cheek, accidentally grazing the corner of his lip.

The world washed away, and there was just Atlas's hand gripping my throat, the air constricting in my lungs, aqua pools sucking me into his penetrating gaze.

What the hell?

His other hand reached into his chest and tore out his heart, holding it out for me to see.

My body shook, dizzy, my hand coming up to my neck.

"Oakley?" Hazel's voice called, and a second later I was back in the front yard, jack-o'-lanterns bobbing in the trees overhead with Aspen curled up to my chest, the tips of his furry ears tapping my chin.

My voice was a rasp, still shaky from the illusion. "Atlas…"

He cut me a silencing glare. Then he pressed a kiss to our son's cheek before turning to my sister. "You get the shot?"

"Got it!" Hazel said, pleased. Oblivious to the illusion Atlas had shoved into my mind.

Anger. Hurt. It was all there. One thing was certain—I'd either misread his emotions or he'd completely brushed aside the lust from when he'd caught Saros and I together.

Atlas got our Pyewacket situated in his stroller, and I went over to pop the trunk of my SUV, setting out the candy and decorations within. Hazel would be handing out treats while we took Aspen around. A Ferris wheel spun at the top of a shoot with a slat at the end. Hazel had found a small enchantment to keep the wheel spinning without a crank. It would scoop up candy and dispense it for the trunk-or-treaters so Hazel could use her floating lens to capture photos from above to share with the neighborhood. When she told me the idea, I knew the other parents would love seeing the giddy and pure moments of their little ones trunk-or-treating.

But I still wished she'd come with us instead.

"You've got this, sis," Hazel said, snagging me in for a hug.

I swallowed the lump in my throat and grabbed a lollipop, sticking it into my mouth before walking down the drive to meet Atlas.

We headed toward Ruby's house first, her sedan down at the bottom of the drive with tiny discs spinning above, glowing like little UFOs. Aspen's eyes lit up as one plopped into the bag attached to his snack tray.

"Thank you," Atlas and I said in awkward unison.

"*Bell, Book and Candle.*" Ruby smiled appreciatively. "One of my favorites growing up."

"Same!" I replied, slightly slurred with the lollipop in my mouth.

"Surprising to see someone so young know the reference." She beckoned behind her, and a set of glowing purple vials floated toward Atlas and me. "Some home-brewed liquid mettle for Mom and Dad."

She winked, and I smiled.

Atlas sloshed it between his fingers, his charming grin seeming to dazzle the coveness. Then he popped off the cap, sniffed it twice, and swigged it down in one gulp, finishing with a satisfied smack of his lips.

"Thanks," I croaked, slightly uneasy about whatever this courage potion would stir in Atlas, considering the last twenty-four hours and the illusion he'd shown me minutes ago.

We continued strolling, stopping by Orion Archer's pickup truck to watch our coven's young witches compete in his trunk-or-treat challenge, an obstacle course he'd set around his house. They hopped across rocks floating over a mini moat, crawled through hollowed logs, and jumped through literal hoops, smuggling any treats they reached along the way. Aspen giggled, watching a little witchling dressed as the Wicked Witch of the West lose her balance and hit the moat with a splash. She screeched, but a moment later, Orion raised his hands and she was dry, as if she'd never fallen in the first place. Giving her a kind smile, he waved her over to her parents while the rest of those competing continued to try to beat his course, seeing who would make it the farthest and snag the most candy.

Up ahead, Blessed Crescent was quiet, number 1 sitting like an abandoned haunted house. Yellow caution tape lined its perimeter, and I watched the families from the prestigious street filter down toward the cul-de-sac. It'd already been decided that the trunk-or-treat would end there, unlike in previous years.

The only event that would take place on Blessed Crescent was the Moonlit Masquerade and only because Atlas had moved in, insisting he would throw the most astonishing party the neighborhood had ever seen. He had told me nothing about his plans for it, but I knew he had hired some fancy event planner to oversee things.

That was if I decided to still attend.

"You gonna drink that?" Atlas whispered, staring down at the vial still clutched in my hand. "Or are you afraid to find out what a little extra courage will invoke while you're with me?"

He nodded ahead at Luna's, where Lynx and Saros handed out faux coffees topped high with mountains of whipped cream to each of the young witches in line. "Shall we?"

It was a dare, but I wasn't in the mood to play games. I dropped the vial into the stroller basket. "I'm good."

Passing the truck, we continued around the court until we were back in front of my driveway. "We should probably talk about what happened yesterday."

He sucked in a breath then shook his head, not making eye contact. "Yes. I think we have to."

Hazel began packing up the trunk-or-treat decorations, hastily coming down to take the stroller. "Why don't we leave you both to it?"

"You told her?" he asked as soon as she was out of earshot.

My cheeks burned with embarrassment, and I began walking toward the yard, hoping he'd follow so we weren't in view of the neighbors or Luna's. "I don't keep secrets from my sister."

"Just from me, then?" he accused through gritted teeth. As we turned the corner for the backyard, he gripped my shoulder, spinning me around until I was pinned with my back against the siding. His elbow rested above us, and he loomed over me, his other hand gently cupping my waist. "Are you happy with yourself?"

"What are you talking about?" I asked, confused. Of course I wasn't happy with myself. I'd hurt him. Hurt Saros. Nothing about what had happened had been good aside from the mind-blowing orgasm.

His chest heaved, and he lowered his face until his lips hovered a few inches over mine. My breath hitched, pulse thumping erratically. "Did you enjoy ripping my heart out with his face between your thighs?"

He was a tempting nightmare brought to life, and while part of me wanted to wriggle out of his hold, the other wanted nothing more than to be trapped in it. Consumed by it. To see what would happen if I let that rage simmering inside him boil over.

"N-no," I stumbled. "Of course I didn't."

"You want him, though..." His voice softened, thumb stroking my jaw before curling down my neck. "*Both* of them."

I nodded, unable to say more. But it was true. I wanted them both. *Needed* them both.

"But not me." It was a statement as much as a question, cracking his usually smooth tone.

It was like a knife to the gut, the belief behind what he'd said. That he actually thought they were the truth.

"I..." The words died on my tongue.

If I said yes, it would be a lie. If I said no, how would I be able to turn away from him without telling him why I'd run off in the first place?

"I see." His gaze narrowed, then his hand slid behind my neck, tugging me so close that the next things he said were like a bruising kiss against my lips. "If you think fucking my team will stop me from wanting you, then you're mistaken."

Heat coursed through my veins at the boldness of his declaration, my body warming beneath his. "It wasn't like that."

His forehead pressed against mine, his mouth still an invisible caress. "You were mine from the moment I saw you at that pumpkin patch seven years ago, and you will be mine until the day I die."

Images flooded me, the world spinning out of reach until it was only Atlas and I, visions of us together on a porch, his withered hand holding mine, grandchildren playing in the front yard. Another of us in the pines, slicked with sweat and passion under the Moon Goddess's copper-belly. A swirl of memories and visions he had for our future collided, overwhelming me until I pushed him away, curling over and dry heaving onto the grass.

Until the day I die.

"Atlas, I can't be yours." I clutched my knees, trying to catch my breath and will myself not to throw up. Tears streaked my cheek but I wiped them away quickly, not wanting him to see. "Not now. Not ever."

I slid down to the ground, resting my back against the siding. As my breathing slowed, I noticed he'd joined me, unclipping his bow tie and undoing the top few buttons of his shirt. "You said *can't*. But you didn't say you aren't."

"A technicality," I heaved out, too exhausted to even snap at him. The energy it took to keep him at arm's length was becoming increasingly more exhausting with each passing day.

"A technicality I'm holding on to like a lifeline until you come to your senses." His palm found my knee, voice softening from its previous fire. "Are you ever going to tell me why you rejected my proposal and then months later ran away?"

His aqua irises reeled me in, threatening to drown me in my lies.

My voice broke. "Are you ever going to give up and let me go?"

The lies were all I had to protect him with. To give my son the father he deserved to grow up knowing.

"Never." He squeezed my knee, and electricity shot up my leg at the touch. Taking my hand in his, he thumbed over the naked flesh of my ring finger until a delicate band with a single glinting gem appeared, along with a shimmering black rune scrawled across my wrist.

I stared at the mirage, unable to take my eyes off the vow marks. The ones I always thought I'd wear.

His.

Sweat beaded at my brow, and my heart beat wildly.

When my hands shook, he released them. The illusion fell, Atlas's brows drawn together in concern. "I can't walk away from us."

"Maybe you can't," I pushed to my knees, body still quivering, "but I already did."

Just as I prepared to stand up and run away from him once again, he dragged me onto him until I straddled his waist, knees digging into the ground. "If I remember correctly, your eyes were locked with *mine* back at Luna's."

Both of his arms banded around my waist, holding me still so I was forced to either meet his gaze or wriggle against the bulge of his trousers to get free.

I did it anyway, wanting to escape the truth that dangled between us, desperate to be seen. But saying the words would be like etching his fate into stone, so I moved against him, making no headway other than building the swell beneath into steel.

"Pretend you don't want this. Fuck them all you want, but *I'll* never be out of your system." My breath caught in my throat, and he lifted his hips beneath me, length rubbing against my seam through the thin fabric of my leggings. And as much as I wanted to scream at him how wrong he was, I knew he was right.

His lips caressed the shell of my ear, Desire thrumming through my veins to everywhere our bodies were touching. "I'm in your blood. Your bones. Your fucking marrow. Just as you are in mine."

The words felt like a hex. There was no enchantment behind them, but they were no less powerful.

Atlas's hands slid up my spine, and he drew me in for a deep, unrelenting kiss. At first, I tried to hold still, to not give in to his pull. But somehow denying myself only made my

Desire more persistent, betraying me and bursting from my lips.

He groaned against me.

I'd been under his spell since we met, and while the feelings I had for Lynx and Saros were intense and real, Atlas was tethered to my heart whether I tried to rip him free of it or not.

They all were.

Pulling away despite being desperate for more, I turned my cheek and pushed off of him.

"I can't," I rasped, running a hand over my swollen lips.

He didn't fight me, and when I glanced back at him, he seemed so small. Sad. Confused. No trace of the self-assured political leader I was used to.

But Lynx and Saros's lives didn't hang in the balance. And I refused to lose any of them.

"I'm doing this because I love you too much, not because I don't."

It was all I could admit before I scurried into the house, locking the door tightly behind me.

ATLAS

"So after months of requests, you all finally agreed to meet. Why now?" I asked, scanning over the supernatural leaders sitting around the circular table.

"Why don't you tell us more about why we're here, and then we'll decide what it's worth to us," said Dante Vivaldi with a smirk, two sharp fangs mostly hidden behind it. Vampires were easy enough to spot even with their teeth retracted. If they went too long without a meal, their eyes began to fleck with red, the bloody shade blotting out the original until they fed.

"As you know, we've been looking into the disappearances on Starry Night Lane." I pointed at the map of Celestial Haven illusioned onto the wall beside me. "While there have been a few on the other covens' streets, we're curious if any of your people have mysteriously disappeared."

Vivaldi's gaze slid from me over to Saros, scanning him quickly, as if sizing him up. Outside of what was in the file, I had no clue what went on during his undercover stint for them. When he'd personally requested Agent Holt, it made me wonder if Saros had kept in touch. I found it odd but when

I asked the High Archon if he knew anything else about it, he said everything worth knowing was in the file.

I begged to differ.

Anyone on Vivaldi's good side couldn't be trusted in my book, so the fact that he and Saros had some unspoken détente automatically put Holt on my radar. If he was going to be with Oakley, around my son, he'd better not put them in danger of coming in contact with Vivaldi or any of his vampire slime.

"Disappearing overnight? Sounds like the Vivaldi Syndicate's MO," Fox Steele huffed out, chuckling along with the two beta shifters behind him. Fox was currently the Alpha Liaison, the one alpha among all the different shifters in Artemis that'd been elected to represent them in any government dealings. Everything said here would be relayed to the other pack alphas, any decisions regarding this meeting put to a vote.

"Yeah, like you haven't had any mate claiming *incidents* that needed cleaning up," Dante replied, shaking his head.

While shifters had been known to get into trouble, they prioritized their pack mentality and the good of the community, honoring traditions above all else. They also hadn't gotten mixed up with any illegal dealings involving mortals, which was more than I could say about Vivaldi.

"Look, bickering will get us nowhere," Lynx offered, and the other leaders all snapped their attention to the empath. They weren't used to hearing from anyone aside from the meeting's government representative—me, their Archon. But I didn't stop him. He was right.

"Have any of your designated areas had issues with people just moving away? Leaving as if overnight?" I asked, gaze trailing over each of them to see if they reacted.

"No," Vivaldi and Fox muttered almost in unison.

"Neither have we," chimed in Niklas Morningstar, the great-great-great-whatever of the original King of Hell. When our government built these pocket districts of safety for supernaturals, angels and demons alike spilled from the mouth of Hell and swooped down from the heavens to live among our people. But Heaven was much too important to deal with the world below them, so Niklas was always sent to represent them both.

Apparently this seemed to only be a coven issue, not widespread. Which at least narrowed things a bit. "So why the change of heart to finally agree to meet with us?"

"If you're willing to ask repeatedly, that means it's a big problem. And if it's a big problem, then you must be desperate." Dante smiled, fully displaying his fangs.

"We're here because he told us to be," Fox said, Niklas agreeing alongside him.

"You all have motive to mess with our community. If you don't want us looking too closely into your activities"—I glanced over to Dante—"or implementing more regulations over your packs"—then Fox—"or sending you back where you came from"—then Niklas—"I suggest you work with us on this."

Vivaldi released an annoyed huff, refusing to admit we had a card to play. "I'm not gonna say I'm sad that some witches decided they don't love *your* little haven and decided to move overnight. Doesn't impact my kind."

"They didn't just *decide*. There's no forwarding address, no discussion with neighbors about being unhappy or having any reason to leave. Just whole households *gone*."

At that, they all leaned in.

"Same houses or different ones?" Niklas asked, thumbing over the swirls carved into the skin of his jaw. They curved down his neck, and then down one arm. At first, most didn't notice them—they were very shallow—but once you did, it was hard to take your eyes off them. Aside from that and his hot-pink irises, he could pass for mortal, not that he'd ever need to. Any mortal that dealt with him wouldn't remember anything about his appearance—at least not until he came to collect. "Could be an old-fashioned haunting?"

"Our pest control team has combed the houses for any sort of ghostly activity," I replied. "Nothing."

He frowned at that but continued stroking his swirls, mulling over the information.

"There is no discernible pattern." I pointed to the map of Celestial Haven, marked with orbs for each disappearance minus Hazel's. While her case we believe was somehow related, it didn't fit the pattern. Besides, I didn't need a bullseye for these fuckers showcasing where Oakley and Aspen were. "This has been going on for a few years now, slower at first but has been getting more frequent. That's when we were tipped off that there was something to look into."

"By whom?"

"Well, we weren't sure at first, but suspect it was a witch doing her own research into the matter."

"Oh yeah, that Ashley Mirabel?" Fox asked. "The one in the paper?"

"Acacia," I corrected. "And yes, that one. We've been slowly getting through the files she'd been keeping, but they are extensive."

"Even if this isn't your problem, until we know the cause, you are part of this community and it could be a problem for you down the road. If they are increasing their pace with targets, what will make them stop with our streets?" Lynx added in, going for the emotional appeal. While it wasn't the tactic I'd go for, or I suspected Saros would choose, I couldn't help but admire it. It was easy to understand what Oakley saw in the empath, even if it made me want to throttle him a bit.

"What do you want us to do?" Niklas asked, looking down at his watch with a yawn.

"Have your demons been making any more deals than usual? Or anything that could ripple out into these disappearances?"

"I'll meet with our Seven and comb through the books," Hell's King replied.

"Thank you, that would be a huge help." Before I'd even finished the sentence, he'd disappeared in a hot-pink puff of smoke.

Always one for theatrics.

I turned my attention to the alpha. "Fox, do you think your pack could sniff around the pines? Our team could go out there but with the festivities happening it would be much easier if you did. See if anything pops up."

"Like dead bodies?" he asked, wrinkling his nose.

"I'm hoping not, but I'm not ruling anything out."

"So now that you've gotten the pets on patrol," Vivaldi started, waving a hand at the shifters, "what are we doing here?"

"As Fox said earlier, your kind are used to making people disappear." I sighed, knowing how ludicrous the words were going to sound. "Any ideas where these people could be going —how they could leave without any clue of a location— would be helpful."

That arrogant smile returned along with the fangs poking down from his gums. "You're asking the criminal to tell you how they commit crimes?"

"We don't *have* to ask. I could always have Agent Holt take a gander." Saros bristled next to me, not even subtly. "I know you two are well-acquainted."

"That won't be necessary," Vivaldi dismissed. "Obviously, our methods are…unique to our kind, so I'll have to think about it."

I nodded. "Thank you."

"Don't thank me. If Agent Holt wasn't here, I'd have ripped your throat out over a threat like that." He said the words as if he were talking about an everyday task like doing the laundry. Not that I feared him, or death for that matter. "Fortunately, I'm willing to work with him on your little problem."

I sucked in a breath before I said anything else to shorten my already dwindling lifespan.

"I'm sure we all have Hallowed festivities to attend to. The link on this card will send a message to me without us needing to meet again." Agent Aleander handed each of them the spelled card as I spoke. "And remember, word about this can't spread. We don't want to terrify the entirety of Celestial Haven unless we have to."

"Yeah," Dante snickered, "would hate to see the housing market go down. Devalue that monstrosity of a mansion you're moving into."

"It's about keeping our supernaturals safe." I ignored the fact that he seemed to know where I lived.

"All supernaturals or just *yours*?" Red had started to bleed through the navy blue of his irises, ready for his next iron-rich snack. "Because you can bet that if these things were happening to our people, you wouldn't be so persistent in your search."

"That's not fair—"

"But it's the truth," Dante added, cutting me off. "Let's

not pretend this is something it isn't. Or that our government is some shining star. We all know better here."

His crimson-spun eyes scanned the room, snagging on Saros a moment, nearly imperceptible.

"I'd watch what you insinuate openly at this meeting," I seethed. "Some might call that treason."

"Some might," he replied, brushing off some lint from his expensive suit jacket before scooting his chair back. "Thanks again for the enlightening conversation. We'll be in touch soon."

And with that, the meeting was over.

CHAPTER 16

OAKLEY

I'd been near silent the last twenty-four hours, focusing on emailing over the photos and graphics for the boudoir displays for tonight's Moonlit Masquerade and doing the final touches on my dress.

Hazel stayed out of my way, not prying when I'd stormed straight to my room to cry after talking to Atlas. I'd spent the rest of the night only coming out to feed Aspen, settle him in his crib for bedtime, and grab a few snacks while I worked on designs. Meanwhile, Hazel was attached to her phone, nearly jolting each time I appeared, as if she didn't want me to see what she was up to.

Slipping the nursing pads into the breast pockets I'd built into my corset, I held it up to the light, inspecting it one final time. Thin spiderwebs of lace cradled the black velvet *V* that ended in two circular cups that covered my breasts. It was the most daring article of clothing I'd ever worn in public, but when Hazel saw the mock-up, she'd insisted I bring it to life. I'd created it with her in mind, but I had to admit, I was obsessed with it.

A whistle came from behind me. *"Damn, sis.* That turned

out amazing. I cannot wait to see how many hearts you stop tonight in that."

Craning my neck, I found Hazel in the doorway wearing her high-waisted trousers and crescent-shaped bra that had a strappy overlay. She wasn't wearing the blazer that went with the ensemble yet, but who knew how long that would stay on.

The Moonlit Masquerade was an adults-only coven affair, held late in the evening while our younger witches were watched nearby at the community center.

"Do I really have to leave Aspen tonight?" I whined, watching him rattle a giant plush bat attached to his play center. He was giggling, smacking it into the haunted doll-house next to it, having the best time.

"Yes." Hazel came into the room, holding my skirt up, its layers of choppy tulle cascading like a mystical black water-fall to the floor. "It's the perfect time to remind everyone of the upcoming relaunch and your models will all be on display. They will expect you there. Even if it's only for an hour."

"I'm holding you to that hour," I said, shooting her a glare.

"Now, if you happen to get swept away, say by some handsome witches..." she winked, "I'm not opposed to picking up Aspen and bringing him home sooner."

"That won't be necessary." I was already dreading being at the party with all of them. Things with Atlas were bad enough without thinking about coming face-to-face with Saros after I'd accidentally borrowed his Recollection and put his job in a precarious situation. He'd probably never touch me again.

Lynx had texted me saying Saros was okay, but I wouldn't

believe it until I talked to him myself, and I was at a loss of what I'd even say.

Hazel sighed, pulling me from my internal meltdown. "Out with it."

"What?" I blinked away my bubbling anxiety.

"You going to talk about what's got you acting so strange?"

"I'm not acting strange," I blurted, realizing as soon as the words left my mouth how much of a bald-faced lie they were.

"Look, you've been weird—weirder than usual—ever since you touched me with Saros's Recollection." Her hands slipped into the pockets of her trousers. "I don't know what you think you saw, but—"

"Aurora," I breathed out, much more inclined to talk about this than my man problems. "I saw you with Aurora."

She sucked in a breath, shoulders raised up tight. We both stood there in silence for a moment, aside from Aspen's giggles coming from his play center, until she finally released her breath and spoke again. "I was not expecting that."

"Why didn't you tell me you were involved with her? Them?" I really didn't see enough to even know what to ask.

"Everyone is entitled to some secrets. Even from their sisters." She shrugged, acting like it was no big deal. "Don't you trust me?"

"Of course I trust you, but I also feel like you've only let me confide in you since you returned. You've told me noth-ing." I lay the corset on the bed before patting the mattress for her to sit next to me. "Nothing about when you were taken. Nothing about since you've been back."

When she sat down, I grabbed her hand, holding it like a talisman for courage to say what had been weighing on me since she'd returned. "You still haven't even told me who you were meeting the night you were kidnapped. Do you know how horrible I felt having no clue where you'd gone? When people asked me where you were going, what you were doing, and I was the shitty sister who didn't have an answer?"

She squeezed my hand. "You had a lot of other things going on, Oakley. You'd just moved here. You had Aspen to take care of."

"That's not a good enough reason." Tears sprang from my eyes. "I almost fucking lost you...and in some ways, I feel like I did. The Hazel before would have told me *everything*. The Hazel before didn't feel entitled to secrets."

"Maybe you just didn't really know the Hazel before?"

"Wow," I said, snatching my hand back as if her words had bitten it.

"I don't mean it like that but, Oakley, everyone has secrets. *Everyone*." Her brown eyes held my gaze in challenge. "Or are you telling me that I know everything that's going on between you and Atlas, Lynx, and Saros, or that they even know *everything* about what's going on with each other?"

"Th-that's not the same and you know it!"

My face heated. We were talking about *her* right now. Not me.

Not *them*.

"Isn't it?" She got up from the bed and knelt by Aspen, taking the orange plastic balls decorated like pumpkins and dropping them down the spiraling tower. Then her attention returned to me, hands continuing to play with her nephew. "Even you have secrets from me, from everyone you claim to love and care about. It doesn't make you a bad person, and it doesn't mean you love them any less."

Fuck. I was getting tired of everyone seeing right through me lately.

I released a long sigh. "Will you at least tell me what was

going on with Aurora? Did your relationship have anything to do with Acacia's murder?"

"Fine. I'll tell you. But keep your judging to a minimum because I already know how this is going to sound." She cut me a glare, and I nodded at her request. Who was I to judge anyone else's love life? "I met Aurora and Fitz when I sold them their house. They helped get me the exclusive deal with Celestial Haven, and with their status in the community, they were an amazing set of allies as I was getting started. It was all professional going into things." My side-eye came out unintentionally and she scoffed. "You said you wouldn't judge."

Wiping the look off my face, I tried to really listen to what she was saying. "What changed?"

"A few months later, they invited me to a moonluck to get to know the neighbors and to get my name out there." She swallowed thickly. "After everyone left, I was about to drive home, but they insisted I stay since it was so late. Said I could use a guest room if I'd like... Or..."

"That's when you started sleeping with them?" I tried to finish for her, hopefully making the sisterly share less awkward.

"Just Aurora. Fitz is much more into watching."

A full-body shiver crept up my torso, and I cringed. Fitz was one of the last people I wanted to think about in that way.

Once I collected myself and looked at Hazel again, she frowned.

"Sorry," I grimaced with a shrug. "In the memory, she said she loved you. Did you love her?"

"I don't think so." Her voice was low and guilt-ladened. "I really don't know. And that's probably what makes me feel the most shit of all. I thought we were just having fun. I knew they were married and committed to each other, and I'd much rather stay commitment free—not all of us want to deal with all the emotional baggage like you do three times over."

"Thanks," I said, teasing her with a glare.

"I guess that's why I didn't want to believe she'd killed Acacia. Maybe I wasn't in love with Aurora," her eyes dropped to the floor, "but I loved how I felt being coveted by someone so..."

"Self-important?" I huffed.

"Powerful."

Aspen started fussing, and my breasts swelled to sate his hunger. I adjusted my bra, trying to manage the discomfort. Of course he'd start crying right as she'd finally begun to really talk to me.

Hazel picked him up from the play center and carried him over to me, then grabbed my nursing pillow, fitting it around my waist carefully. I lifted my shirt up and unclasped my bra, Aspen latching onto my nipple quickly.

Once he was situated, I looked back up at Hazel, wondering if I'd just lost the rest of this moment.

"There was this magnetic pull from them. Knowing they wanted me in their world... It was a high being desired by people like that. Made me feel alive."

"I can understand that." I sighed with relief, from both the pressure in my chest abating and also that she'd continued talking. "I'm sorry for prying. I know it really wasn't my business, but I'm glad you told me."

"Thanks for not judging." Her smile didn't meet her eyes.

"Who am I to judge? My sex life is a dumpster fire." I chuckled.

"True," Hazel teased, laughing with me a moment before dissolving into seriousness. The big sister tone returning just as quickly. "I have a feeling everything's going to work out, sis."

"Is this feeling just a feeling or more of a *knowing*?"

Is she saying what I think she is? Has something changed in her vision? Has she seen something with Lynx and Saros?

"It's a knowing," she said, and I started to release the tension coiled in my chest, "but not in the way you're thinking. More like sisterly intuition."

Well, what good was that?

"I know you're disappointed, but I learned my lesson before. Truly." She placed a hand on my shoulder.

"Hazel," I pleaded, "can't you do a reading?"

She shook her head. "No. Not because I can't, but because I won't."

"But—"

"I love you too much to keep watching you stifle your own happiness by trying to outrun fate."

Trying...

Leaving still hadn't been enough.

"Before you freak out again, there hasn't been another reading." She sighed, clearly frustrated that I would worry regardless. "Fate isn't promised and neither is tomorrow."

Hazel headed toward the door, stopping in its frame to glance over her shoulder. "Take advantage of whatever joy you can in the present or you'll be left with regret."

The way she said the last word felt like a knife had been slammed into my ribs, but somehow the advice seemed to cleave her just as sharply.

"Hazel?" I asked, wondering what *regret* she spoke of.

"I'll watch Aspen once you're done so you can finish getting ready."

And just like that, her own armor of secrets had been put back on.

CHAPTER 17

OAKLEY

"Hubba-hubba," Hazel crooned at me. She adjusted the lapels of her cropped blazer while I grabbed the last few items for the diaper bag. Then I stood, fluffing out my skirt and taking a deep breath.

I didn't like having any tension between us, especially now that she was back.

"You look incredible, Haze," I said with a smile. Legs for days, the sleek trousers hugged the curve of her hips, and crisscross straps draped over her bra, accentuating her chest.

"Yeah, my boobs look amazing in this bra thanks to you."

Hazel was always self-conscious about being small chested. Meanwhile, I would give anything to donate some of my assets to my older sister.

We all had our crosses to bear, it seemed.

As I looked down for one final appraisal, I realized this was definitely the most dolled up I'd been since having Aspen. Swathed in delicate lace and tulle that left very little to the imagination, I felt like walking sin.

Our heels clacked against the garage floor, Hazel nudging me out of the way to push the stroller. Pressing the key code with my finger, the garage door groaned, lowering behind us. Some of the other neighbors were already out in their masquerade finest migrating toward the foggy hands curling in a seductive come-hither motion toward 5 Blessed Crescent.

A few, like us, were headed toward the Coven Community Center to drop off our little ones first. Ruby and some of the other neighbors were keeping watch of the witchlings tonight.

A stunning teenager with blonde waves ushered us in with a radiant smile. "Happy Halloween!"

"Happy Halloween," Hazel and I replied in unison.

"Chrys," Ruby's voice called from deep within the community center, "come help me set up the snack station."

Chrys, as in Chrysanthemum Wells, Aurora and Fitz's daughter. I hadn't met her yet, only having seen her from afar a few times when she drove off to school. She waved us to follow her into the large meeting room. It was all set up with different crafts and stations for the witchlings to enjoy, a play area with puzzles and toys, and a reading corner with festive books scattered around a rocking chair.

"Wow." Aspen couldn't enjoy most of the things here yet, but this would be wonderful as he got older.

"We've set up a bunch of travel cribs and cots in the side rooms for when they are tuckered out, so make sure to enjoy yourselves," Chrysanthemum said quickly, rattling off details about the stations and activities they'd prepped for the young witches. She pointed over to the refrigerator in the center's kitchenette. "You can put any milk for him in there. I left some Sharpies there, so make sure his name is on it, along with any special instructions. We have all been trained in warming spells to help get them to the exact specifications your witchling might want."

"Thank you so much," I replied, taking it all in, more at

ease leaving Aspen here for a few hours. I could suddenly breathe better. Hazel got us signed in while I headed to the fridge, opening the freezer to stick the bags of milk in before dropping his diaper bag in his designated cubby.

When I got to the sign-in table to meet up with Hazel, she handed Aspen over to me to give my goodbye kisses while she slipped on an iridescent-onyx beaded bracelet, matching the one around his wrist, onto her own.

"I've got this, sis." She waved her wrist at me. "Let Auntie Hazel take care of her bestie. I have a feeling you'll have three distractions tonight."

I shot her a glare.

Ruby handed me one more bracelet. "Don't worry, we've got an extra, but I still think you should take her up on her offer." The coveness winked, sending heat creeping across my cheeks.

I wasn't ready to think about those three distractions yet.

We waved to Aspen on our way out the door, both donning our spelled bracelets in case we were summoned. The autumn air wrapped around us like a frigid blanket as we followed the foggy hands beckoning us toward number 5.

I hadn't been to the house since Atlas moved in. Somehow the space looked more imposing than before, like a towering glass castle fit for a political king, as if the house itself had somehow shifted to match its new owner.

The moment we stepped onto the long drive, I felt the presence of being watched. My attention darted around, wondering if others were walking up with us, but there was no one. Just the fog and the clack of our heels against the pavement.

Despite the event being a masquerade theme, we'd been instructed on the invitations that our masks would be provided for us. Now, as we got closer, I saw there were dozens of masks—some animalistic, others decorative, and a few just plain spooky—dancing along the fence.

"Manifest your mask and then pluck your poison," came a cheery singsong voice, pulling our attention to a young witch holding a clipboard, raven hair swirled atop her head like a 1950s pin-up girl.

"You must be the event coordinator." Hazel extended her hand with a smile. "I'm Hazel and this is Oakley."

"Clio," she replied, shaking it. "Nice to meet you."

My sister could charm the pants off, well, anyone. I could too, if I wanted, considering Desire was my gift, but I usually tried to keep it at bay. Hazel's thumb stroked Clio's hand, lingering there until I cleared my throat.

"Oakley...as in Aspen's mother?" Clio asked, finally ungluing her focus from my sister. "Such a cutie. Atlas is always showing me photos during our meetings."

My heart floated and sunk simultaneously. "That's me." I gave her an awkward wave. "So, what do we need to do?" I asked, trying to get us to the party and away from the topic of my ex.

"Place your hands in front of you and call your mask forth," the event planner instructed.

Hazel held her palms out, lifted toward the sky, and I followed.

Thoughts cluttered my mind, worry bolting through me over how things would go tonight, obscuring my ease with my magic. A moment later, a calming hand landed on my shoulder and my scattered thoughts cleared.

A chill ran up my spine, my hands now cradling something metallic.

"It suits you," Lynx purred in my ear, hand still on my shoulder. Looking down at my palms, there was a delicate mask embellished with diamonds along the nose and brow line, three rows of glittering chains dangling from the center out to the mask's edge.

Clio was already finishing up tying Hazel's on, its delicate black filigree making her cherry-red lipstick pop even more in the darkness.

"May I?" Lynx asked, lifting a hand toward my mask. He was dressed in a deep-charcoal shirt, the top three buttons undone, with black pinstripe trousers. He donned on a mask representing his namesake, an onyx lynx with pointed ears painted with golden crescents and embellishments.

"Thank you," I said. My breath caught when I spun around and almost bumped into Saros. He wore a black owl mask, its beak and feathers carved in fine detail. Somehow even the faux fowl matched his furrowed brow, embodying his serious disposition.

"Oh, the things I wish I could do to you right now, Wicked," Lynx whispered over my shoulder while his fingers meticulously tied the ribbon at the back of my head. I didn't miss the way his hand trailed down my arm when he stepped away, or the curl of his cat-like smirk beneath his mask. A flood of his lust washed through me, electricity zinging straight to my core, making me zip up my thighs.

"Doesn't Ms. Brooks look ravishing tonight, darling?" Lynx asked, keeping up appearances. A few other coven members came up and began summoning their masks.

Saros's throat worked, his voice was a rasp, scraped away of its usual baritone. "She does."

"Shall we?" Hazel cut in, pointing over to a dozen floating vials and assorted treats. "Clio said we are to pick one and it will transport us to the celebration."

"And don't forget to drop your cell phones in the bucket. You can retrieve them on the way out," the event coordinator instructed from over our shoulders.

Anxiety simmered at my fingertips, now clutched around my phone. I took a deep breath, reminding myself that I had my wrist band if Aspen needed me. So did Hazel. And we were only a short walk away.

I tossed in my cell, and the others followed suit, Saros with only the slightest hesitation, probably not loving being disconnected in case something came up with their assignment.

There had to be at least forty phones piled in the small bucket. It would be fun to comb through them later.

The last few stragglers sidled up next to us, quickly picking things from above. One snatched a purple glowing vial and chugged it down, vanishing a moment later, the empty glass swiftly finding its way to the recycle bin. An iridescent unicorn-masked witch, whom I believed to be Sage, snatched a cookie with orange flecks strewn within, eating it in three bites before disappearing from view.

"Nothing's labeled." Unease coiled within Saros's words.

"Chop-chop," Clio said, glancing up at the empty house.

Where was everyone?

Hazel reached up and grabbed a bright-yellow vial, drinking it down in one gulp. "See you in—"

Poof!

She was gone.

A shiver ran down my spine, but I knew nothing Atlas could put together would hurt me. He'd already said the evening would be unlike any other Halloween event of the past, and he did love theatrics. I reached up for a sleek black apple, turning it over in my palm. It was smooth, the outside polished to such a shine that I saw my reflection on its skin. I looked so like and unlike myself... Saros's evergreen irises peered at me over my shoulder. Stepping closer, he reached above my head, and I stilled at the brush of his chest against my back.

Pulling down a small bowl with thick purple soup swirling inside, he sniffed it, wriggling his nose. "Purple carrot soup?"

"My favorite!" Lynx said, and his faux husband handed over the bowl, billowing lavender smoke rising from its lip.

"Go ahead," Saros directed him, and without another word, Lynx chugged it down.

Poof!

He was gone.

As I brought the apple to my lips, Saros gripped around my waist, taking me by surprise. He held me tight, like the idea of me disappearing set him on edge. Quickly grabbing a green vial from above, he brought it to his lips but didn't drink.

Instead he waited, watching me.

My teeth pierced the apple's onyx skin, its usual burst of tartness tinged with something magical. Bubbles flitted across my tongue, then my vision began to spin. I shut my eyes, not wanting to become ill.

I held onto Saros to steady myself until the world felt like it had stopped moving, but when I opened my eyes, I was clutching the arm of a man who definitely wasn't Saros.

Aqua irises peered through the slits of a silver wolf mask, Atlas's smooth voice coming into focus. "You didn't really think you could tell me you still love me and just run away again, did you?"

Atlas's chest heaved, looking somehow more feral than the silvery wolf depicted on his mask.

"Please." I looked up at him, body shaking while I clutched the bench I sat on. I was in the dining room of his house, half the walls around us composed of glass. "Stop making this so hard for me."

"Did you or did you not say you still love me?"

"I did," I replied, distracted by the fog whirling above the yard. Was that where the party was taking place? I hurried over to the glass, trying to find the others. "How did I end up here?"

Crowds of witches wandered through a rosebush maze, the same fog that had called us to the party blanketing it. When it thinned in spots, I could make out those below, but many areas were completely obscured. Private coves with sleek lounge chairs and various installations ranging from cages to leather swings to St. Andrew's crosses were strewn throughout.

A witch with platinum hair in a horned mask was strapped by her wrists and ankles to the ends of the leather

X. Knelt before her was Sage Harlow in her unicorn mask, horn pressed between the witch's thighs. Another witch held a deep-plum candle, an assortment of them lit on the table set on the opposite side of the cove, dripping wax down the trapped witch's shoulders. She shook against the restraints and then vanished—the fog blocking them from view.

Another spot opened within the thick blanket, showing Hazel, who'd already discarded her blazer, chatting with some neighbors and toasting with bubbling shots. When one of them turned, I stared in shock, looking at myself.

No wonder my sister wasn't concerned that I hadn't shown up at the party.

"You illusioned me there?" I asked, annoyed at his forethought. "Where are Lynx and Saros?"

"A temporary fix to be able to talk to you." Atlas's chest pressed into my back, and my hands shot out, bracing the cool glass. "And they are fine. Just enjoying the party with everyone else. This isn't about *them*. This is about *us*." His whisper curled into my ear like a sensual secret, the bulge in his trousers semisolid against my ass through the thin layers of tulle.

The glass dimmed to the house's privacy setting, its chill dissipating. My breaths became shallow, ensnared by his presence, the thud of my heartbeat amplifying at the knowledge that we were truly alone together for the first time in months.

It was something I'd been avoiding. A gravitational pull I'd tried my best to ignore for both our sakes.

With a snap of his fingers, projections of the boudoir shots reflected off the dark walls of his backyard maze, Full Moon Emporium's logo marking the spaces between. It was beautiful, mesmerizing. When the logo went away, an address popped up on the screen. The one for the space at Mystic Square.

"What the fuck? We didn't walk through the space."

His reflection frowned, obviously expecting a different sort of reaction. "I looked it over and video chatted with Hazel for approval."

"What about *my* approval?" I stammered, face flushing with heat. "What about what *I* want?"

My attention darted to the banister and then his hand was on mine, interlacing with my fingers and keeping me against the glass. My stomach tightened at the contact, Desire flooding my veins, seeking *more*. He turned me to face him, and I sucked in a breath, his aqua pools drowning me in their depths. "Why don't you quit pushing me away and tell me what you want, Oakley?"

I shot some Desire through his arm, hitting him like a brick. He moaned, bending in half—all the distraction I needed to untangle myself from his web. I hurried toward the staircase, jolting when bars swung across the wall.

"Is this a baby gate?" I asked, glaring at him as I gripped the bars and pulled on them.

Atlas shrugged. "Looks like babyproofing the house came with a few extra perks."

They were locked in place, so in terms of keeping our son from the stairs, it was amazing. But right now, I wanted to rip them from the walls and get the hell out of here. My resolve to keep him at arm's length was disappearing with each passing second.

"I just want the truth." His hands were clenched by his sides, lips flat. "Just give me that and you can go to the party. To *them*."

The truth. The one I'd been dancing around. Was it fair to hold Atlas's fate lodged in the back of my throat? How could I even say the words? Everything I'd done to try to change things had seemed to only bite me in the ass and make it worse between us.

"I saw you die." The confession blew out of me, taking all the air from my lungs with it, my voice merely a rasp.

His gaze narrowed into slits, and I wished Lynx was here to tell me what was brewing beneath the surface of this witch that held so much captivating power over me.

"Well, technically Hazel did and shared her premonition with me." I stepped away from the gate, leaning against the half wall that lined the staircase, continuing on before he stopped me from getting out what I needed to say. "I don't care if you don't believe in what she saw. I couldn't live with myself if being together meant your death. That's why I came here. That's why I left Salem. I'm trying to build a life for Aspen and keep his father safe."

"Why didn't you just talk to me?" He slowly walked toward me, taking the spot next to me on the wall. His tone was soft. Sad. But there was no telling me the premonition was wrong, or that I shouldn't have listened to Hazel. No anger.

What the hell?

"Why aren't you shocked?" I asked, glaring at him. "I just said I saw a vision where if we stay together you die."

He remained silent, a hollowness haunting his eyes.

An icy tingle streaked down my spine, goosebumps prickling along my skin. "Did you know about the vision? Did she tell you already?"

Had she gone behind my back and shared his fate with him after everything I'd done—how hard I'd worked to keep it from him?

"I didn't know about Hazel's vision." The lines on his face hardened. "But I did know about the hex on my family."

"Hex? What?" I croaked. "Why have you never told me about it before?"

Sure, there were hexes and curses out there, but I'd only heard of them being outlawed. I'd never met someone who had actually been the victim of one. Most of the time they could be reversed with the proper sort of magic.

"If people knew my grandfather and every male in his line had been hexed by the Moon Goddess herself, do you think we would have been able to lead the supernatural community since its inception?"

By the Moon Goddess herself? What did his grandfather do to piss her off? We'd always been told she was a benevolent goddess, watching over us. Helping.

Not there to harm or hex.

"But you couldn't tell me?"

He'd wanted to marry me. We had a witchling together. This would have affected me no matter what. But instead, he'd kept it a secret all these years.

Tears stung my eyes, building in their rims. I grabbed my corset, running the spiderwebs beneath the pads of my fingers, needing to tether myself to something.

"I wanted to, Oakley. You have no idea how much I did. But how do you tell someone you love that you're destined to die just as your life's meant to begin?" He spun himself to stand in front of me, clasping my hands in his. Thumbs grazing the edge of my palms. "There was never a good time to share that, and I didn't want to lose you."

If the hex had passed from his grandfather to his father and then to him...

"Aspen..." My hands shook within his. "What's going to happen to our son, Atlas?"

"Nothing." He squeezed my hands, steadying them. Taking a deep breath, he rested his forehead against mine.

"That's why I never told you. The hex dies with the family member that willingly accepts their fate. My grandfather, my father, they used every trick in the book to thwart theirs. I'm not."

He traced along the chains of my mask, and I unintentionally leaned into his palm, the tears I'd held tightly streaking beneath the delicate metallic links. Cradling my jaw in his hands, he lifted my chin when I tried to drop my gaze. "The hex will never touch our son. I'd never condemn my child to that fate."

All the air had been swallowed from my lungs.

"But you'd condemn *me* to watch you die?" My heart rattled against my rib cage, anger the only thing keeping me from shattering. My hands balled into fists. "You asked me to marry you knowing this and not telling me."

"And look what happened when you learned of my fate," he seethed, catching my wrists before I tore away from him. "You fucking ran."

"To stop it. To *change* it." My voice quivered, along with every part of me, my chest cracking, heart splintering into a million tiny pieces.

He'd known. Had known the entire time we'd been together and yet he refused to warn me, even when he'd planned to marry me, even when I'd been carrying his son. He'd taken fate into his own hands, and I fucking hated him for it.

His gaze hardened before he released me from his grasp, staggering back a few steps, eyes darting around the room. "Maybe it was selfish of me not to tell you, but I wanted to steal every moment I could *while* I could. I'd do it all over again. The only thing I regret is not fighting more for you to stay."

Drawn by some invisible force, I dragged my feet forward,

still keeping a healthy distance between us. "Why didn't you?"

"Because I knew what would eventually happen." He wrung his hands together. "When you left, I thought maybe it was better if I just let you go..."

"What changed?" I asked, trying to steady my breaths but the words still came out ragged.

"Nothing." He prowled toward me, herding me backward in a circle until my ass bumped into the edge of the long dining room table. Nudging his knee between my thighs, he lifted me up and sat me there, his hands caging me on either side. "That's the problem. I still love you just as fiercely. Every day that passes feels like one more stolen from being with you and our son."

Hadn't I spent the last month trying to enjoy every moment with Lynx and Saros, knowing it wouldn't last? Why was the idea of enjoying what Atlas and I could such a painful concept?

Which was truly more tragic: getting to love someone ephemerally or living out your days never experiencing the full beauty of its wonder?

Atlas leaned forward, hips bolted between my thighs, nose touching mine. His voice was so low, it felt like a wanton caress. "In case I haven't been clear enough, I'm done with you pushing me away."

"Atla—"

He stifled my final plea with a brutal kiss that smothered my objection, tasting of tart cherries, dark punishments, and hidden desires.

And this time, I didn't try to stop him.

I didn't want to.

As much as I wanted to fight fate, I was tired of fighting *us*.

My body trembled, aware of every brush of his hand as he dug through the layers of tulle until he finally reached my thigh, continuing to kiss me. When his fingers traced my seam, nothing obstructing his path, he growled. "Coming to the Moonlit Masquerade bare beneath this skirt... Who were you planning to fuck tonight, Oakley? Them? Or Me?"

Possessiveness wove through his words and his fingers pushed inside me. I swallowed, adjusting to the fullness, unsure how to answer. He pumped his hand, palm grazing my clit with each stroke, and my breaths became shallow. "Is that what you wanted? To have them take you right in front of me, like at Luna's?"

My hands balled into fists at his words, but my body slicked with heat.

"What if I did?" My chin rose in challenge.

He stopped abruptly, and I shifted my pelvis, seeking more friction. After he removed his fingers, he lifted them up into the slip of moonlight. They were glistening. "This. Is. Mine."

Bringing them to his lips, he sucked them into his mouth, and I growled in frustration, desperate to be filled, to find that release. My Desire was as eager as my body was for him, pulsing from my fingertips, leaking onto Atlas with nowhere else to funnel.

He groaned. Hand coming to his buckle, he undid his belt, tossing it off to the side. Then he unbuttoned his trousers, peeling them off along with his underwear.

"Atlas," I panted, part of me knowing we should stop, that this would only complicate things—the other part wanting this more than anything.

Lust leaked steadily from the tip of his tan shaft, hastened by my wayward magic. He dragged me closer until I was flush against his length, then he rubbed up and down my seam, the crown of his cock stroking my nerves. "I'm going to fuck you now and remind you what it's like to be *mine*."

Gripping me tightly, he lifted me off the table. I yelped in surprise, forced to wrap my legs around his waist as he carried me until my back slammed against the cool glass. He whispered into my ear, curling his pelvis into me, slickness building where he teased. "You want that, don't you?"

The words wouldn't come. That would take logic. Sense. And I didn't want either of those things. That would end this right here, right now, and I wasn't ready for that finality. So instead of words, I nodded my silent confession, then coiled my magic around his cock, notching it at my entrance.

There was nothing tentative when he shoved himself deep inside me, driving forward every punishing inch in one thrust. I bit down on his shoulder to stifle my scream. He held me in place as I throbbed around him, pulsing with anticipation. I lifted my mouth off his flesh, leaving behind two crescent-shaped bite marks.

"More." I dug the heels of my boots into his back and urged him to move.

He inched himself out of me in painfully slow increments as I wriggled against him, desperate for friction. When I nearly thought he would fall out of me, he slammed in to the hilt, and I bit down on his shoulder again.

"Greedy little witch, aren't you?" he teased, retracting his hips before punching straight into my womb. I cried out, hugging him tightly, savoring the piercing fullness of him. "I'm not fucking you like *that* tonight."

But it's what I craved. Fast and wild. Unthinking. Because the alternative meant—

"You'll take my cock nice and slow," he whispered, nipping along my throat. "We've waited too long not to savor this."

Holy shit.

Rocking my hips as much as I could pinned between Atlas and the glass, I gained the friction I sought, enjoying each graze of his body along the sensitive bundle of nerves.

Plunging himself into the depths of me, I held on tight, tilting my pelvis to meet his thrusts. My thighs began to quake. I was so damn close...

"Ah, ah, ah," Atlas tutted, his gaze brutal and punishing before he was out of me, setting me down, leaving my body too hollow. Too empty. But before that moment had truly even passed, he flipped me over, pinning my hands against the glass, whispering over my shoulder, "Admit that you're mine and I'll let you come."

My chest heated, anger bubbling to the surface. "If you won't, then I'll do it myself, or I'm sure one of them—"

He growled in frustration, taking his hand off my wrists. Just when I was about to walk away and show him how serious I was, he gripped either side of my waist, wrestled my skirt higher, and slammed into me, picking up the pace. Then he snaked one hand along my hip before circling my clit. It was electric, rough, and I shook as he slapped into the backs of my thighs.

I whimpered, watching the bounce of my reflection against the glass, fog rolling over the party below us. Atlas ramped up his rhythm without losing any of the delicious depth, as if he wanted to drill himself in all the way and stamp himself on the sensitive nerves tucked inside me. "Tell me you're mine."

My fingers grasped for purchase and I released a guttural cry, body detonating with his punishing movements. Heaving against the window, I slid my hand across it, finally noticing the clear glass under my fingertips.

Clear.

Not darkened.

Oh my Goddess.

I looked out at the crowd. The fog had eased up, exposing the witches enjoying the revelry of tonight's party. Some were talking, others dancing, a few strewn across lounge chairs or tucked away, writhing together.

"You love that they're watching me fuck you, don't you?"

Before I even saw the sienna and evergreen eyes, I knew who he referred to.

Saros's hands clenched at his sides. Throat bobbing.

Lynx had put his arm around him, as if trying to send some calm in his direction.

It didn't seem to be working.

"The way you're clenched around my cock tells me you do," Atlas growled, continuing his strokes. "Looks like I'm not the only one that doesn't enjoy sharing."

I couldn't believe he had done this. It had all been a ploy to, what? Prove his claim over me? To hurt Lynx and Saros?

I pushed off the glass and turned to face him, directing him back onto the bench. He set his legs on either side of it and I straddled him, sinking onto his cock until I was flush with his lap. His expression was triumphant as his magic pulsed up through my chest and out through my fingertips.

If he wanted to show me that I was his tonight, I would show him exactly what that would need to look like.

I spread my legs wide, pushing the heels of my boots into the ground, lifting a few inches up Atlas's cock before slowly descending. Twisting my gaze toward the window I spotted Saros and Lynx. They watched every rise and fall of my body, and I kept my attention pinned on them. Atlas kissed my neck, nipping along my jaw—thinking he'd won.

He had absolutely no fucking idea.

If he wanted me, it would be on my terms or he wouldn't have me at all.

I waved my hand and four forms appeared between us and the window. I was on my knees, riding Lynx's cock, Atlas filling my other hole as they thrust into me in a steady rhythm. Saros stood in front of me, fucking my face, tears streaming down my cheeks, breasts bouncing, our sweat-slicked bodies writhing together.

"What the fuck, Oakley?" Atlas rasped, eyes darting from my illusioned Lynx and Saros to the ones watching from the yard.

Raising and lowering myself in Atlas's lap, I slipped my hand toward my sensitive bud. He smacked it away, eyes locked on the image of the four of us, toying with my clit. I continued riding him, shifting the bodies and contorting them into different positions, showing them all fucking me, together, in pairs, alone.

"You love watching them fuck me, don't you?" I cooed, twisting his earlier words and crooking my finger under Atlas's chin to meet my gaze. He ground out a series of curses, his thick release pouring from him in hot spurts. Rolling my hips in his lap, he continued to fill me, and I lowered my lips to his ear. "The way you just filled me with your cum tells me you do."

Atlas slid out of me, focus glued to the illusion still animated in front of him, his release spilling down my thighs. I clenched them together, adjusting my skirt, eyes never leaving Saros and Lynx.

I couldn't read Saros, but Lynx— I knew he would under-stand. He always did. Emotions never lied.

I wished his power was the one cradled within me right now. That I could know, with just a glance, what they were all feeling.

All I heard, though, was the rustle of clothing and the sound of a zipper while I descended the stairs. But the look in Atlas's eyes at Luna's, the look in his eyes tonight, told me his truth, whether he wanted to admit it or not. He *was* turned on.

He'd asked what I wanted. The truth was that I wanted it all.

Them all.

But there was no real way forward for us until we could admit it to each other, fate or not.

"Great Goddess! Did she just do what I think she did?" Lynx asked as we watched Oakley storm away from Atlas.

"Fuck him and then used his power to illusion us all taking her in front of the coven?" I shifted on my heels, trying to ground myself because that vision she created felt so damn real. "Yes, Lynx. That's exactly what she did."

"I'm really glad Hazel was off with that event planner and didn't see all that."

Wish I'd been off anywhere else myself...

Maybe then I wouldn't have been saddled with a semi-hard cock and a heavy dose of confusion. It was clear there were still a lot of feelings between those two—not sure whether more hate, love, or denial—but where did that leave us?

"Wild! I think she made it pretty clear what she wants," Lynx said, not even trying to hold back a smirk.

I envied his ever-present optimism, but I'd seen enough of the past to know better. People wanted to believe they'd evolved and learned, that things would improve. Instead it usually just cycled.

Once in a rare moon someone had the stuff it took to break it.

"Maybe he's not the ideal addition to what we've got going on, but she wants us," Lynx continued, and I knew he was reading me. "We need to go find and talk to her."

But I was pinned to the spot, still staring up at Atlas who paced back and forth before zipping up his trousers. The logical part of me agreed that I should go find her, just like I should have the other day after Luna's. Maybe if I had, things wouldn't be so...I don't even know between us and I'd be assured that what we had wasn't fleeting. I'd be certain she was still choosing *us*.

As certain as Lynx seemed to be.

Must be nice to never have to read between the lines. I could see anything from someone's life, but the context? That was always a fucker to decipher.

"Saros."

My attention snapped to Lynx. He'd already moved a few feet away, staring at me, but I was still rooted in place like a schmuck. "What?"

"You okay?" he asked, tilting his head. Taking a step forward, he held out his arm, as if to ask if he could touch me —use his Empathy. "I'm getting some mixed emotions and I'm not sure which one to—"

"Don't manage me, Lynx," I ground out, retreating from him. The words came out more bitter than I intended. "Sometimes emotions just fucking *are*. They don't always need to be fixed, they just need to be had. Allow me to have mine in peace."

His eyes went wide. "Don't you want to find Oakley? Hear her out?"

"I don't think I'm much in the mood to listen. Right now I've got a lot on my mind." Working through the maze of thorny roses, I avoided them until I remembered this was all an illusion, as real as Oakley's foursome fantasy she'd shoved in Atlas's face. I inhaled deeply, then walked through the wall in front of me, Lynx following.

"Why don't I go see what Oakley says and then we can meet at home?" he offered, gripping my hand tightly with his own. I braced myself for the flood of calm, but it never came.

At least he'd given me the space to stew.

"Sure." Though I doubted a thirty-minute head start would be enough to let me figure out what the hell was going on.

He headed around the house, peeking into the glass door before glancing back at me, as if wanting to give me one more chance to change my mind and follow him. I waved at him to go ahead before continuing down the long driveway.

From Blessed Crescent, I spotted Luna's with its light on and rolled my eyes. Lynx must have forgotten to turn it off when he closed up earlier.

When I reached the cul-de-sac it was quiet. The chirping of crickets the only sound aside from the masquerade in the distance. Stepping up into the truck, I reached for the button and flicked it off before a sting pinched the nape of my neck. "Wha—"

"Well, this was easier than I thought it would be." As he spoke, images slammed into my mind, knocking into each other like bumper cars. *A musty hallway. A bloody gray suit. Computer screens. A room with no windows. Throbbing pain.*

Then everything faded to black.

((((●))))

"Rise and shine, Agent Holt."

The familiar, yet abrasive musk of bleach mixed with iron clogged my nostrils as I opened my eyes. Slumped over the back of a metal chair, my chest ached. When I moved to sit upright, the muscles of my shoulders tensed from the restraints cuffing my hands behind my back.

I'd been here too many times to question where I was. I knew it all would be white: the walls, floors, chairs, everything down to the cuffs on my wrists.

Most people believed SNO-OPS was where all the terrible secrets of the government played out, but they would be wrong. There was a darker, more sinister spot, tucked beneath the department's underbelly. Somewhere, most agents, including my very own partner, never ventured.

The Casket.

"Agent Aleander, what's the meaning of this?"

Through the only window in the room, two people were slumped over chairs, unconscious. Aurora and Fitzgerald Wells. Fitz was bleeding all over the white floor from his face and knuckles.

He'd tried to fight them off.

Aurora's eyes were vacant, poised on the floor ahead of her. I recognized that look all too well. It was the same one my mother had when my father would *correct* her. Like if she stared at that one speck of dust somewhere on the ground, she could mentally escape from this moment. Like it wasn't really happening.

If they'd hurt Aurora already, I couldn't see it. But they would. It was rare for anyone to completely escape the trauma left behind from their time buried in The Casket.

Pain was quite a motivator. Find someone's weak spot and they would do just about anything. If the government didn't already know someone's, it was usually my job to dig around and find it.

But the physical pain? That was left to an enforcer.

Currently, it looked like that would be Festus, Agent Aleander's lackey and occasional side piece, though he thought he was stealthy enough that no one else at SNO-OPS knew.

"I tried to do this the nice way. Tried to put a little pressure on you and light a fire to get the information we needed," Agent Aleander said, his breath hot over my shoulder. "Unfortunately, your continual refusal forced me to get creative."

My gaze narrowed, hands tightening into fists. "What are you talking about?"

"I think you just need some motivation." Agent Aleander strode across the room and out of reach, pressing the invisible panel built into the wall. "I considered using Agent Carver, knowing you two have a history, but then tonight, like some blessing from the Mother Goddess herself, an even better opportunity fell into my lap."

That's when I truly saw the person sitting there, tethered to that white chair. One surprise I never could have prepared myself for.

Oakley.

I thrashed against my bindings, kicking and screaming despite the fact that I'd been in this room a thousand times and had seen a thousand people do the same thing with no success. "What did you do?"

"Really, I didn't need to do anything." Agent Aleander picked at some dirt from beneath his fingernails. "I just happened to catch that spectacular *show* back at Archon Thorne's place. Falling for the sister of your open case vic and witchling momma to your boss? Classy, Holt. Didn't know you had it in you."

He leaned down right in front of me, so close I was tempted to headbutt him but wasn't willing to be knocked unconscious again until I knew Oakley was away and safe. "Even better that she's got such a unique ability."

Fuck.

He knows.

"Let her go!" I seethed, mind sprinting to all the worst-case scenarios of how far they'd go to see her gifts in action. Because while the supernatural world might believe we were serving some noble cause, they'd never been down in The Casket where the blood and muck and dark secrets flowed.

But I had. And I'd vowed I'd never come down here again.

I guess in a way I got my wish. I wasn't here as a predator anymore—now I was the prey. And I could have lived with that. But as I watched Oakley stiffen, attention shifted toward the door that'd no doubt opened to her cell, I refused to let them prey on her.

"Now, now. We need to know what's hiding away in the Wellses' mental vaults," Aleander continued, calm like we've been trained to be. He had a hollow sort of tone, like he didn't have any skin in the game. But I knew better. He wouldn't have brought us here otherwise. "And if you're not willing to use your ability, Ms. Brooks can borrow it for a bit and help us out."

Can borrow it for a bit?

Rage pooled in my ribs, and I unleashed the next words in a fiery growl. "If headquarters finds out about this—"

He chuckled. A sound that was all too wrong for him. "Oh, aren't you cute. I wouldn't be wasting my time if there weren't more important people wanting this intel."

"Who put you up to this?"

"Let's just say the Archons may believe they run the show, but they'll be begging for a piece of power soon enough." He smiled with a smugness that I wanted to claw off his face with my bare hands.

Maybe I would later if I got the chance.

He sighed. "I'll give you an hour to mull it over. Then I'll need to know who will be up for getting what I need done."

"And what if we refuse?"

"As of right now, no one knows about Ms. Brooks's *special talents* other than Festus and me." He pulled out his phone and swiped through it. "But one message to my contact and I'm sure they'd love to get their hands on her. Push those limits to see what she's capable of with that power-stealing snatch of hers." He shook his head with a *tsk*. "You think I just *happened* upon you all those years ago to recruit you?"

I could have sworn my heart stopped beating, recalling when I'd first met Aleander at the shelter. It was after I'd run away from home at sixteen. After I realized some cycles couldn't be broken from within. Sometimes the only option was escape—forging your own path.

"You were so eager to find a way to be of use," he said, shaking his head. "Just think of all the uses we'd have for *her*."

"Go to Hell, Aleander."

"Oh, I'm planning on it." He smiled so wide it looked awkward against his jaw. "I hear the lust demons there can fuck for days."

Striding toward the door, he pressed another invisible button.

Five. Four. Three. Two. One.

The door slid open, and Aleander stepped through, glancing over his shoulder. "Talk to you and your little power thief soon, Agent Holt."

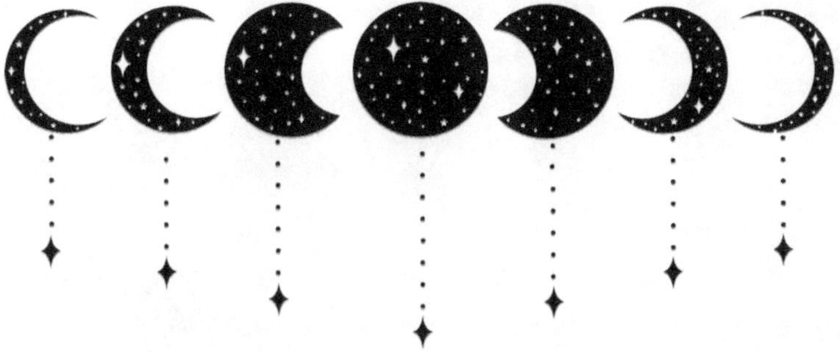

 What had been an illusion versus reality?
They didn't seem to care too much, returning to their revelry.

Meanwhile, Archon Atlas Thorne stomped across the
pristine floors, slamming the door to his office behind him.
The heat coming off him was enough to flip on the fan from
his home system as he sat there stewing.

Pulling out the box from his pocket, he flicked it open,
staring at the small gemstone ring inside, brows drawn
together like a pair of angry curtains.

Should I have stopped her from leaving?

No. That definitely wouldn't have improved the situation.

Oakley Brooks hadn't seemed to appreciate the baby gate
maneuver. Though in the end, hadn't the Archon gotten what
he wanted? The towels currently mopping up the table and
wiping away the handprints smearing the glass would make
one think so.

But witches were confusing.

Complex.

After wringing his hands together for a few minutes, Atlas
slicked back the wayward pieces of his hair and pocketed the
box. Picking up the silvery mask he'd discarded, he headed
down the stairs, ready to play host to his guests.

There was no sign of Oakley on the lower level of the house, so I headed back toward the yard, searching through the maze of thorny black roses and the festivities still in full swing.

Nothing.

She probably headed home to get Aspen fed and in bed.

I rifled through the bucket and pulled out my phone, calling her to find out where she was. It rang over and over, in time to the buzz coming from the very same pile I'd just grabbed mine from. Walking over to it, I dug through, finding her phone blinking brightly among the dozens within.

Flipping through my contacts, I dialed the next best bet to get ahold of her.

"Hey, Hazel. I tried calling Oakley but there was no answer, and I realized she left her phone here at the party. Should I drop it by, or does she want to come get it tomorrow?"

"How should I know?" Hazel asked, unease prickling her tone. "I haven't seen her."

"What are you talking about?" I jolted at Atlas's stern

voice behind me. He reached around and snatched the phone from my hand, pressing the Speakerphone button.

"I left early to get Aspen home and to bed. I told her I was leaving," Hazel said through the line.

"Of course you did." Atlas groaned, though I wasn't sure why.

"You're saying you don't know where my sister is?" Hazel's voice jumped up an octave, wobbling a bit. I didn't need to see her to know she'd be outlined in lime-green fear.

This was one of those moments I wish I could turn to my gift to calm her, but my words would have to do. "Don't freak out, Hazel."

She huffed out a sarcastic laugh. "That's rich saying that to someone who was chained to a pipe for weeks."

"Let me see if she's with Saros," I offered, trying to reassure both of them. Atlas rolled his eyes as I grabbed the phone back. "I promise I'll text you an update, but if you see her first, please text us."

Before I finished hanging up, Atlas had his phone out, holding it to his ear. A loud, persistent ring echoed from the bucket.

"Do you think he and Oakley could be together at Luna's?" he asked, looking wary, blueish-gray smoke filtering around his feet.

"Without their phones?" My brows drew together. "Saros was pissed when he left. Maybe he could forget it if he wanted to be alone, but Oakley? I don't see her leaving without her phone even if she was angry."

His jaw ticked. "You're right about that."

"I'll stop by Luna's on my way back to the house. See if by some chance they are there."

"I'm coming with you."

"And leave your own party?"

"They are having plenty of fun without me. The amplifier should hold my illusion through the night." He waved at Clio, circling his finger in the air to let her know to keep things going. "If you think I'd ever put a party before Oakley, then you have no idea how much she means to me."

"Oh, believe me," I watched the swirls of pink spiral around him like a hazy tornado, "it's very clear to me. Or do you forget who you're talking to?"

We sprinted down the drive. The lights were off in Luna's, but it didn't hurt to check anyway.

I kept pace a few ahead of the Archon the entire way to the truck, and I couldn't lie, it had a pinch of self-indulgent pride blooming in my chest.

Unlocking the back, I opened the doors and switched on the light.

It was empty.

"They aren't here."

"Fuck." Atlas brought his fist to his mouth, biting on it as if to stifle the wisps of red around him.

"I have an idea." I sprinted toward the community center, Atlas jogging after me.

When we got inside, only a few lights were on, a small group of young witches watching *Halloweentown* on the projector screen. Ruby was sitting with them until she saw us. From how quickly she stood up and shuffled over as quietly as she could, she could tell something was wrong.

"What brings you both here?" she whispered.

"The bracelets the parents had tonight, was there any sort of tracking enchantment on them?"

"Of course there was." She said it like not tracking all the parents in the coven would be the real ludicrous thing.

"I know Hazel already picked up Aspen, but we need you

to track the one that was on Oakley Brooks tonight," Atlas urged, speeding through his words with impatience.

She pulled out a large orb, a map stretched out within its depths. When she held her hands over it, she tapped in a code, probably whatever identifier was associated with the bracelet. "Hmm."

Placing her hands on the orb, she expanded their distance, zooming out on the area. Then tried again. When that didn't do anything, she did it once more, looking at a larger plot of land in the dome's reflective depths.

"This is strange." Her brows knit together. "These were spelled to have no distance limit. I've never heard of something that could hide its location, but the signal just keeps bouncing around."

Fuck.

"There's one place I know of that could work that sort of signal interference." The words were brittle when they left my lips.

Apparently, he'd drawn a similar conclusion. The red around him still floated, but lime slips of fear swam through it. "Think Saros is with her?"

"I can only hope." I swallowed hard. "Either way, there's no good reason for her to be in that part of headquarters." Another thought popped into my mind. "Our vow marks are embedded with trackers." I lifted my arm, looking to where the star in my constellation had been laced with the rune. "Let me check his."

I pulled out my phone, scanning over it with the camera. My Maps opened up, the signal zigzagging around the screen.

"See anything?" Atlas asked, trying to snoop over my shoulder.

"It's ping-ponging." My ribs pinched together, chest constricting. I gripped Atlas's arm, giving Ruby a wave while I walked with him outside of the community center. As soon as we were away, I tugged him close. "We need to get to The Casket."

Atlas's knuckles were white, his usually smooth tone rippled with distress. "What would they be doing there?"

"I don't know, but it can't be good," I replied with a shake of my head.

"Explain to me on the way," Atlas said, putting an arm around my shoulder and turning me toward the pines.

We wandered deep into the woods. This was the farthest I'd ever been in the pines. We were nearing where the shifters and vamps tended to dwell, stopping when we reached the large mouth of a rocky cave. "Where are we going?"

"To get her back." Atlas nodded at the dark tunnel ahead. "And Saros."

I followed him inside. He clutched my shirt with one hand as we continued forward, the moonlight dissipating with each step. Then he halted, rustling in the darkness, but he never released me with his other hand, his grip deadly tight.

Whatever he was doing, it didn't seem to be working.

He growled in frustration.

"You know, if you wanted to test the waters, you could have just asked," I teased, trying to lighten his prickling energy. It was the only thing I saw in the pitch, outlining him within its clutches.

"Let's save the jokes until after we've found them," he replied sourly.

"Okay, no joking..." I trailed off, figuring we might as well kill time while we waited for whatever it was he needed to happen. "Are we going to talk about earlier tonight?"

"Not sure what there is to talk about with you," he said, brushing me off, his tone threaded with annoyance. "This is between Oakley and me."

"Is it?" I nudged. "Because I'm pretty sure she made it clear she wants to be between all of us."

A ribbon of powdery sugar wafted through the darkness.

Got ya.

"I suggest you shut your mouth before you end up pinned to one of these trees and I go get them myself."

Guess someone isn't ready to be honest yet.

"You forget I can see how you feel even when you don't want to acknowledge it."

The hand gripping my shirt tightened its hold. "What's that supposed to mean?"

"It means I sensed the lust coming from you when she showed us that illusion." Unlike Oakley, Atlas's lust was less powdery and more like a chocolate chip cookie straight from the oven. Warm. Decadent. "You liked it."

"You don't know what you're talking about." He cleared his throat. "I was only feeling that because I was fucking the witch I love, who happens to be Desire-blessed."

"Oh, she was full of desire. And you." I winked in the darkness at my own humor. Someone had to make this impatient guy less uptight. If we had any chance of getting them out of The Casket, we'd need to keep our heads on straight. "It's okay to admit it was hot to see her with us."

The cavern began to rattle, shaking beneath us, and the hand clutching my shirt tightened once again, bunching the fabric in his fist, as if worried he'd lose me.

What the fuck was this?

"If it fires you up and our witch is satisfied, who really loses in that situation? No one," I continued, trying to steady my own feelings more than anything else since I had no clue where we were going.

The floor beneath us began to loosen, like we were sinking deep into it.

"She's not *our* witch," Atlas deadpanned. "She was mine first."

"What are we, toddlers?" I asked, chuckling in the darkness. "What are you so afraid of?"

The ground shook again, settling wherever we were.

"We're here," he said, releasing a breath, like he'd never been more grateful to be done with...whatever sort of magic this was.

"Never thought to let us use this when we had to go to headquarters?"

This would have been much less annoying than flying mortal airlines between states.

"Only Archons and a select handful have access to these transporters. No one else is supposed to know about them." He pressed a button, holding his finger on it until a door slid open to the basement of headquarters. "One of the perks of the job."

"Of course it is."

I mean, it made sense. It was easier to get between territories with some secret system. But it would have been nice to share the perks when we'd been away those few weeks to work on the case.

We walked for a while, turning down hallways and moving through stairways until we got to Atlas's office. It was huge, overlooking the bustling Salem District. Highways tangled around each other, swerving off into different neighborhoods. Arbor Sanctum perched up in the distance, where Oakley and Hazel had grown up. Billboards and skyscrapers poked up within the cityscape—including a large one for Pierce Protections that I recognized by the large silver star on its side.

Atlas sat at his desk, pulling out drawers, looking for something. "Explain to me where Oakley is exactly and what is The Casket? What goes on there? We have only been told things on an *as-needed* basis."

"The Casket is where in-depth interrogations are done..." I swallowed thickly. "Torture."

"Are you telling me that the mother of my son is being tortured right now?" A crimson swirl lashed out like a smoky snake, wrapping around us.

"I don't know," I said, taking a deep breath. "Until we get closer, I won't be able to sense her emotions. And even that could be hazy because I won't be able to pinpoint that it's Oakley until I have eyes on her."

"How do we get there?" He laid the blueprint of the building in front of me. "What's the layout?"

"I've never been there myself." But that didn't mean I didn't know where it was. I had a general idea.

"But Saros has." Atlas filled in the blanks.

"Yes. And that's the last place he'd ever want to be." I scanned over the rendering, thinking of where I'd met him on those days when we were young and he seemed especially distraught after work. "He spent years forced to use his Recollection on unwilling participants."

"What would they want to do with Oakley?"

"I don't know." I shrugged, trailing my finger along a hallway I remember seeing him coming from, though I didn't remember there being any doors at the end of it. "Maybe use her as leverage to get him to finally pull memories from Aurora and Fitz?"

"Then he better pull those fucking memories."

"You don't get it." My gaze snapped up to his, scowling at him. "Saros spent years digging through people's minds for whatever the government wanted. Sometimes scrambling them beyond repair. That's not easy to live with."

"If he cares about her as much as you claim, he'll be able to live with this."

I tapped on the spot where The Casket was buried beneath us. "Hopefully it doesn't come to that."

"Got any bright ideas to get in?" he asked, rolling up the blueprint and shrinking it down to throw in his pocket.

"Bright? Not really." There wasn't going to be any good way out of this. If Saros and Oakley were in The Casket, someone on the inside had ordered this. The fact that Atlas, one of our Archons, was here with me and clueless didn't give me too much confidence. "Effective? Sure."

"Then let's go."

This would easily end all of our careers—something I was willing to part with. Atlas, he had much more at stake. But he didn't hesitate to head toward the door, the fear dissipating until the air around him silvered with resolve.

That told me everything I needed to know.

Our witches were worth more than it all.

CHAPTER 21

OAKLEY

The last thing I remembered doing was storming out of Atlas's house and heading toward the yard to find Saros and Lynx. Now I was somehow in an all-white room with a single window seemingly looking out onto nothing.

A strange sound came from outside the room, and the door slid open before shutting just as quickly.

"Where am I?" I asked the large wrath demon when he walked into the room. "What am I doing here?"

His skin was red, jagged scales rippling up his brawny arms. All bulk and unforgiving muscle, the nastiest scowl on his face. Crossing his arms, he stood there in silence.

My hands were bound behind my back, and panic streaked up my throat as I fought against the restraints. Tears welled in my eyes. I needed to get home. To get to Aspen. Was he still at the community center? Was he safe?

"Please let me go. I don't know why I'm here, but I have a son who needs me."

I tried to send out any magic I could—not that I thought I'd be able to kill this guy from an awkwardly timed erection, but I was desperate enough to try anything. There was nothing running through my veins, aside from a large dose of fear, not even a hint of magic. Whatever cuffs were strapped around my wrists prevented me from doing more.

The demon must have noticed because his face turned from stoic to slightly amused.

Glad one of us finds humor in this situation.

I looked down at my dress, my legs wrapped on either side of the chair, mortified. The tulle was shoved up in all the wrong places, itchy and uncomfortable, and Atlas's earlier claim was sticky between my thighs. My breasts were like rocks, starting to throb.

My body stilled when the door slid open again, and another man stepped in. He looked familiar but I couldn't place him. He was in a polished gray suit and had unusual eyes, a combination of orange and blue that somehow was unnerving.

"Please let me out of here. I need to get back to my son," I pleaded, trying to move against the restraints. They somehow felt tighter than before, and my wrists were raw, rubbed against the thick metal.

"Patience, Ms. Brooks." His voice was annoyingly calm, making me feel anything but. "I promise your witchling is at home and completely safe."

Somehow his promise wasn't too reassuring, what with me being tied up to a chair with no clue where I was or why I'd been taken.

"I remember you." My gaze narrowed. "From the hospital."

His lips lifted into a tilted smile. "Ah, I guess I made an impression."

"I wouldn't say that," I seethed. "I just remember every detail of the day I got my sister back."

"What a happy reunion that must have been." The overeager smile was still there as he circled me. "I should properly introduce myself. The name's Aleander."

The wrath demon continued to stand by the door, arms crossed and silent. For whatever reason, they wanted something from me. "I'm sure you still have questions about your sister's capture. Why Aurora went after Acacia. Why she was so quick to confess her crimes."

"Guilty conscience?" I shrugged, not sure where this conversation was going.

"Do the Wellses strike you as people with guilt on their minds?" Aleander asked, condescension coating his words. "And here I was thinking you'd impress me today."

"Sorry to disappoint." I glared at him, the pain in my wrists turning to numbness from pushing against the binding so much.

"You can make it up to me." The tilted smile returned along with my unease, nausea clawing at my gut.

"What do you want?"

"It's really quite simple. Mrs. Wells and her husband have answers we need. Answers that could alter the course of supernatural history." *What the hell is he talking about?* "You will help me get them."

"I don't know how you think I can help."

"It seems as though Agent Holt needs a little reminder of what his job is."

Panic scratched at me again, shredding at my insides until I was a tangled jumble of anxiety and fear.

"Where is he?" I pleaded, pulling at the restraints that only seemed to cinch tighter around my wrists, cutting off my circulation. "Where's Saros?"

"I've been giving him a little time out to think. It's taking a bit of *convincing*." He shrugged, and my mind quivered over what that really meant. "But if he's not willing to dive into their memories, I'm hoping you'll consider doing it yourself."

"What—"

"I saw your little *display* at the Moonlit Masquerade." *Holy Mother Goddess above.* "It seems as though you have a very *unique* skill set. I did have a few questions, though. Do you have to actually fuck someone to steal their ability? Would a simple blow job suffice? I'm sure there are worse ways to borrow another's power. How long do you have access to an ability once you take it?"

My mind raced, body instinctively recoiling at his questions, mortified that he'd been watching. He'd seen.

When I didn't answer him, Aleander continued, "Maybe that's a little too personal, but I'm sure headquarters would covet someone with your ability."

How stupid was I? Saros had warned me. That's why he'd been so afraid to be with me. And he'd had every right to be afraid.

I was fucking terrified.

"However, there's no need to mention it to them so long as I get the answers I need from the Wellses. Whether they come from Agent Holt or yourself, I couldn't care less."

"I need to see him. Now."

My heart rioted in my ribs, thumping against it like a prisoner wanting release. The room was feeling smaller with each passing moment, filling my head with dizzying heat.

"Of course." Aleander nodded to the wrath demon, who pressed a blank space on the wall. The door opened after a few seconds. "I'll have Festus bring him in."

When the wrath demon returned, he was dragging Saros with him. He looked like he could barely stand, his face bloodied.

"Goddess above," I gasped, body trembling at the sight. "Unbind him."

But he did no such thing. Instead, Festus stood there holding him upright by the wrist cuffs like a puppeteer supporting his marionette.

Someone had to know we were missing, right? What if they didn't and no one was coming? I had no idea how to get us out of here, and Saros's head was bleeding everywhere. What if this was where it all ended and I never saw Aspen or Hazel again. Not to mention Lynx and Atlas.

"You aren't really in a position to make demands right now, Miss Brooks," Aleander said, shaking his head. "But I'm sure I can figure out something."

He snapped his fingers, and in a flash Saros and I were seated on the hard floor, cuffs interlocked. The chair gone.

How the hell did he do that?

"I'll be back in fifteen." Aleander gave us one final look that felt both predatory and arrogant—and not in the charming way Atlas could pull off. "Festus will be outside the door to make sure you don't do anything foolish, like try to escape."

"Let her go," Saros slurred, blood dripping from his lips as he heaved out the words. "You don't need to involve her."

Aleander pressed the wall, and seconds later the door slid open. As it started to shut, that tilted grin returned. "Follow through, Agent Holt, and I'll release her. Unharmed."

I didn't have to be able to read Saros's emotions to know that neither of us believed him one bit.

CHAPTER 22

OAKLEY

"Everything's going to be okay," Saros breathed out, still not looking at me.

"How can you say that? You're bleeding everywhere, no one knows where we are or has probably even realized we are missing, and I need to get to Aspen—" Warmth spread over my breasts, the milk that'd been swelling within finally letting down into the nursing pads within my corset.

Great.

"I'm sure Hazel's got it covered. You have milk stored for him, right?"

I nodded, slightly reassured at that despite the tightness in my chest.

He's with Hazel. She'll keep him safe.

Saros's evergreen irises were dull when they finally met my gaze. "You're going to get out of here. I'll do what he wants."

"What information is he looking for?"

"Something in Acacia's research made it seem like either Aurora or Fitz knew about the disappearances, but instead of giving that information to headquarters, they've kept it secret." He looked down at our entwined cuffs, then scooted closer to give himself more slack to use his sleeve to wipe away some of the blood on his face. "That secret was why they'd killed Acacia."

"I think Aurora was in love with my sister." As soon as the words left my mouth, something shifted in his expression, like he was surprised but maybe that he shouldn't have been. "Could she have known Acacia took her and did it for revenge?" I asked.

"Maybe. But I'd be more inclined to think they'd do something to save their own skin." He stopped wiping the blood off his face, revealing rough gashes. "Besides, if that were the case, why didn't she free Hazel when she killed Acacia?"

This was true. Aurora didn't seem like a selfless person, but my sister obviously saw something in her. I didn't get the impression they'd had a one-off fling from the memory I'd been privy to or how defensive Hazel had been when they'd arrested the Wellses. "So Aurora's memories would tell us what happened that night and why?"

"I'd have to dig around for the why. Filtering through maybe hundreds of memories to find the right one without their cooperation..." He inhaled deeply and sighed. "It's one thing when they agree to show something to me—those memories stay at the surface. When there's something someone wants hidden...that takes digging. And doing that to someone's brain, someone's memories, can mess with their minds permanently."

His gaze dropped, and all I wanted was to reach out and stroke his cheek. He was so close, our bodies inches away from each other's, but I held myself back, unsure where we stood after everything.

"What happens when you touch someone?" I asked, hesitating a bit to clarify what I really wanted to know. "When you touch me?"

"I see whatever traumatic or horrible memories are lying just beneath the surface, influencing or impacting them in that moment." He held his palms up, hoisting up my attached wrist cuffs with his. Waiting. It was a silent offering, and my breath caught as I slid my palms to meet his, even though I knew he couldn't see anything with whatever spelled the thick cuffs. "That's not how it is with you."

My eyes drifted up. "It isn't?"

"No." The corner of his mouth twisted into probably the best smile he could muster, blood and gashes marring its edges. "When I touch you, the most beautiful moments of your life flash before my eyes. And it's like I can't breathe."

I understood those final words all too well, feeling as if the air had been sucked out of this tiny white room. For a moment, I could almost pretend we weren't in this awful predicament.

"There's only three other people that's ever happened with."

"Lynx and who else?" I asked, trying to do the math in my head.

"That's a topic best kept for another time. When we aren't chained together in a cell." His fingers laced with mine and he pulled me closer, our foreheads touching.

"Then why so much concern over the transference? Of being with me? Why avoid touching me when you see the good?"

Saros's words rushed out in a whisper, sending a shiver through me. "I was concerned... What if the magic isn't the same for you? What if you touch me and only see the worst and darkest parts of my life? The things I've done. The people I've hurt. What if it changes how you see me?" His throat bobbed. "And I struggled every time we touched because...I always risked seeing you with someone else."

"Atlas?" I croaked.

"Yes. Him and Lynx." His thumb brushed along mine. "I'm so envious. Not because I didn't want you with them or couldn't handle loving you alongside them, but because I knew I wasn't able to give you what I so desperately wanted to. In the present, the mind subconsciously draws on past experiences, so it's like a front-row seat to your sex life. And while you deserve every ounce of pleasure you've gotten and will get—I'm selfish enough to admit that I wanted to be the one in those memories feeling your body respond, swallowing those cries of ecstasy with my lips." Releasing my fingers, he brushed away the tears I hadn't realized streaked my cheeks. Then he peppered hauntingly soft kisses where the ghost of them remained. "After what happened between us at Luna's, I wasn't mad that you came. Scared you'd touch me and what you'd see, yes. But when I realized Atlas had been there, it felt like another moment that didn't belong to me."

"It did belong to you." I caught his mouth with my own, my tongue tangling with his like our hands locked together by the cuffs. Copper tinged where the corner of his mouth bled and I pressed a kiss there before continuing, "I mean... I can't lie, I'm apparently really into the idea of being shared, but it was when I saw he was turned on by what you were doing to me that I lost control. I felt horrible afterward for not warning you."

I steadied my breathing, not wanting to panic anymore so we could escape this situation and get back to Aspen and crew. But I didn't know how we would get out of this room or if we even would, and I refused to let him believe he meant anything less to me than he did.

I took his hands in mine and guided them to my heart, ignoring the hardened swell of my chest. "There will always be enough Desire and love running through me for some to belong to you. As long as you're okay with it also belonging to someone else. And I'm really sorry about what happened earlier at the masquerade with Atlas. That was not my intention, I just needed him to know what I wanted."

"And what is that, Midnight?" He brushed his fingers over my heart, sending a shiver down my spine.

"All of you," I admitted. "Though, I'm not sure if it's possible."

He sighed. "The truth is sometimes messy. But it also makes things clear." He shook his head, as if remembering what had happened in all too vivid detail. Heat crept over my cheeks.

"And you're not mad?"

"At you, Midnight? No. I just wish it hadn't landed you here."

"Aleander would really risk scrambling the Wellses' minds for that intel?" I asked, eyes darting up to the door and picturing the wrath demon probably still poised outside of it. "Even people who are that high profile in the community?"

"What would anyone say at this point? They've been arrested for murder. Claiming they are mentally unstable wouldn't be that hard of a sell."

That was true. No one would be fighting for them. The only one who'd said anything since they'd been arrested had been Hazel. "So you're going to do it?"

"I don't really see another choice." His forehead rested on mine again. "Not one that doesn't put you at an even greater risk. Aleander *can't* tell his contact at headquarters about you."

There was another way... A way I could take some of this burden from him.

My hands quivered, gripping his. "If they removed my cuffs... If you showed me how to—"

"No." His tone was firm. Stance clear. "The next time I make you come, it will be over and over and not under some fucked-up time limit in the place I hate most. I'm getting you out of here."

"There's got to be something I can do to help," I pleaded. I couldn't just sit by and wait. My body hurt and my mind raced over getting out of here safely and back to Aspen. If Saros left me here, I'd go crazy. "We're in this together."

He pulled me close, making it look like a lover's touch, but the purpose in his eyes said more. "Actually, there might be something, but it probably sounds crazy."

"Tell me."

"It involves using your gifts." The evergreen of his irises brightened with something akin to mischief.

"I'm in." I clasped his hands in mine, whispering low. "Just tell me what to do."

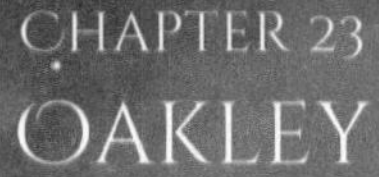

CHAPTER 23

OAKLEY

Saros squeezed my hand at the *swish* of The Casket cell door.

"It's time," Aleander said, entering the room. "What's your decision?"

"I'll do it." Saros's tone was gruff, confident, and I clung to it, knowing it would help me soon enough. "So long as you let Oakley go."

"Very well." Aleander pointed over to Festus to escort him. "As soon as you're done, we will.

"I'm going to need you to take *these* off," Saros said, lifting his wrists, "and she stays with me so I can ensure she's okay."

He nodded to Festus who unclasped Saros's cuffs.

"Hers too." Saros pointed to me, clenching and unclenching his hands.

With Aleander's nod, Festus removed mine next, and I rolled my wrists, savoring the heaviness of the rough mystery material finally gone, my arms now completely bare minus my aspen tattoo. I was so glad Hazel had insisted on getting a bracelet for herself when we'd left Aspen at the community center since mine was nowhere to be seen.

Saros and I had to play the timing just right for this to work.

"Now shall we?" Aleander said, leading the way out of the room. Festus followed us, and I shot some Desire his way, glancing over my shoulder to spot him shifting uncomfortably. Then I shoved out every bit of Atlas's ability I had access to. Thankfully, he'd been amplified when it transferred to me, otherwise this wouldn't have been possible.

By the time Festus adjusted his untimely erection and got back to walking behind us, it was done.

"Alright, Agent Holt, have you decided who you're going to start with?"

I stared down at my blood-soaked sleeve and dark, calloused hands, ones that didn't truly belong to me, hoping beyond hope that this worked. "Auro— I mean, Mrs. Wells."

Next to me stood my true reflection, Saros illusioned with my likeness. He placed a seemingly tentative, delicate hand on my shoulder.

When we got into the Wellses' room, Fitz had already been taken elsewhere. Aurora sat in her chair in the center of the otherwise empty room. Festus was with Saros in the corner, Aleander standing opposite of them.

"Tell me, Mrs. Wells, why did you kill Acacia Mirabel?" I asked in my illusioned voice, hoping I'd nailed Saros's inflections. "This is the only time I'll ask nicely."

"My husband was just taken away broken and bloody and we are locked up Goddess knows where. I think we are past the point of doing things nicely," the former coveness replied, any smoothness in her tone completely vanished. "If you want more, you're going to have to hunt for it."

"Very well." I took a deep breath, recalling Saros's instructions, hoping I did this right. "Don't say I didn't warn you."

I stood in front of her, my hands threading through her

oily blonde strands and gripping her scalp. My eyes focused on hers. I'd never been more grateful for Atlas and his gifts than I was at this moment.

In a blur, Aurora and I stood in the pine forest, just the two of us on some imagined astral plane. The pines felt like neutral territory, and I needed to buy us some time for Lynx to hopefully find us, since Saros was confident he would have a way to track him through their vow runes.

"Aurora. I need you to listen very carefully. I don't honestly give a shit about you killing Acacia. She kidnapped my sister, so as far as I'm concerned, her death is no loss." Her eyes went wide, realizing who she was really talking to, but the surprise also came with a relieved sigh. *"Look, I've never liked you. Not even a little bit."* Her lips pursed, definitely not shocked by this revelation. *"But apparently my sister cares about you. She still doesn't want to believe you'd kill someone. I'd like to believe she is a pretty good judge of character, so I need you to tell me, was she wrong and you really are as heartless as everyone thinks? Or is there some good in there?"*

Aurora's throat bobbed a moment at the mention of Hazel, but then the queen bee returned. *"What do you think?"*

Aleander cleared his throat in the background, reminding me we weren't really here. These pines were just in our minds, our bodies, however, were still trapped in The Casket. "See anything yet, Agent Holt?"

"Not yet. It's going to take some time. If you think you can do a better job, then you're welcome to come try," I called out, giving my best impression of Saros's grouchiness.

"I saw Chrys earlier tonight."

Aurora's blue eyes snapped to mine. *"You did?"*

"Yeah. She was helping with the witchlings for the Halloween festivities."

"How was she?" she asked, biting her lip. Maybe no one had been able to get answers from her, but I knew how it felt to be a mother desperate for her child. As desperate as I was to get us out of here and get home to Aspen.

"She's doing okay. Such a sweet young witch." I smiled. *"Now, if you didn't have anything going for you, I don't think I'd be able to say that."*

"I'm glad she's okay." Aurora's throat bobbed and I knew the topic was hitting its mark.

I cocked my head. *"I'm sure she'd be doing better if her parents weren't locked away for murder."*

Her gaze narrowed. *"What do you want?"*

"You're willing to go to jail for life. Possibly have your brains scrambled. What gives?" It was the one thing I never understood. People like Aurora and Fitz Wells didn't just willingly cart themselves off to prison. Their selfishness was based around surviving and surviving well, at all costs. *"You'd really give up a life with your daughter, with your son, for this?"*

"They deserve better than either of us."

"Maybe they do." I shrugged. There was no disagreeing with that. *"But sometimes what we want and what we deserve aren't the same thing. And I can tell you that the young witch I met tonight would rather see the best in her mother than the worst."*

The hard lines around Aurora's eyes softened.

"Is there anything you can give me that would help the case but doesn't mess with whatever it is you're hiding?" When she hesitated, I continued, *"Help with this investigation. Cooperate. Atlas can work to have your sentence shortened. He has sway. We both know he does."*

She exhaled loudly. *"Acacia was getting too close to the truth. When Fitz and I realized Hazel had gone missing, I confronted her about it. She'd been watching the street for a long time. Research-*

ing." Disgust coated her words. *"She denied it, of course. But we needed to see what she knew."*

"And what did she know?"

"Too much." Her lips thinned into a straight line. *"Though we never were able to get past the wards to where she kept every-thing, we did try."*

"So you killed Acacia, knew she had Hazel, and did nothing to help her?" I asked, trying not to let my anger rise up at her words. I needed to stay calm to keep this illusion going. Furrowing my brows, I combed through her hair, hoping it still appeared like I was rifling through her mind as Saros.

"How could I explain where she was without tipping people off about what we'd done?"

"You're horrible," I hissed.

Maybe I wasn't as good at being calm as I'd thought.

"It probably doesn't sound like it, but I really did care about Hazel. I was relieved when they found her." Her tone was apologetic, but that didn't negate the fact that she was truly the selfish bitch I'd always believed.

"She could have died if she'd been left there much longer."

"The bodies stacked on top of my conscience weigh me down below any moral compass you could try to keep me on."

What did that even mean? *"What bodies? Those that disappeared?"*

Aurora said nothing more, keeping her mouth clamped shut. I gripped her shoulder, making sure her eyes met mine. *"Are you behind the disappearances?"*

She shook her head. *"No."*

"But you know who is?"

Her tone was clipped. *"You're asking the wrong question."*

"What question should I be asking?"

The sound of the door sliding played in the back of my mind as she responded, *"The better question is what."*

The illusion fell, a commotion snapping us from the fantastical forest in our minds and into the present. I dropped my hands from Aurora and turned, watching Saros spear his elbow into Festus's big, pointy nose. Lynx was rushing through the doorway with someone else behind him.

Atlas.

His aqua eyes trailed over my body, as if checking to make sure I was okay. I nodded quickly to him in answer.

Aleander staggered backward in surprise, noting when Saros and I swapped places. "What the fuck did you do?"

He *swished* through space, manipulating it however his gift allowed, until his arm was wrapped around Lynx's throat, cutting off his air supply.

"No!" I screamed, trying to get to him. Atlas grabbed me first, though, pulling me out of the way.

One moment Lynx was gasping for air, the next Aleander's body had calmed and he released him, eyes glazed, face slack.

"Get what you needed, Midnight?" Saros asked as Lynx disarmed the giant wrath demon who now looked more like a giant cuddly lovebug. His huge meaty arm came around Saros, dragging him into a hug.

"It won't last long," Lynx warned, eyes darting to Atlas and then the door.

"We need to go, Oakley." Atlas held out one hand, using the other to still clutch me, making black smog fill the room, then he dragged me outside, leading me down the hallway.

I resisted every step. "We can't leave them."

"They are perfectly capable of handling themselves," Atlas said, directing me down another hallway and toward a stairwell. "They'll need to make sure Aleander and Festus are subdued. It's you that I'm worried about."

Boots pounded behind us, and we ran for the stairwell,

quickly bounding up it until we reached a landing. Then we sprinted along a few hallways before turning off to head through another door, heading down a few levels. When we got to the next landing, Atlas pulled me close, conjuring more smog in the direction we'd come from as bootsteps thundered down the stairs.

Swish.

It was the only sound I heard before Atlas released me with a gasp.

"Oakley…" His gaze trailed downward, my eyes following it to the serrated knife partially lodged into his side.

His illusioned smog began to dissipate, revealing Aleander standing behind him, hand still wrapped around the knife's thick handle. He twisted it in deeper, making Atlas grunt.

"Thought you could get away that easily, Ms. Brooks?" he taunted before ripping out the blade. Crimson spilled from Atlas's side, the scent of iron filling the air, dizzying me.

I was going to be sick.

He groaned, eyes darting back down to see the wound for himself.

"Run," Atlas urged, aqua eyes pinched in pain when they drew back to mine. One hand braced his abdomen as he released more smog in my direction.

Swish.

Aleander's arm banded around me, squeezing so hard I could barely breathe, the crimson-coated blade clutched in his fist. He held it out at Atlas, dragging me backward with him. We ascended the stairs one at a time, my legs trembling violently with each step.

Atlas staggered forward, trying to get to me, smears of red painting the yellowed wall he used to support himself.

"Atlas!" My throat was scraped raw, screaming his name over and over, hoping someone, anyone, would come. "Atlas!"

Bootsteps grew steadily closer, Lynx and Saros shouting my name from above. I craned my neck, Aleander releasing me just as Lynx dove for him, and both of them tumbled down to the landing.

I ran toward Atlas, reaching for him. He lost his balance and tipped forward, collapsing into my arms and taking me with him to the floor.

My eyes stung, Atlas's heavy body pinning me beneath him, as leaden as the sharp ache lancing my heart. "A-Atlas."

A sputtered cough over my shoulder was his only response.

Warm blood spurted from his wound, soaking through my dress. I tried to roll him off me so I could staunch the bleeding, but his limp body was too heavy.

The agent stilled, eerily silent as Lynx's brows knit in concentration. Saros grabbed Aleander's head, holding him in place until blood seeped out of his ears, trailing in twin rivers down his cheeks. Saros shifted his grip, wrapping his hands on either side of his handler's neck and twisting it quickly with a sickening *crack*.

Aleander's body crumpled in a heap on the ground next to us, his haunting orange-blue gaze colliding with mine.

A second later, Saros lifted Atlas off of me, and Lynx came around to help me sit upright, looking me over with concern. When his eyes drifted to Atlas, his hands tensed. While he was drawing ragged breaths, the blood continued to pool from his abdomen. I shook at how much red coated his clothes and my own.

This can't be happening.

Not now.

Footsteps echoed around us, but I couldn't take my eyes off Atlas, off the way his skin was much too pale, or the way the aqua of his irises dulled into a glassy sheen.

I hadn't been able to stop fate.

And now Atlas's hex had come to claim him.

CHAPTER 24

OAKLEY

I scooted myself closer, pulling Atlas into my lap, his head resting on the layers of my tulle skirt. A dark puddle expanded across his black shirt faster than his fumbling fingers could staunch it. I tried to ignore its iron stench. "This can't be happening," I whimpered.

"We knew this was coming," he rasped, voice cracking above a whisper.

"N-no, it's not." My gaze flicked up to Saros and Lynx, pleading. "He needs more time."

Lynx scrambled to his knees and ripped off his shirt, using it to put pressure on the wound, trying to stop the bleed. Crimson seeped through the material, spreading much too quickly.

It wasn't enough.

Atlas shushed me, slowly moving his hand toward mine. "It's okay." He squeezed, so weak. "There never would have been enough time."

"B-but it was supposed to be on our wedding day," I sputtered, tears streaking my cheeks, falling onto Atlas and my dress below. "Not in this terrible place."

"The only thing I see is you... That's all that matters." He gave a rueful smile. "That you're here."

Using his borrowed gift, I waved my hand over myself. The tattered, blood-soaked dress was replaced by a beautiful purple gown. I held his hand and refashioned the onyx gemstone ring along with the runes. Ones we'd never get to wear.

He smiled, bringing my knuckles to his lips and pressing a kiss to them. "More beautiful...than I could have imagined."

His eyes began to flutter, the grip of his hand slipping away from mine. I clutched it harder, tethering it in my grasp. Wishing I could somehow tether him.

"P-please don't go." My entire body shook as I leaned down and kissed him, his lips barely returning it. Resting my wet cheek against his and slipping my hand over his heart, I whispered, "Aspen needs you. I need you... I love you, Atlas."

And I did. Maybe I'd thought I could exist keeping my distance from him, but that was when I believed he'd be somewhere living. Thriving.

Not this.

Not a lifetime *without*.

"You have to let me go." If I hadn't been so close I would have missed his words.

"No." I refused. Begged. "Stay."

"My love for you will last far beyond death." The rattled rise and fall of his chest slowed with each frail pull of air, grains of time slipping away far too quickly. What I wouldn't give to halt him within the hourglass, stopping him from meeting this fate. "Promise to hold our son close. Make sure he grows up knowing...all the good times."

The corner of his lip flicked upward, the ghost of a smile.

"I promise," I rasped. It was all I could manage to get out.

He'd accepted his fate. Embraced it long before today. And

somehow, despite the shadow of his hex, he'd always fought for a brighter world for those around him.

The world needed that light.

Tears streaked my cheeks, watching it flicker out.

He choked out a gasp and released my hand, eyes becoming vacant and glazed over, two glassy marbles. The tan in his complexion was gone, his pallor matching the chill of his skin. I scanned over him, Lynx's entire shirt saturated in crimson, his hands still shaking as he held the shirt in place.

Our illusions had vanished, Atlas's gift dying with him.

"No!" I screamed, banging my fists into his chest, trying to jolt him awake. Grabbing his shoulders, I shook him. "Please. I can't lose you."

No. He couldn't be gone.

Not like this.

Curling into him, I sobbed, the force of it shaking his body against my own. I gasped for air, nose pressed into the creases of his shirt, needing to breathe him in one last time. The usual crisp linen scent was flooded out by the metallic stench of blood.

Lynx slowly removed his crimson-coated hands off of Atlas, placing one on my spine, stroking up and down in slow, gentle movements.

"Oakley," he whispered, attempting to pull me up toward him. "We need to get you safely back to Aspen."

"I-I can't." I clutched Atlas's shirt tighter, splotching it with my tears.

A feminine hand slipped over his chest, and I jerked upright. Aurora knelt next to us in her hideous puke-green jumpsuit.

"Don't touch him!" I grabbed her wrist, pushing her away from us.

She stood her ground, sliding her hand back to his heart

and nudging me out of the way. "Do you want a chance to save him or not?"

"What are you doing?" I asked, watching her hands hover atop Atlas's chest. She nodded to Lynx. "Put pressure in the wound again."

Light pulsed under her palms until sweat beaded her brow.

"Incarnation," she whispered. The answer to a question I'd had since I met the bitchy coveness.

Her gift.

"You can bring people back to life?" I asked, hoping this was true. That maybe Hazel had seen something I refused to —some good in her.

"Not people." She lifted her hands, and Atlas's chest rose up to touch her palms. His stare was still vacant but a bit less glassy. "Inanimate objects."

"So you can't bring him back?" *Then what was the point of getting his heart to beat again?*

"His body should hold on a little longer at least. You won't have much time."

I lowered my gaze, noticing the slight rise and fall of his chest, his breathing shallow and abnormally slow. He was no longer dead, but no longer alive either. It was something in between but it was still something.

"How much longer?" Saros asked, brows knit tightly. I didn't see Aleander's body in the stairway anymore.

"Fifteen, maybe twenty minutes."

My eyes met hers, trying to understand, wanting to know how I could use this to save him. "What happens then?"

"He'll die." She said it so detached and with such a look on her face that I got the impression she'd tried this before.

"Did you do this to Acacia?" I asked.

She nodded. "I knew I couldn't bring her back for good,

but I'd hoped it would be enough for her to tell us how to get Hazel out." She swept her hands over Atlas's nearly still body. "As you can see, she wasn't able to say."

Saros started down another flight of stairs, the sound of his footsteps grabbing my attention. "Where are you going?"

"To make a phone call." His face was all seriousness. I knew better than to ask more.

There was more commotion above us. Someone would eventually come here looking. I had no idea how Aurora had gotten out of The Casket, but I didn't really care right now. I just needed her magic to work. To give us some time.

"We need to get him somewhere safe," I said to no one in particular, not sure where we would be able to take him.

Lynx lifted him over his shoulder, then started toward the stairs that Saros had gone down. "I've got a way."

CHAPTER 25

OAKLEY

Lynx guided us to a large portrait of Atlas's grandfather, the founder of the Council of Magical Welfare. His emerald eyes and confident smirk glinted back at us, and I didn't know whether to take it as a blessing or an omen that we had to cross his threshold to save his grandson from a hex he'd brought upon their family.

My hands were shaking as I placed one on Atlas's back, needing whatever Saros had planned to work. I'd do anything. Pay any price. Whatever it took to keep him for our son and me.

Once Saros caught up to us, he simply said, "Get us to the pines."

Lynx nodded, apparently understanding, and stepped through the painting, the rest of us following. My eyes stayed locked on Atlas's limp body, my heart locked on the frail hope that Aurora hadn't been full of shit and that we could keep him here somehow.

I couldn't accept anything else.

We were spat out in a cavern tunnel, a few holes above spilling moonlight into the dim space.

Strange.

Lynx halted and turned to me. "While we still have some light, look in his pockets. There should be some sort of stone or talisman that gets this to work. Didn't see what it looked like when we came here but it should get us back to the pines."

I fumbled through the pockets of Atlas's trousers, finding nothing before combing through his jacket pockets. When my hands flitted over the angles of a small box, I flinched, releasing it, knowing I couldn't bear to open it and find the ring I'd illusioned onto my finger moments before.

The one he'd all but begged me to wear and be his.

I jolted out of my thoughts as my fingers grazed over something hard and cold, and I plucked it out, examining the polished dark-gray stone inlaid with crystal shards. This had to be whatever Lynx was asking for.

"What do we do with it?" I asked as he ushered us farther into the cave.

"Here," Lynx finally said after a few minutes, though I had no idea where *here* was without any light in the darkness.

He fumbled for the stone in my hand and clutched it tightly, muttering a few words too quickly for me to understand. Then after a beat, the ground began to shake beneath us.

"What the fuck's happening?" Hands clutched onto me, but I had no idea who they belonged to within the pitch surrounding us. We lowered through the cave floor, like grains of quicksand, landing within another dark cave.

"Come on," Saros said, starting to jog toward a dark figure in the distance. "We don't have much time."

"Time for what?" I asked, but he was too far away to hear me.

My chest ached, my skin feeling too tight as I followed

Atlas's limp body slung over Lynx's shoulder while he sprinted after Saros.

There was a rustling sound in the trees, and I glanced back, suddenly realizing Aurora wasn't with us anymore. In fact, I hadn't seen her since before we'd entered the cave.

But I didn't have time to worry about that because, when I faced forward, a well-polished suit and devilish smirk stole my attention. While I'd never met him myself, I'd seen his face in the papers before.

Dante Vivaldi, Vampire King and nefarious supernatural crime boss.

Saros and Lynx continued through the tree line, meeting up with Dante. Lynx laid Atlas on the ground, and the Vampire King knelt next to him, staring at his throat.

Hundreds of pines loomed over us from every direction, as if to witness what was about to happen. A few howls broke up the silence in the distance.

"What is he going to do?" I whispered to Lynx who'd come up beside me.

"Keep death from reclaiming him." He swallowed thickly, eyes pinned to the vampire and his few friends who were standing slightly farther out.

"Permanently," Saros added, glancing over his shoulder.

Holy shit. He was going to turn Atlas.

Would that even work?

My gaze darted up to the moon. The Goddess felt more like an unwelcome audience than a comfort now. "Will this interfere with the hex?"

"What hex?" Lynx and Saros asked in unison.

I spent the next minute rushing through what Atlas had told me, why I had left and why he hadn't stopped his fate. To save our son.

Saros rubbed the stubble along his jaw. "He's dead. Effectively accepted his fate."

He's dead.

I knew Saros didn't mean it to come off so brusque, but if this didn't work... Atlas was gone. Forever.

How would I keep going?

What would I tell our son?

No. I needed to focus on doing whatever I could right now so I wouldn't have to learn those answers.

Vivaldi appeared before us. He pointed to Atlas's throat and his forearm. "He has some strong-looking veins here. Have a preference?"

I shook my head. "Whatever will save him."

He nodded, then bit into Atlas's forearm. Blood seeped down his wrist as the vampire drank from him. Using a sharp fang to slice into his own forearm, he dribbled the blood into Atlas's mouth. I'd never seen how vampires sired others, only the fictionalized accounts on television. It wasn't something their community openly shared. Vivaldi's tongue lapped around where he'd bitten Atlas before he repeated the process of biting him to take more blood and feeding him his own, licking the wound, and starting over.

"How do you know him?" I whispered to Saros.

"My first undercover assignment," he said, watching everything the Vampire King did, as if he didn't fully trust him. "I had a favor to call in."

"But you don't even like Atlas." The last few days had been horrible between them. If he only had one favor to call in from the King of Vampires, surely this wouldn't have been his first choice.

"I've seen how much he means to you." He cupped my hands in his own, his Adam's apple bobbing as he paused.

Then he drew his evergreen eyes to mine. "And I know how much you mean to me."

"Thank you." My voice quivered. There were so many things I wanted to say but I didn't know where to start. Saros had saved our lives tonight, and now he was trying to save Atlas's.

"It's done," Vivaldi said, a seductive lilt caressing his words.

I looked down at Atlas. His chest was still rising and falling, more prominently than before. Vivaldi shut his eyes, placing two dark bloodstones over them. The bleeding had stopped, his arm had already healed, leaving behind two small fang marks. I lifted his bloody shirt, the skin beginning to stitch itself back together where he'd been stabbed.

It's working.

"Do you think he's going to be okay with this turn of events?" I asked, my hand fidgeting in his.

"If it were me and I got a second chance to live a life with the ones I love, I wouldn't be too picky about the circumstances," Saros replied. Being a vampire, sired by their mob boss leader—that was going to be a tough transition for Atlas and all we'd ever known, but we'd have to cross that bridge when we got there because Saros was right.

"So what do we do now?" I asked, flickers of hope bursting to life in my veins.

"I will wait with them." Saros looked over at Lynx. "He'll take you home to Hazel and Aspen. Go get showered, feed him, and then come back. It'll be a while from what I remember."

"But—"

"Come on, Wicked." Lynx put his arm around me. "Let's get you ready for when he wakes."

When. Not *if.*

Relief washed through me.

Atlas would live. Forever.

And when he woke up, I would be here to savor it with him.

CHAPTER 26

OAKLEY

"Are you really okay letting her go?" I asked, looking back toward the cave we'd emerged from earlier, wondering where Aurora had escaped to. The wind whistled and whispered within the trees, as if they were telling secrets to one another.

When I'd returned to the pines an hour ago, I'd told Saros everything I could remember that she'd revealed during our time illusioned away on the astral plane.

"She gave us some answers. Now we just need the evidence to prove them," Saros said, not letting on any more than that, but it seemed like something had clicked into place for him. "Once they work through the last few wards, the answers should be there."

"Won't you get in trouble for her escape? She did help kill Acacia, after all." While I wasn't too sad about Acacia's demise, I didn't want this to crash down on Saros and Lynx.

"Aurora saved Atlas by exposing her gift." He leaned back against the tree trunk we were seated in front of, hands clasped and resting on his knees. "But they would have learned of her Incarnation ability soon enough, and we both know how bad that would have been for her."

"What about Fitz?" I asked, brushing away clumps of pine needles before sidling up next to him. I'd given him a few inches of distance between us, still unsure how he felt about touching me, even though I knew it no longer showed him my worst.

"That'll be a problem for another time," Saros said with a shrug. "No one has contacted us, so I'm guessing we aren't the ones being looked at for Aurora's escape or the...interrogation."

"Who do you think put Aleander up to this?"

"I have no idea." His tone turned hardened, his brows drawn together. "But I sure as fuck intend to find out."

We sat there in silence, and stared at Atlas's rib cage continuing to expand and contract. Lynx had been watching over him, a hand on his shoulder. He'd wanted to make sure to keep him calm when he woke, trying to pour as much into him as possible. I also had the sneaking suspicion he wanted to give Saros and I some space to talk.

"Hey." Another thought came to me now that we had some time where we weren't on the move. "You said there were two others like Lynx and I that you saw the good moments when you touched them. Who were they?"

He turned to face me, taking my hands in his. "I didn't have the greatest childhood. My father... Let's just say he ruled with an iron fist." His focus dropped to where our hands were clasped together. "He'd never laid a hand on me, but my mother...that was a different story.

"The first time I ever discovered my gift was when I was fifteen. I'd gone to give my mother a hug goodnight and images flooded into me. Her most treasured memories." His face contorted in pain, as if he were reliving them all over again.

"What did you see?" I asked.

"They were all memories of us as a family. Or ones of my father bringing her gifts, showering her with attention after his *episodes*." He took a deep breath, and I squeezed his hand, waiting for him to continue. "I hated my father. Hated how he treated her. Hated how she just forgave him over and over again.

"After the first few times, I started avoiding hugging her. I couldn't take watching through her eyes how much she loved him. Her abuser. It made me sick.

"I left home when I turned sixteen. That's when I stayed away from the full moon, letting my magic dwindle, living among the mortals. Aleander found me in a shelter outside of Salem, told me there was a way my gift could help other supernaturals. That there were people who needed me to save them." Saros pinched the bridge of his nose. "That's when I moved to the capital and started working for SNO-OPS... handling their cases that needed my *expertise*."

Tears welled in my eyes, ribs pinching in my chest, heart aching for the boy he was—all he deserved. He'd gotten so much less. "Saros, that's horrible."

"It was. I went back when I was older and had a handle on my gifts. My mother had apparently fled a few months after I left. It was just my father at the house. He actually wanted my pity." He chuckled darkly. "It was the one time I didn't regret showing someone the worst of their life. I forced him to relive the pain he inflicted over and over until it eventually scrambled his mind. Never saw him again."

"What about your mother?"

"I have no clue where she went. I've looked for her off and on over the years, but there's been no sign of her." He shrugged. "I'm just glad she got out of there and that I found him before he found her."

"I'm so sorry, Saros." I rested my head on his shoulder, pressing a kiss to it.

He lifted my chin, evergreen eyes soft like a lush forest grown just for me. I could stare into those eyes forever and never tire of them. "It wasn't until years later when I met Lynx that I found someone that I didn't see their worst. And not again until you. I think my gift only shows me the best moments in those I'm fated to love."

Fated to love.

"So the first time you touched me…"

"It took me by surprise. You scared the shit out of me."

His gaze dropped down before it dragged back up, and I ran my palm along the stubble of his jaw. "Who is the fourth person? You said your mother, Lynx, and me… Who is the other?" I asked it tentatively, so blown away that he'd admitted so much about his past and his feelings. "If you are fated to love someone else, I would underst—"

"It's not what you're thinking, Midnight." He smiled, those brilliant white teeth of his on display. *Goddess, his smile is breathtaking.* "The fourth has me wrapped around his tiny little fingers."

"Aspen?"

"Yes. That first time he reached for me, it was the strangest feeling. The vision itself was mostly a blur but then there was *you.*"

The breath pulled clear from my lungs, heart thudding against my rib cage. It was the only thing I heard over the wind sweeping through the pines.

"It was a simple moment. But the expression on your face… The warm comfort and unconditional devotion radiating in just a single look…" He wiped away the cool tear that'd tracked down my cheek. "It was the most beautiful memory I'd ever been drawn into. All I wanted was to experience that for myself."

His attention dropped to where his fingers entwined with mine, thumb tracing over my racing pulse.

"It terrified me." Then he lifted our hands up to brush his lips across my knuckles. Heat spread down my neck and through my chest at his admission and the reverence igniting his evergreen irises. "But you, Lynx, Aspen... You're my family. Not the one I was born to, the one I was destined to build."

"And Atlas?"

"He loves you. He loves Aspen. Whether you two are together or not, he is always going to be part of our lives." He rested his forehead on mine, then kissed my cheek. "We'll just have to see what he wants once he wakes. I'm guessing he'll need time to absorb everything."

I nodded, cupping his jaw with my palm a few moments. Then my gaze trailed over to Lynx who was still focused on Atlas. His brows were knit together in a way I'd never seen before, both of his hands clamped around one of Atlas's that rested on his chest.

"How much longer?" he called behind himself to the darkness. "I hate that I can't get a sense of his emotions yet. He's alive...everything is just dulled."

Vivaldi swept into view, a few additional vamps behind him. They were large, beefy, and seemed like they meant business. Nerves rioted through me, still unaccustomed to being around their kind. Even the few owls in the treetops hooted ominously before flying from their perches. "It varies from person to person. There are a multitude of factors: age, health, circumstances around their transition."

"You promise this will work, though?" I asked, refusing to give up on Atlas coming back to us, not caring that it might look a bit different than before. My heart would always beat for him, even if his no longer would.

"I've never had performance issues before." The Vampire King chuckled, gazing at me from under hooded eyes. The red in them bled out, glowing in the darkness. I gulped, and he shook his head, pulling a flask out of his pinstripe trousers. Once he'd taken a few sips, the red muted, filtering into a shade of crystalline blue. "You really should lighten up, Red. Life's too short and immortality is too dull to not have some humor mixed in."

"Remind me to be a ball of laughs for you after he wakes up, then." I glared at him, which only seemed to amuse him further.

"Is there anything we should expect?" Lynx asked. "Anything to make this easier for him?"

"He will have an insatiable thirst and need at least one tether to feed from tonight and on the full moons through his newly sired immortality."

"What does being a tether entail?" I asked Dante, luring his crimson-flecked gaze.

"A tether is a vampire's lifeline. Someone he will regularly have access to as he transitions through the course of his newblood phase. Once he's no longer a newblood, in a year or so, he won't need to solely rely on his tethers to feed, but your connection will be critical for him. The bond, both emotional and physical, will remain throughout his immortal life. Yours as well if you choose to join him."

"I'll tether him," I said, without giving it a second thought. I had the man I loved back. What was a little blood-letting?

"I really don't think you should be doing this, Midnight," Saros said, tone firm, concern seeping through his words.

"You can't be depleted all the time. Aspen needs you already to help sustain him."

I moved closer to Atlas and Dante, awaiting the next instructions and fidgeting with my fingers. "It's not your choice to make."

Lynx grabbed my arm. "Maybe not, but we're making it anyway."

Dante rolled his eyes. "So who's going to do the honors?"

"I am," Saros said, cutting me a glare.

My eyes went wide. "You?"

"And me," added Lynx.

I stood there in shock.

"We're in this together, Wicked." Lynx pulled me in for a kiss.

"It'll be safer for us on the full moon when we are all trying to replenish our gifts. To have three tethers will ensure he will always be able to find any of us, and we will be able to help him through his transition," Saros added matter-of-factly.

"Well, I must admit, I'm a bit envious of the Archon that he has three hearts ready to bleed for him," Dante said, his sensual lilt licking up my spine. "Sounds like he will have a most memorable full moon feasting."

"What's that supposed to mean?" I asked, my curiosity piqued.

"There'd be no fun if I ruined the surprise of it all." He huffed. "Speaking of, seems like the acolytes have finished preparing his passage back to join the undead."

Atlas's nose began to wriggle as we knelt down next to him. Dante instructed me to take off the bloodstones from over his eyes. I set them off to the side, and Saros moved himself between me and Atlas, allowing me to stay near enough but not so close that he couldn't protect me. While I wanted to push him out of the way, there was a part of me that was nervous, unsure what to expect in these first few moments of his transition.

What if it didn't work?

What if the hex still affects Aspen?

Even though Saros had reminded me that Atlas had fulfilled the terms of the curse, had died, that didn't bring me the sense of comfort I needed. Not yet at least.

Lynx held his hand tightly. "Everyone try to remain calm so I can push emotions into him if needed."

I gripped Saros's shoulder with one hand, using the other to brush back Atlas's hair. His eyes fluttered open, two glowing crimson irises searing into me.

CHAPTER 27

ATLAS

T he stars shone so brightly. The acolytes perched on them like wayward angels watching down on us from above.

What the hell?

Am I high?

I squinted, spotting an acolyte waving down at me. Another beside her was glaring, as if not sure what to make of us below. I'd never seen them so clearly before. Coming from a line that had been hexed by their maker, I knew they were more than a myth, but the reality of their existence... My mind tried to wrap itself around it.

Thump-thump. Thump-thump. Thump-thump.

There was a hollowness in my stomach, my body weak and empty like a shell. This hunger...it was different somehow.

"Atlas?" Oakley's voice cut through my thoughts, and I blinked a few times, shaking my head. The last thing I remembered was running with her down the stairs. How did I end up in the forest?

"Oakley?" I rasped, coughing a few times and pushing up

to my elbows. Saros was in front of her, Oakley gripping his shoulder, peeking around at me.

Thump-thump. Thump-thump. Thump-thump.

Where was that sound coming from?

"I thought..." My brow knit in confusion, taking in Saros's protective stance, Lynx's hand on my shoulder, and the others situated around us. "What's he doing here?" I asked, glaring at Dante Vivaldi who knelt next to Lynx, two of his large goons poised imposingly behind him.

A rush of calm flooded my veins, though the hunger was still present under the surface.

"He's here to help you," Lynx said, squeezing my shoulder. I realized he was the source of the foreign calm flowing through me. I gripped his wrist and pushed him off me. Lynx hissed, clutching his hand with the other one. Oakley's eyes narrowed on the handprint bruise now blooming there.

What the fuck?

Thump-thump. Thump-thump. Thump-thump.

I lifted my hand, shaking out my fingers. Had I left those marks? There was no way.

"What's going on? What is that sound?" I pushed all the way up to sit, and Saros guided Oakley back with him as he retreated a step. My hand came to my throat. "And why is this scraped raw?"

Thump-thump. Thump-thump. Thump-thump.

"Atlas..." Lynx started. "Why don't you let me help you?"

But when he moved to step forward, I hissed. He whipped his head away, and my gaze caught on his pulse fluttering like a hypnotic butterfly, coaxing me closer. My tongue darted over my lips, snagging on something sharp. Bringing my finger to my mouth, I tapped the source, piercing its pad with a sharp sting. I jolted, snapping my hand away and bringing it up for inspection. Blood bubbled up from the prick, and I quickly lapped it up.

The strange *thump* quieted a moment, and I savored the silence.

Oakley winced, chest heaving. A web of blue and purple veins crept delicately across her cleavage—

A dark arm moved to block my view.

Thump-thump. Thump-thump. Thump-thump.

I stood up quickly, taking a step toward her, but Saros tucked her behind himself. My head was dizzy, and I wasn't sure if it was confusion or the burning ache in my stomach. The only time I'd had a break from the incessant drum, from the hollow feeling deep in my gut, was when I'd lapped at my finger. I lifted it into the light. There was no sign of where I'd bled earlier.

I swallowed down my panic, pulling out my phone and turning on the camera, holding it up to my face.

Glowing red irises stared at me, a set of fangs peeking from my upper lip. "No. No. No. This can't be happening. You should have let me die. The hex—"

My attention snapped up to the coppery orb, meeting the gaze of the Moon Goddess for the first time ever. Though I'd known the reality of her, seeing her now was no less awe-inducing.

She was skyclad, skin the shade of illuminated honey, nearly camouflaged in her rocky throne. Long raven tresses cascaded from her head, blending into the night sky, stars woven in their depths. She watched me, lips peeling up into a knowing smirk.

"Died with you, right?" Oakley asked, tone rattled with fear.

My chest felt lighter than it ever had. I wasn't sure if that was from whatever had happened to me, or finally being released from the curse that had plagued my family for generations. But when I looked up at the Moon Goddess, I somehow knew the hex was gone.

"Yes," I croaked, tears pricking my eyes at the knowledge I'd been able to keep our son safe.

Oakley released a loud exhale, smiling. Tears streamed down her cheeks as she pushed Saros aside to take a step closer to me.

Thump-thump-thump. Thump-thump-thump. Thump-thump-thump.

With each movement, the beat of her pulse called to me, beckoning me to taste her blood.

To feed.

I stumbled backward until I hit a felled tree trunk, feet brushing through the thick blanket of pine needles. Oakley's chestnut eyes looked up into mine, pleading, tiny flecks of copper shimmering through them that I'd never noticed before. "I know this is terrifying, but living without you was worse."

"You have *them*. You would have been okay," I said, voice less raspy but with more gravel in its sound than I was used to.

"They could never replace you." Oakley rooted herself firmly in place, not coming any closer but not retreating either. "You each have a piece of my heart, and I'm selfish enough to want to keep you all."

My hands shook. I was weak, but I thought back to when I'd moved Lynx's hand away and the bruises that still marred his flesh. "What's happening to me?"

But I already knew. I was turning into a monster.

A vampire.

"You need to feed." Saros was so calm it unnerved me. I frowned. "Come here, lover boy," he said, dryly.

He held out his wrist, then slid up his sleeve, exposing the veins running along his forearm, slightly covered by the constellation tattoo.

Thump-thump. Thump-thump. Thump-thump.

"Seriously?" My brows pinched together. "You?"

"I drew the short straw." He chuckled. When I didn't look amused, he continued, "You aren't sinking your teeth into Oakley until we know it's safe. I'm the only one of us who's been fed from before, so I already know what to expect."

Why would he do this?

My eyes slid to Oakley, memories of the masquerade fading in and out, so fuzzy they felt like a lifetime ago. How much time had passed since then?

"What happens when I drink from them?" I asked Vivaldi, wanting to understand what I was getting into.

Thump-thump. Thump-thump. Thump-thump.

"Their blood will give you power, and feeding from them tonight will tether you to them. You will be able to always sense them. Even hear each other through a mental connection. You'll be bonded to them. Eternally."

Eternally.

Because I was now immortal.

I'd died. Come back. I'd broken the Moon Goddess's curse, and now I had a chance, albeit not the one I would have ever expected, to have Oakley, my son... A family. "And you're really okay with this?"

"You want her?" Saros asked, stepping next to Oakley. "You're stuck with us."

"Both of us," Lynx added, coming to her other side.

"What about my gift?" I asked, attempting to cast. Nothing happened. "Am I still a witch?"

"You are and you aren't," Dante explained. "You still have your gift, but it will be amplified. You still have magic, but you will need to feed to maintain your strength and be able to use it."

Thump-thump. Thump-thump. Thump-thump.

Saros stepped forward with his hand extended. Hidden among the constellations, small scars peppered the flesh, sets of twin marks where he'd been fed on before. And he was right, I would rather keep Oakley safe. The truth was, we all would. And three men to fight for her and our son might not have been how I imagined our family looking, but that didn't mean this couldn't be better than any illusion I might have conjured.

They loved her. I loved her. And she loved us all fiercely—fiercely enough to let me die to save our son while refusing to lose me. She would have been okay with them. Safe. But my greedy witch wanted more than that. She wanted it all.

And she fucking deserved it.

I took Saros's hand, his jaw tensing as I did. I knew he'd see my memories, the worst memories. I'd been briefed on it before ever working with the agent, so I'd never touched him. Hopefully whatever he saw would only be momentary while he let me feed.

Opening my mouth, I rested my fangs against his fluttering pulse, then slowly sank them into his flesh. When that coppery tang touched my taste buds, it was like a bolt to the brain. Laced with a subtle smoky undertone and peppery notes, it was divine. Like the first sip of water after wandering the desert.

My eyes clamped shut, savoring each gulp of iron-rich salvation.

"How will we know he's had enough?" Oakley's voice quivered, and I snapped my gaze to her, continuing to drink. She was transfixed, biting her lip in a way that had me wanting to bite it for her.

"His eyes will return to their normal shade and his fangs will be able to retract if he wishes," Vivaldi said, observing from afar. "You will probably feel a bit of *fang-fever* after he's fed from you."

Fang-fever?

I'd have to ask more about that later. Right now, I was using all my concentration to figure out what I was doing and trying not to be disgusted with myself at how satisfied I was consuming blood.

This was going to take some adjusting to.

After a few minutes, Saros gripped my throat, making me hiss, but my fangs popped out of his flesh. I was still starved, but before I could object, a paler wrist was shoved into my mouth. Instinctively, I dragged my teeth down Lynx's forearm until they found the perfect raised vein to descend into. Along with the powerful earthiness of his blood, serene calm washed over me. His Empathy. I was grateful for his assistance. The last thing I wanted to do was hurt any of them, not after everything they'd done for our family.

It was important to me that they all trust me. And I'd have to relearn how to trust myself. I had to admit that part of me was scared out of my mind for what this new life would entail.

But I would figure it out. I wouldn't waste this second chance.

"Anything else we should know?" Lynx asked with a languid sigh, eyes fluttering. Was he actually enjoying this? Maybe this was fang-fever?

"He will need to feed and rest a lot over the coming days," Vivaldi said, gaze meeting mine. "Much like a newborn witchling."

Oakley chuckled, her smile radiating beneath the moon's glow. "Lucky for him, I'm a bit of an expert with newborns."

Then her hand reached out and clasped around my throat, surprising me in more ways than one.

"My turn," she said, thumb grazing the column of my neck.

She lifted to her toes to kiss the corner of my mouth, and when she pulled back, a little blood trailed from her lips. With a growl, I gripped her ass and dragged her closer, kissing her until I'd lapped it all away.

"We're watching you." Saros's warning filtered through my thoughts, startling me.

I arched a brow, not surprised in the least that he could get in my head.

This would be interesting. I took a deep breath, seeking that tether in my mind before pulling on it.

"Oh, I'm counting on it," I replied, a smirk lifting my lips before I sank my fangs into the base of Oakley's throat.

While Saros and Lynx's blood had nourished me, building up my confidence enough to feed on Oakley, her taste was addictive, silky with hints of plum and clove. It was as if every ounce I consumed of her was rushing through my bloodstream and heading south. She sighed, resting her palms on me, magic leaking from them.

Fuck.

This must be fang-fever.

Desire thrummed through me, a heady buzz, and my hips searched to close the gap between us, every part of me begging to have her in this moment, savoring her clamped around me while I drank from her.

But I wouldn't. Not yet.

I was still much too strong for my own good, and I wouldn't touch her until I knew it was completely safe to do so.

Swallowing down the ecstasy of her life essence and

magic, I looked at Lynx. *"How are my eyes?"*

He squinted a moment until his response finally came through our shared connection. *"Good."*

"Good." Lapping up the last bits of blood, I retracted my fangs. Oakley stared at me in equal parts lust and awe when I pulled back. She wiped her hands on her jeans, then shoved them into her pockets, as if embarrassed she'd released her magic as I'd fed.

"Find the tether that binds us and tug," Saros instructed her aloud. "It should be like having a radio frequency dialed in just for the four of us."

Interesting.

"Sorry," she finally responded through our connection. *"Guess I got a little carried away."*

"I intend to get carried away with you more later."

She smirked. *"It's a date."*

"One you'll be chaperoned for," came Saros's stern voice.

"Don't tempt me with a good time," she replied playfully, huskiness and need flavoring her tone. Her eyes fluttered and she zipped her legs, the fang-fever seeming to affect her.

"Wicked, we are always going to tempt you with a good time." Lynx flashed us a devilish smirk before putting his arm around her and pressing a kiss to her forehead.

The echo of someone clearing their throat broke through the silent woods. "Now that you seem to have it handled, I must depart." Vivaldi motioned to his goons. "Business to attend to and such. Archon, come and find me when your thirst has settled. There will be much we'll need to discuss."

Before I could reply, the three of them walked off into the darkness, disappearing into their territory—a place I'd need to familiarize myself with soon enough.

For now, though, I'd enjoy this chance at a new life.

For Oakley. For Aspen. For us all.

CHAPTER 28

SAROS

I stared at the orbs hovering in front of the board, now with the addition of Aleander and whoever had put him up to getting answers from Aurora. I knew it couldn't have been sanctioned by SNO-OPS, and the fact that Atlas didn't know meant the government wasn't publicly backing this. Just some small devious facet within,. either its own operation or a few corrupt people placed in strategic spots for their hidden agenda.

Crack.

The sound of Aleander's neck snapping rang in the back of my mind. I didn't regret it. Not for a moment. But taking someone's life still took a toll. Each time I'd hoped it would be the last.

One of the shittiest parts of having a photographic memory: I never forgot anything. And those moments, especially the horrific ones, replayed with so much vibrancy when I was alone and it was quiet. It was hard to get them out of my head.

My breath stuttered, and I looked over the orbs, moving Aurora's to the edge of the board with a flick of my wrist.

No clue where she'd gone to, but my gut told me she wouldn't be a problem, and my gut usually wasn't wrong. I didn't regret letting her go. I knew what would have happened to her had headquarters found out about her Incarnation.

Knock, knock.

Knock.

Knock, knock.

Pulling out my phone, I looked at the time. 12:23 a.m. My jaw clenched.

Who would be knocking at this hour?

I put my leather SNO-OPS cuffs on, still unsure if we were in the clear over what'd happened at headquarters. It was hard to believe we'd gotten so lucky.

Shuffling to the front door, I spread my fingertips on the wood, tapping at the invisible wards to lower them. I opened the door, my other hand clenched in a fist, ready to unleash if someone unwanted was on my doorstep.

Oakley stood on the porch, illuminated by coppery moonlight and wrapped up in her fuzzy black robe and pumpkin slippers. In her hands were two mugs, steam wafting up from them carrying the smell of apples, nutmeg, and caramel.

"Salted caramel apple cider," she said with a smile, holding one out in offering. "I may have added a quarter shot of bourbon to them."

"Did you text? I would have come over if you needed me for something."

"I didn't. Everyone is fine and sound asleep back at the house. I just figured maybe you could use some company..."

There were twin marks at the base of her throat. Atlas had fed recently. While the effects of his mealtimes, along with the full moon's arrival, had gotten us a little lust-addled, none of us had acted on it. We'd all been on edge and in survival mode, trying to navigate this new normal and find out what had shaken out at headquarters.

The way her eyes were glued to my lips as I sipped my cider, though, had me wondering if that was about to change. I swallowed the anxious lump at the back of my throat. She had come here to be alone with me. Did that mean—

She floated her mug to set it down on the porch rail before stepping out of her slippers.

Was this for real, or had I fallen asleep after staring at the board for hours?

I need to stop reading so many spicy fantasy books.

As the robe fell around her shoulders, dropping past her waist and falling onto the dimly lit porch, my breath hitched. She was in a black ensemble, the bra connected by a strip of fabric that went down her center into a pair of briefs, a galaxy of stars scattered along the mesh.

The mug slipped from my hand, and Oakley caught it before it shattered on the porch and floated it to sit next to hers. "You like?" she asked, taking a few steps closer.

"I think it's obvious I more than like." My eyes darted around the neighborhood. The streetlamps hovered over the cul-de-sac, but it didn't look like anyone was out, most witches tucked away in the pines to recharge. "You sure you want to do this out here?"

"Do what?" she asked innocently. With a wave of her hand, my dick sprang to life, ready to break free from my jeans.

Definitely not dreaming.

"Mischievous tonight, aren't we, Midnight?" My hands slid to my belt buckle and I arched a brow at her. However, instead of taking off my jeans, I strode forward and patted the porch rail. She eagerly shuffled over and turned toward me, then I lifted her up and set her onto the dark wood, nudging her legs to either side of me. The heat of her core pressed against my jeans.

My mouth crashed into hers, and I reached down, finding her bare. Her lingerie was missing a strip of fabric.

She was the sexiest witch and tonight, I'd have her all to myself under the full moon.

I swiped my hand through her glistening folds, and our tongues stroked each other's while I circled over her clit, her breath catching. When she grabbed the support beam, wriggling against me and panting against my lips, I nipped at them and plunged two fingers deep inside of her.

She needed to be soaked and ready for what I had planned. I only hoped that when I made her come and my magic transferred to her that it wouldn't ruin things between us.

If she sees my worst, will she still want me?

"Don't let go, Midnight," I instructed, tapping the support beam. Then I knelt before her, bringing her thighs over my shoulders, parting her with my tongue. Keeping my eyes on hers, I lapped up her glistening desire. She moaned, her nails digging into the wood. *Good.* I wanted her to leave those marks, a memory made beautiful reality in the divots she'd engrain there.

"Oh Goddess, Saros," she whimpered, her free hand grabbing the back of my neck. Jerking her body against my face, she tensed around my fingers. "*More.*"

I beamed, admiring my handiwork, the lust dripping between her legs. "Look how responsive you are."

Continuing to pump in and out of her, I twirled my tongue against her sensitive bud, making her legs shake around me. She nearly lost her balance, sending some Desire straight into my chest, and I growled out, gripping her thighs to steady her.

Chuckling at our near mishap, she bit her lip as I stared up at her, drinking in her glow in the full moon's embrace. The tumble of her autumn hair moving with the crisp breeze, the sprinkle of tiny freckles peppering her flushed cheeks.

Absolute perfection.

She crooked her pointer finger under my chin, then guided me to stand.

When I did, she tugged down the waist of my jeans until my cock sprung free, a bead of precum already seeping from its tip. Pressing her palm into my chest, she pushed me so I staggered backward, my ass hitting the cushion of our love seat floating a few feet above the porch. I scooted until I was flush against the backrest.

Grabbing the exposed bar across the top of the swing's woven netting, she straddled me, her knees on either side of my thighs. She positioned herself with my cock beneath her center, holding on to the bar for support. Instead of lining up with her, though, I gripped around her waist, dragging her up and down my length, coating myself in her lust, making sure to hit her sensitive nerves until she was quivering in my clutches.

"Don't stop," she moaned, writhing along my cock, building friction the way her body wanted. While images flared in and out of her mind, sensual and intimate with some familiar and unfamiliar faces, I kept my physical body linked to hers, grounding myself in this moment.

This was my last first time with someone—there would never be another for me—and I wanted to savor it.

Most people were lucky to have one great love of their life. I had two.

And apparently also a vampire I was bonded to for eternity.

"Use me. I want you soaked," I whispered in her ear. "I

know enough to know I'm your biggest." While watching the witch you love with her past lovers wasn't ideal, it had been an ego boost in that respect.

Our bodies writhed together in an intoxicating rhythm. Gripping the bar with one hand, Oakley sent some of her Desire into my lap with the other, lining my tip up with her entrance. I braced her waist, guiding her slowly. Her breath hitched when she'd lowered about halfway, and I kissed her feverishly. I groaned as I filled her. She was so fucking tight. "Feel that? Every inch is yours."

She whimpered while I nipped along her neck. Then I lifted her up slightly before watching her sink onto my shaft.

I tapped the love seat, and it began to gently sway, each push forward carrying us to the slip of coppery moonlight.

My jaw stayed clenched until her muscles relaxed around me, then I eased her lower and lower. I brought my hands to her hips and assisted her up and down while she braced herself with the bar overhead, kissing the beautiful dip between her breasts and along her sternum.

Tapping the swing again, it swayed a little faster, while Oakley continued to slide up and down, tight and wet. Warm and perfect. "Watch how wickedly you swallow my cock, Midnight."

Her eyes lit up, a vision of Lynx playing at her mind, the two of them on the hood of her car. There was no jealousy filling my veins, though, just my replenishing magic. They were so damn sexy together, everything I could ever fucking ask for as his hips drove in and out of her. "You want Lynx to watch me fuck you?"

She didn't say anything but kept riding me, as if she were too nervous to answer.

"Tell me."

She bit her lip. "I want them both to watch. See how good I take you."

"Good would be an understatement," I agreed, lifting my hips a bit, making her breath catch.

She paused there, flush with my lap, cradling me in her body as deep as I could go.

"But right now, I just want you, Saros," she rasped. "Just you and me."

"It's you and me, Midnight," I whispered, sliding my hands up her back and pulling her closer to me so I could kiss the twin marks on her neck. Oakley moaned.

"I'm taking you here," I said, pressing my hips up into her again and hearing her moan against my cheek. I thumbed along her bottom lip. "Then I'm going to take you here." I slipped my other hand down her ass, hovering over the tight ring of muscle. "And finally, I'll take you there so you're ready for us all to fill you the next full moon."

She whimpered in response, seemingly intrigued by that idea.

I knew I fucking was.

Tapping the swing one more time, I amped up its pace, driving my hips into her each time she lowered herself onto my cock. She clutched the bar, knuckles pale, body beginning to quake.

I strummed her clit in quick, dulcet pulses, her eyes rolling back in her head. Then she shut them, lips parting to whisper my name like a sacred chant. "*Saros, Saros... Saros.*"

"Open your eyes," I said, pausing until those beautiful chestnut irises met mine. She was so close, and I didn't want to miss a moment, needing to etch this into my memory.

Her breathing was frantic, panting as she continued to ride me, to grind into my stroking fingers, the swing moving us both. "I-I'm about to co—"

"Come for me, Midnight," I commanded, never more ready for something in my entire life. Never craving someone's pleasure so badly.

There was no more denying her or us. I would take every breath of her ecstasy, and I would give her all of mine.

"Oh my Goddess."

I drove my hips deep into her, sending her over the edge, her tight warmth squeezing my cock. Moonlight glittered along her skin, and I clenched my jaw, growling out my release and painting her womb. My body absorbed the aftershocks of her pleasure, coming with so much force that my cum seeped out from where our bodies were still joined.

Oakley's eyes went wide the moment my magic transferred to her, and I braced myself, hands tensing around her waist. I tried to swallow down my fear, voice coming out in a rasp. "Tell me what you see."

"You, watching me from Luna's when I first moved into town." She kissed me, a smile peeling at the edges of her lips.

The sharp pinch in my chest released, pressure stinging behind my eyes as relief washed through me. "When you were in those leggings and maroon sweatshirt? You were fucking beautiful. I was embarrassed that I was staring too long because you were probably with someone and I was supposed to be married."

She tightened around me, making me wonder what she was seeing now. "Where'd you go, Midnight?"

I brushed her hair out of her face, trying to take in this moment.

"The study." She wriggled against me a bit for friction, my cock still hard, still wanting more. "You saw Lynx and I in the windows. Watched us."

"I never claimed to be a good witch." I chuckled. She arched a brow at me and hugged around my neck beginning to slide up and down me again. "Goddess above, you feel incredible."

Standing up, I gripped around her thighs, kissing her as I carried her toward the door. I waved a hand through the wards, the door swinging open for me to cart her over its threshold. My body buzzed from the moon's replenishment, but that paled in comparison to the thrill of finally giving my witch everything I could.

No more meager scraps. No more holding back.

Never fucking again.

I would have all of her, and she'd have all of me.

I set her down in the entryway, drinking in every captivating freckle and curve. I couldn't wait to have her again. "I'm so glad you see the best of my memories. You make up most of them."

"I think it's time we make some more," she said, peeling off her lingerie until she was completely naked. "Don't you?"

"I do," I agreed, dragging her to the bedroom. Tonight, we would make our highlight reel for decades to come.

CHAPTER 29

OAKLEY

After three uninterrupted hours of beautifully messy sex, Saros slept peacefully next to me. Grabbing my phone, I swiped through in case Lynx or Hazel had texted that they needed me back home.

There were no messages; however, I did have a few emails. Two were spam, but the last one was from the HOA. Unlike the monthly newsletter they sent out, this one didn't have a fancy header, just a message.

Dear Brooks Household,

This is a gentle warning that your festive decor will need to be removed in two weeks' time. Failure to do so will break your contractual agreement with the HOA that was signed upon move in. Your property will be inspected within 24 hours of the new moon. Thank you for your understanding in this matter.

Keep Starry Night stellar,
Your HOA

I groaned. "Seriously?"

The decorations were adorable and had taken days to put up. Plus, I still had a few weeks until the deadline. Wasn't it a bit presumptuous to assume I wouldn't be taking them down? I knew the rules.

Saros yawned next to me, then rolled over to where I sat. A flash of Aspen's tiny fingers wrapped around his filled my mind, bringing a smile to my face.

"Thought I heard you groaning," he said, taking in my pleased expression.

"I got an email from the HOA warning me to take down the Halloween decorations," I replied, rolling my eyes. "So dumb."

He shifted onto his stomach, pushing up to rest on his elbows. Then he reached over for his glasses on the nightstand and put them on, somehow looking more handsomely astute with them. "Do you need help getting them down?"

"No." I kissed his forehead. Images from the last few delicious hours played in my mind, making my thighs clench. I was sore everywhere but greedy enough to still want more. It was rare to have time alone, even rarer to have that and feel reassured that Aspen was fine and cared for. But I trusted Lynx and Hazel with him—Atlas, too, despite his current *condition*.

"But that's not the point," I continued. "Why do they even get a say?"

"Because they are the HOA." He shrugged, his hand drifting over my thigh, stroking up and down, up and down. More moments flooded my mind of him turning me into the puttied state I was now in after innumerable orgasms. I'd probably have his Recollection flowing through my veins for a week.

I took a deep breath, trying to focus. Saros was smiling

smugly at me, all too pleased about the transference now that he wasn't concerned I'd see his worst memories.

"But who are they?" I asked him. "Do you know anyone on the HOA? Do the other streets have them?"

"No. They like to remain anonymous." He pressed a kiss to each of my thighs before he sat up next to me. "I'm not sure about the other streets, but there's a reason why Starry Night has won awards every year. It's supposed to be the safest, most aesthetically pleasing, most coveted coven to be part of."

"Well, don't you sound like you drank the Kool-Aid?" I chuckled. "Besides, we know that isn't true or there wouldn't be disappearances."

He combed his fingers through my hair and brought my head down to rest on his shoulder. I nuzzled against him, savoring the contact. A few sensual moments from last night raced into my mind, making my thighs clench.

Clearing my throat, I squeezed the comforter, trying to ground myself using some tips Saros had shown me. "Don't you think it's strange that they meet once a quarter and make all these rules for our street and we don't even know who they are?"

His brow furrowed, body stiffening against me. "Show me that email."

I scrolled down to it and held the phone out for him. His eyes jolted to the board a moment, and I squinted in the darkness, trying to figure out what he was noting. "What is it?"

"Hold on a sec." He swung his legs over the bed and snapped to turn on the light. Picking up an orb, he flicked his finger across its glassy shell. Images flared each time he did, moving too fast for me to make them out. When he finished with one, he moved to another, doing the same thing with the next four orbs.

"What?" I crawled over to the edge of the bed, watching him.

"I remembered seeing similar wording in the emails we checked for the folks who disappeared," he said, flipping through another few orbs. "I didn't think anything of it because your sister didn't have one. She didn't fit the pattern, though."

"Because she wasn't part of it," I added, filling in the blanks for myself.

"Exactly." He pointed at all the orbs, back in their situated timeline spots, each with a similar-looking email. "Every witch who disappeared received at least three warning emails. They came once a week, and stopped after the new moon. After they had vanished."

I stood up from the bed, walking over to read each one.

Dear Lark Household,

This is your third and final warning to remove the flock of ravens from your lawn. We have had numerous complaints from residences along Starry Night. Failure to do so will break your contractual agreement with the HOA that was signed upon move in. Your property will be inspected in 24 hours. Thank you for your understanding in this matter.

Keep Starry Night stellar,
    Your HOA

"So the HOA could have something to do with the disappearances?" I asked, squinting at another orb.

Dear North Household,

This is your third and final warning to repaint your front door to its original evergreen. Bubblegum pink is not an approved color. As listed in the *HOA Code of Conduct* under Section 4.51: *All door color changes must have prior approval.*

Failure to do so will break your contractual agreement with the HOA that was signed upon move in. Your door will be inspected in 72 hours. Thank you for your understanding in this matter.

Keep Starry Night stellar,
    Your HOA

"It definitely doesn't seem like just a coincidence." I continued to read through. There were warnings ranging from color or structural changes to leaving up birthday decorations to letting the grass grow to *obscene* lengths. Each final notice came within weeks of the disappearance, the household always vanishing as if into thin air after the new moon.

The new moon within the lunar cycle was attuned to fresh starts, emptying your life of things that didn't serve you. While anti-magic—magic that actively harmed others like hexes and curses—wasn't allowed, it didn't mean that someone couldn't have been performing it. The new moon was meant to help banish negative and toxic elements from your life, but if someone had the right ability for it... Could they be illegally casting anti-magic using the extra ritual power of that sacred night?

Could the HOA be behind it?

Saros already had his phone out, swiping and tapping a few times before putting it to his ear.

"Who are you calling?" I asked, eyes wide. The clock read 4:12 a.m. Who in their right mind would answer the phone right now?

"The Locksmith," Saros replied, phone still held to his ear, a faint ringing whispering through the other end of the line.

"Locksmith?"

"Yeah, my contact at headquarters. The one who helps decipher things and break through wards like the one Acacia Mirabel had on the evidence we sent in."

"Think he has something?" I asked, wondering what kind of hours this power locksmith worked where Saros thought nothing of calling him in the middle of the night.

"Hey, Theo," he said, voice in its serious business baritone. "Anything new on the Mirabel case? ... I need you to search for any notes about the HOA."

He waited, silence filling both ends of the phone.

A moment later, I heard Theo's distant voice, but it was too quiet to make out what he was saying.

Saros's brows furrowed. "That's all there is?" He ran a hand over the bottom half of his face, as if frustrated. "Not sure if that helps us, but if you spot anything else, let me know."

"What'd he say?" I asked once he'd hung up.

"He said she had a map of the neighborhood where she was denoting possible HOA members." He shifted things around on the board, clearing out the bottom right corner. "He's sending it over to me now."

The door creaked down the hall, and Lynx's soft voice filtered into the room. "Hey, it's us."

Us.

I turned, spotting Aspen in his arms, a gummy grin with his one tiny tooth peeking up above his bottom lip.

"There's my sweet little witch," I cooed, taking him from Lynx and nuzzling his nose with mine. Then Lynx gripped my chin and pulled me in for a kiss, one that had my toes curling against the carpet. "How's Atlas doing?"

"Well enough he decided to come along for the trip," Atlas said, coming in from the hallway.

"Did anyone stop you on your way over here?" I asked, nerves jolting at the idea that our secret could be found out.

"You know they did." Lynx chuckled, shaking his head at Atlas. "But it was the perfect test run to ensure his Illusion is up and running after the full moon last night."

His attention snagged on Saros standing in front of their case board. Moving closer to it, he looped his arm around Saros's waist, glancing at me from over his shoulder. "This wildling was hungry, though, so I figured I'd bring him to you and see how things were going. Didn't want to interrupt, but I checked first to make sure we wouldn't be disturbing anything."

"Speaking of," Atlas sat next to me on the edge of the bed before brushing some tangles out of my face. His hand lingered over the base of my throat, a familiar tingling sensation ghosting there, along with the memory of last night when he'd fed from me. "Someone looks beautifully flushed from a night of enjoying themself."

Heat crept across my cheeks, and Lynx waggled his brows at me from the corner of my eye, making me shake my head at him.

"Well, you're both just in time," Saros cut in, thankfully taking the attention away from my blushing. "I think we might have just gotten another lead in the case."

"Are we still working the case?" Lynx asked.

"Look, I am seeing this through until someone says otherwise. No one has come after us, which makes me think we still have our jobs."

Atlas nodded in agreement. "I've taken Aleander's spot as your handler, according to headquarters, so why not? Besides, don't we want to get to the bottom of this?"

"Fair enough." Lynx shrugged, squinting at the board. "Whatcha got?"

"Locksmith just sent the map Mirabel had in her files. She was trying to narrow down the HOA members." Saros ran his hand over his phone, then waved it toward the newly opened corner of the board. "Oakley got an email from the HOA this morning with a warning, and I remembered seeing similar emails when we combed through the victims' inboxes."

"I think I remember seeing some too." Lynx picked up each orb, reading through the text. "So each victim got at least three warnings leading up to the new moon before they disappeared? Did Aurora say anything about the HOA when you talked to her?" he asked me over his shoulder.

I'd already sat down on the bed, taking a deep breath when Aspen latched, trying not to let the Toothy Terror get the best of me. "No, she didn't— *Shit!*" Aspen bit down on my breast with a smile, and I yelped, causing them to turn around. I tapped his cheek with my finger, giving him a stern look that was very difficult to do when he was just so stinkin' cute. Atlas chuckled next to me, probably entertained that his son was also a biter now.

Once I'd gotten him relatched, I tried to recall what Lynx had asked me. "You know what? She did say something odd. When I asked her if she knew who was behind the disappear-ances, she said I was asking the wrong question. She said I should have asked *what.*"

"*What?*" Atlas repeated.

"Hmm." Saros ran his palm along his face again, scanning over the board. "That is odd."

"Are you noticing what I'm noticing about this map?" Lynx grabbed Saros's phone and walked out of the room, opening the front door. A few minutes later, he walked back into the bedroom. "Every house she noted has a silver star in the front window."

"Have you ever talked to Wade Pierce before?" I asked them, only having briefly seen the CEO of Pierce Protections once.

Saros shook his head. "Not in months."

"I've been trying to arrange a meeting, but Pierce is always busy traveling." Atlas rolled his eyes, pulling out his phone and swiping through it before typing out a message and sending it off.

Saros peered out the window before shutting the blinds, as if nervous we were being watched.

"I'm supposed to train Laurel this afternoon," Lynx offered, hands sliding into his pockets. "What if I do some digging while I'm at their house?"

"Won't she notice?" Saros was looking over the map again, face contorted, deep in thought. "And didn't you say they have cameras in every room?"

"Well, nothing like a well-timed distraction," Lynx replied with a shrug, giving me a smirk.

Atlas's focus was pinned to the map. "This is definitely promising." He nodded a few times and then turned his attention back to the rest of us in the room, a confident twinkle in his eyes. "I think it's time we find out who's in the HOA."

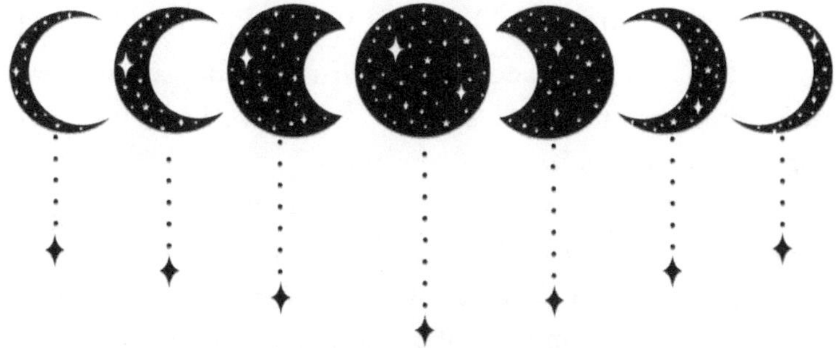

When Lynx Caven of number 16 arrived at 4 Blessed Crescent, Laurel Pierce was busy shaking up her pre-workout elixir in the kitchen. Silver door opening with a groan when his foot hovered over the *Blessed* doormat, he stepped inside, already looking up at the cameras nestled in each corner.

Clearing his throat, he walked back into the kitchen, smiling at Laurel as she sipped her drink. When she offered him one from her Brewrig, he accepted, taking the shaker cup and drinking the elixir down in two gulps.

"Shall we?" he asked, nodding toward the home gym. Laurel led the way, and he began giving instructions for their session.

Ten minutes into it, he excused himself to use the bathroom, scanning over each door he passed. When he was finished, he crept to one door, opening it slowly before peeking inside and shutting it just as smoothly. Across from it sat another door, whose handle, when he went to jiggle it, wouldn't budge.

"What are you doing?" Laurel asked, poking her head out of the home gym space. Lynx's hand jolted back.

"Oh, I was hoping to see more of those cool gadgets Wade was telling me about. He'd mentioned them at the town hall and said he'd show them to me next time he was in town." He stuffed his hands in his pockets, leaning against the wall. "Any chance it'll be soon? The self-regulating system and upcoming upgrades just seem so cool. I've been trying to convince Saros to get one for our house."

Laurel walked over and rested her palm on the door, opening it. "Go ahead. He has all the models in there with their specs. Boys and their toys! To me, it just looks like a bunch of techy mumbo jumbo. I'll hop on the dreadmill for five."

"Awesome! Thanks, Laurel."

She returned to her workout, beginning her walking mystical tour of Ireland on the dreadmill.

A moment later, the doorbell rang. When she answered it, Oakley Brooks was there. "I'm so sorry to bother you, Laurel, but I wanted to personally invite you to the opening of Full Moon Emporium as a thank you for modeling."

"I'll definitely be there. I was just getting my workout in, thou—"

Oakley reached into her pocket and pulled out two talismans, dropping her voice down to a whisper. "Listen, I know Wade is gone a lot for work. This is a new prototype I've been working on for long-distance couples."

Laurel pushed the door open further, waving her in. "What does it do?"

"Let's just say the next time you and Wade want to have some far-apart *fun time*, if you mail him this and keep the other, you'll be able to experience *everything* together," Oakley said with a wink.

"Oh, that sounds nice. But Wade isn't really into long-distance affection..." Her face shot down to the ground.

"He will be once that's around his neck. I imbue an aphrodisiacal enchantment into each one. It'll latch onto his desire, and you two will be long-distance love bunnies before you know it." Oakley smiled, and Laurel returned it, pocketing the talismans.

Meanwhile, in the other room, Lynx fumbled through drawers, using his phone to break the ward on the one at the bottom of the desk.

Need to keep all eyes on this.

The *click* of the lock on the office door had him issuing a slew of curses. Shaking the papers until they shrank down, he stuffed them into his shoe. Then, he went to the computer, clicking through the screens before taking a few pictures.

The air grew thick and heavy in the room. The heat set on full blast. He wiped his brow with his sleeve.

When Oakley went to use the bathroom, Laurel tried to unlock the office door, but it wouldn't budge. She tried again, calling out to Lynx, "Did you lock the door?"

"No, I thought you did?"

"It's fine, I'll just override the system. Wade showed me how to."

"That would be great," Lynx said, eyes darting around.

No, it most certainly would not.

Laurel walked through the house, finding the main panel. It was blinking, error messages popping up each time she tried to tap on it.

Only a few more minutes and Lynx Caven wouldn't be a problem.

Hand clamped around his mouth, he struggled to breathe. He pulled out a set of leather, government-issued cuffs, shaking them to regular size before using them to break the window.

Laurel ran toward the room at the crash. She pounded on the door, but Lynx was no longer there to respond.

There wasn't much time to warn the rest of the HOA. Numbers 5, 7, 10, 12, 11, and 17 were alerted just as Lynx's hand touched the circuit breaker.

Our time had run out.

CHAPTER 30

LYNX

I coughed, sputtering for clear air, frantically scanning over the yard for the circuit breaker that powered the panel. Sweat beaded at my brow, and I inhaled deeply, my fingers finally landing on the switch next to the faded silver star. Tugging it down, my attention darted to the house, sprinting through the lawn toward the front door to make sure that Oakley was safe and it had worked.

The blinds were closed in the large black mansion, silence haunting the air like an ill-timed specter. I stepped on the mat, waiting for the silvery door to groan open on its own.

It didn't.

What if Oakley was locked inside? What if something had happened to her while I was disabling the system?

I moved the wicker chairs out of the way to try to peer inside the windows. There was a *snick* of the front door and I finally caught my breath. Relief washed over me when Oakley stepped out onto the porch.

"You okay?" I asked, quickly scanning her for any staticky gray distress. There was none, only pale-blue relief and swirls of pink as she nodded back at me. I dragged her into my arms, gaze darting to Laurel who was dazed, staring back at the inside of her house, bracing her elbows in a fog of bitter confusion and rippling sadness.

"Everything's going to be okay," I reassured her, putting an arm behind her to guide her toward Atlas and Saros who were waiting for us at the end of the drive, ready to find out what she knew. The evidence from Wade's office that I'd photographed and texted to Atlas and Saros should give us more to go on too.

It fucking had to.

(((●)))

AFTER I'D SHUT DOWN NUMBER 4'S HOME SYSTEM, I STUDIED THE photo of Mirabel's map on my phone and sprinted from house to house, pulling the circuit breakers. Meanwhile, Oakley ran over to Ruby's place to alert the coveness. The neighbors were baffled, wandering out into the street, curious what had happened to warrant turning off their beloved home systems. The natural leader she was, Ruby led them to the community center, giving them a full rundown.

We'd effectively disbanded the HOA, the moniker actually standing for Homes *Ownership* Association, self-coined by the network of houses on Starry Night Lane—one of the many random bits of information I'd gleaned from Wade's desk.

So fucking creepy.

I'd never been happier that we'd opted out of having the system installed when we moved in.

Atlas finally heard from Wade Pierce after Laurel had contacted him from our custody in a panic. The tech tycoon pretended he had no idea why his technology had *"short-circuited,"* and Pierce Protections started damage control, ordering the swift removal of their panels until they could ensure they were no longer installing *faulty* equipment.

Two weeks had passed since then, and while we believed whoever had orchestrated Oakley and Saros's kidnapping had covered it up, we were hesitant to meet at headquarters to discuss anything involving the case. Though we still didn't have all the details, we were hoping there would be some evidence within Acacia's files. Saros had personally requested that the Locksmith, Theo Graves—a trusted old friend from training—notify us of any updates before taking it up the chain.

Today, he'd contacted us to say he'd been able to unlock one of her more intricately warded orbs and we were eager to see its contents.

According to the official SNO-OPS report, Aleander had died in the field on assignment. No further details listed. The only people who knew the truth were us and Aurora Wells—not that she'd be coming out of hiding to divulge that.

The reality was, until we knew the information Theo had and who had been behind Aleander's actions, we couldn't count on the supernatural government or its usual channels of operations. Atlas would be taking a careful look at all the Council of Magical Welfare leaders at their next quarterly Summit.

For now, we were glad to have gotten to the bottom of who, or rather *what* had been the cause of the disappearances.

We knew enough from Oakley's discussion with Aurora that there was more to it that Wade wasn't telling us. But the missing files I'd found and snapped pictures of in his study paired with Acacia's research could help us fill in the gaps.

Sitting at a mortal bar, I waved over the young guy behind

the polished countertop. "Three Four Horsemen shooters for us— Actually, add one more while you're at it."

Saros and Atlas cut me a look that had me shrugging. It wasn't often I got to come out to the mortal world I'd grown up in anymore. Ordering an old favorite was the least I could do with the opportunity.

Theo arrived in his signature mortal outfit: jeans and a red hoodie pulled over his head. As a shifter, he didn't look any different in his human form, but he was always nervous to be out among the magically-unblessed.

The bartender shoved the four shooters in front of me, and I dropped the cash on the bar, leaving a generous tip.

"Cheers." I slid the drinks to each of my companions and then tapped my glass on the bar top, picking it back up and chugging it down. They each followed, obviously not used to this tradition. Theo grimaced, sputtering out a handful of coughs. Saros smacked his lips together, and Atlas sniffed his a few times, wriggling his nose before drinking it. He'd fed from Saros just before coming here, so his fangs were retracted, at least temporarily, but he was stuck wearing his sunglasses inside, looking like a character from *Men in Black*.

Theo nodded to Saros. Standing up from his stool, he came around and clapped his hand on Theo's shoulder. Then he squeezed it and smiled like they were dear friends, which they were, but right now he would be seeing everything Theo had, pulling those memories of what had been on that final orb. I prayed to the hidden Moon Goddess above that whatever it was, it would help us with the case.

"Glad you popped in for a drink, brother," Saros said in his smooth baritone, actually sounding more charming and less grumbly than usual. "Be in touch soon."

"See you soon," Theo replied, shaking each of our hands before heading out.

Saros sat between Atlas and I again, sharing what he'd seen through our link. *"Within each panel was a piece of dark-gray slate that had the capability to absorb and harness very powerful magic, including the power of the witch it belonged to. Apparently, Fitz was Wade's first investor, the first panel Pierce Protections installed outside of its own home.*

"The panel absorbed Aurora's Incarnation. When Wade found out, he put a failsafe rune on the stones so they couldn't absorb specific gifts, only general magic."

"So how did we end up with the HOA?" I asked, trying to put the pieces together.

"While Wade did failsafe the systems from taking on more abilities, he didn't deactivate the Wellses' system, instead finding a way to channel it into his algorithm. Acacia never discovered how exactly, but it seems as if he thought it would help the homes run more efficiently to have more houses learning from the witches within them. She didn't believe he had anticipated them connecting with each other within their own network."

"I don't know what evidence we will be able to find that will confirm it, but we can look back through the stuff I grabbed." I clasped my hands together. *"If Wade knew about it, I don't see him being very forthright with that information."*

"Was there anything more about the people that disappeared in her file?" Atlas asked, leaning closer.

"She suspected they are either sucked into the slate pieces themselves or were channeled through them somewhere else. A group of geologists she had worked with on the East Coast are currently studying the fragments, trying to determine how to locate the witches and if they need an extraction team."

"Sounds like a trip to the East Coast wouldn't be a bad idea in the future," Atlas suggested.

Saros and I nodded silently in agreement.

Standing up from the bar, we headed toward the door.

Working for the government while holding on to this information felt unnatural, but I would do it until we knew more. There were more lives at stake now than just our own. "So what's next?" I asked as we stepped out into the crisp autumn air.

"Let's mull over what we've learned and see how the Archon Summit goes," Atlas instructed, adjusting his tie. He pointed at the shop a few doors down. "For now, people are safe without the systems. That has to be enough until we can find out more."

CHAPTER 31

OAKLEY

"When will the guys be back?" Hazel asked, Aspen playing happily in her lap.

"Soon." They had used Atlas's traveling talisman to visit the capital. "They were having an offsite meeting with their tech guy."

"What's going to happen when Atlas has to attend his quarterly Archon Summit?"

"I'm not sure." I inhaled deeply a few times, trying to ignore my anxiety about how things were going for them right now. I couldn't hear them through our shared connection from this far away, but I would have been able to sense if there'd been an emergency of some sort. "Hopefully his amplified powers will hold any glamor he illusions. We'll make sure he has enough magic after this next full moon, and one of the guys will have to go with him."

"Have you heard anything from Aurora?" I asked Hazel, and her eyes briefly snapped up from Aspen, dark-brown irises glaring.

"You really think she would contact me?" She tickled Aspen, smiling at him, though her tone was slightly annoyed.

"It wasn't that deep, Oakley. But I appreciate that you think it was."

"I don't know. When I brought you up during the interrogation and how you didn't think she was capable of killing Acacia, that seemed to shake her."

"Yeah, but she *did* kill Acacia." Her voice rattled, body tensing a moment before she relaxed back into playing with Aspen.

"People do desperate things if they're scared enough." I got up from the floor, setting the crystals and herbs that I'd been preparing aside and joining her on the couch. "You won't ever see me rooting for Aurora, but I don't think she was as bad as I'd originally believed."

"Honestly?" Hazel's lips were a flat line, and she brushed some strands of her brunette waves behind her ear. "I'm hoping our paths don't cross again. The fact that she knew I was in Acacia's hidey-hole and was more willing to let me die than take the fall doesn't make her too endearing."

"I mean, imagining her living her life on the run in that awful puke-green jumpsuit is pretty satisfying," I teased.

Hazel chuckled with me, shaking her head. "I'm sad I missed it."

"I'm not." That night had definitely made for one of my worst. Being taken, seeing Saros broken and bloody, watching the life bleed out from Atlas...

I shuddered. *Everything is okay now.* "I'm so glad you were here with Aspen. I knew he was safe with you. If anything had happened—"

"You're not allowed to finish that sentence," Hazel said, effectively cutting me off. She lifted my witchling up, handing him over to me before she grabbed her phone and swiped to check it. Then she tucked it in her back pocket and hugged around us both. "I'm just glad you guys figured it out."

She stood up from the couch, looking eager. My gaze narrowed.

"Ready to go walk through that space at Mystic Square?" Her tone perked up as she pointed to the garage. "I know you delayed the opening a bit, but the brick and mortar Full Moon Emporium will be the perfect place to host the next moonluck."

"Yes, it will," I agreed with a smile.

"So why don't we go check it out?" She waved her arm for us to come along. "Finally do that walk through?"

Following her out into the garage, I bounced Aspen on my hip. "Sounds great."

After getting Aspen in his car seat, we took the seven-minute drive to the edge of the neighborhood near the docks where the aquatic supernaturals dwelled.

Mystic Square was a small outdoor mall with about a dozen storefront spaces. Between Vivaldi's Restaurant—a fancy supernatural fusion spot with a hidden speakeasy-esque backroom that was known to be the headquarters for their operation—and Booked & Brewed bookshop was the empty space. Faded remnants of the old record shop sign and crackled paint overtop its doors were the only clue as to what had been there previously. I tried to imagine seeing Full Moon Emporium's sign up there in a few weeks. Hazel was getting it made as a grand opening gift.

"Wow," I said when we got inside, feeling a bit breathless, my eyes glossing with tears. "This is perfect."

It had a wide-open space with a perfect nook for lounge chairs for those waiting on their spouses and a row of small booths that apparently used to be listening stations that would become dressing rooms.

"Right?" Hazel agreed, clearly pleased with her find. "The minute I opened the door, I saw it."

My attention snapped to her. "You saw it? Like...*saw* it."

"Yes," she said with a smirk.

I was shocked. "I thought you weren't going to share your visions with me anymore?"

"I think I'll make the occasional exception," she replied, running her hand over the spacious countertop. I could imagine beautiful displays with crystal talismans hanging from them on one side, the register on the other.

"Any others you'd be willing to make?" I asked curiously.

"Hmm... I might be convinced." She shrugged, continuing to point out different features for another fifteen minutes. Then we walked through the next steps to prepare for the upcoming moonluck. We wouldn't have everything situated in time, but it would be enough to kick things off for the shop. There even was a small back room that I could use to create my designs in and a corner I could gate off for Aspen when he was at the shop with me—and any other kiddos that came in while their parents were browsing.

"What do you think?" Hazel asked, hands flipped up in question. "Is it love?"

Taking one final look, I beamed at her. "It is definitely love."

It was really happening. Full Moon Emporium would have its own beautiful space in the neighborhood that Aspen and I could call home for good.

((☾●☽))

When we got back to the house, Hazel waved me to go ahead inside, opening Aspen's door to get him out of the car. Stepping into the living room, my mouth gaped at the candles floating around the interior, along with a wine-colored velvet dress hanging in the air, its train stretching to the floor. "What's this?"

"Another exception," Hazel said, carting Aspen in her arms. "Put this on while I get him changed.

I grabbed the dress and darted into my room, hands shaking as I ran them over the soft material and pulled it over my head. I heard Hazel wrestling with Aspen, meeting them in the living room to find him in a little black playsuit with a burgundy velvet bow tie pinned to the neckline and a matching vest.

"I predict you should head to the backyard," Hazel teased, and I noticed that she was already in a tailored black suit with a wine-hued corset peeking beneath it.

What the hell was going on?

The candles that floated in the living room parted, trailing out back. Hazel waved her arm for me to follow them, still holding on to Aspen. I stepped out onto the porch in my bare feet. The hexagonal arch had been decorated in black and burgundy roses, their thorny stems wrapping around the wooden shape.

And in front of that stood my three handsome witches.

Lynx wore a wine-colored suit with a matching tie, a white button-up beneath it, and Saros was in a black suit with a maroon shirt, no tie. They both smiled at me before my attention glided to Atlas. He'd retracted his fangs, or illusioned them away. Either way, he looked as I'd remembered him, wearing a black shirt with trousers and a vest that matched his son's.

"Oh my Goddess," I rasped. Everything was beautiful, but I was so confused seeing them here all dressed up. "I thought you weren't getting back until tomorrow?"

"Then our surprise went as planned," Lynx said proudly,

winking over his shoulder at Hazel. When I turned my attention to her, she just shrugged, bouncing along with Aspen.

"Do you like it?" Saros asked, voice gravelly, his nerves like pebbles scraping his usually smooth baritone.

"I do." I eyed them curiously. "Is there an event happening here tonight?"

"You could say that," Atlas replied with a charming smirk.

Lynx took a few steps forward, extending his hand. "We're here to make you ours, Oakley."

"All of ours," Saros added, walking toward me to give me his arm as well.

I rested my palms on both of their forearms, and they escorted me toward the arch, my heart beating wildly in my rib cage.

"If you'll have us, that is," Atlas said with a bow. For the first time ever, he seemed nervous. He reached into his pocket and pulled out the ring—the one he'd proposed to me with before, only two more stones had been set into it. "I know this wasn't the family I envisioned for us and I admit it took me by surprise, but I've realized that sometimes the real dream is the one we can't see for ourselves. I may have traded one curse for another, but at least I can live with this one. With you and our son. And there are no two men more worthy to stand alongside us than these."

He handed the ring to Saros, who clutched it clumsily in his shaking fingers. "Midnight, the first time we touched, I knew there was something here. It scared me more than anything. I always thought I'd finish this case and just want a life of my own, but through your love, through Lynx's... This is the family I want to make the rest of my memories with."

A tear spilled down my cheek, and Atlas brushed it away.

Finally, Lynx took the ring, giving Saros a kiss, seemingly moved just as much as I was by his words. I was speechless.

"Wicked, somehow you left your mark on me before we'd even met." He looked over his shoulder where his oak tree spanned his beautiful body currently hidden from view. "Once we did, I knew this day would come. Of course, I didn't think we'd become bonded eternally by your formerly hexed vampire ex," we all chuckled at that, "but there's no one else I'd rather spend my days with than our family. No one I'd rather spend my nights with in the pines. We're all better together. Wouldn't you agree?"

I finally dug up some words. "I would."

"So what do you say, Wicked?" He flashed me a devilish grin. "Ours until eternity runs out?"

I nodded, eyes flitting over all of them. "Yours."

Rich purples and crimsons painted the sky as the sun continued to set and we held each other's hands, preparing to say our vows before the Moon Goddess watching from above.

"Moon Mother, bless our sacred union," Atlas said, looking up at her. He stared so intently it made me wonder if he could truly see her on her copper throne. She had been the one to curse his family, but when he called to her, it was not in anger but in gratitude. "Bless us with loyalty, always vowing to put our trust in each other."

"Bless us with love and a vow that we will always lead with it," Lynx said, looking up at her before his eyes glinted, scanning over the rest of us.

Saros squeezed my hand, evergreens shimmering with the promise of tears. "Bless us with commitment and a vow to carry our family above all else."

Their collective attention turned to me. These witches would go to Hell and back for me, for Aspen, for my sister, and for each other. Goddess, if I wasn't the luckiest witch alive. "Bless us with the desire to bring out each other's dreams and let's vow to always find the best in one another."

Keeping our hands interlocked, we moved them to the center of our circle, Hazel coming next to me, holding out her palm to bless the union as our witness. Her eyes lifted to the Moon Goddess. "Four hearts entwined until eternity."

"Until eternity," Atlas vowed. A star-shaped rune appeared on his wrist, shimmering like a thousand faceted diamonds.

"Until eternity," Lynx repeated, the same mark replacing his temporary one.

Saros's lips peeled up in a grin, that gorgeous smile coming out to light the early evening. "Until eternity."

His mark joined the constellation crawling up his forearm.

"Until eternity," I said, wrist searing until my vow mark sat like a beautiful star perched in my Aspen tree. "And forever after that."

I kissed each of them, the moon beaming down on us, its warmth blotting out the autumn breeze.

Spinning around, I grabbed Hazel, tears spilling down my cheeks as I hugged her.

"I couldn't be more thrilled for you, sis," she said, kissing my cheek before wiping away my tears. "Now get together for your first official family photos."

She spent a few minutes taking pictures of us all together, some shots with Aspen before setting the timer and getting one of everyone. Afterward, I waved the guys inside, wanting a moment alone with her.

"I can't believe it," I said, looking around at the perfect wedding ceremony. "But I have to know... Did you see this?"

"*If* I did, I can tell you that reality is so much more beautiful than anything my foresight could conjure." Hazel put her arm around me, placing her hand on my heart. "Now go begin your life together as a family."

"You're my family," I said, lip wobbly, more tears stinging the backs of my eyes.

"And I always will be." She pressed a kiss to my temple, then nodded toward the house. "But ours just got a whole lot more love."

I placed a hand on her shoulder. "Thanks for everything."

"The best thanks you can give me is a beautiful life."

I smiled, leaning my head against her chin. "I think I'm going to have just that."

The guys were inside, laughing as Lynx pulled out a giant cup of dirt and a handful of spoons.

Arms wrapped around each other, we headed inside before we all took turns feeding each other chocolate pudding and enjoying Aspen's giggles beneath the moon.

I didn't know what tomorrow would bring for our family, but I was ready to spend every day fighting for them.

Until eternity.

EPILOGUE

OAKLEY

"I wouldn't be surprised if you were asked to host every moonluck, Oaks." Hazel popped by the counter to grab a few more apple-raspberry elixirs to bring around to the neighbors while they scoped out Full Moon Emporium. There was still much to do to get the shop fully up and running, but we'd already had a bunch of preorders for the designs we'd displayed around the shop and sold out of every enchanted talisman in stock.

"Want another full moon reading, Oakley?" Ruby called from the table she'd set up in the lounge area.

I sighed, dragging Hazel over with me. "I'm good, though maybe you'll finally tell me what was on those extra cards?"

She waved her hand over the deck and held up two cards. The Magician and Strength. "One for each of your husbands, it seems," she said with a wink.

As I looked around at my witches, they were pretty accurate assessments of the three. The Magician represented having the power to manifest what you wanted into existence. Even the powerful-looking witch on the card with his green eyes and messy black hair reminded me of Atlas.

Strength, the card with a silvery knight and her beast, actually had more to do with mastering physical emotions, and the Hermit pulled on his great life wisdom.

An eerily apt representation. I could have brushed off the cards. However, if I'd learned anything about premonitions from the last year, it was that they often weren't wrong—but that didn't mean there was nothing we could do to hasten them toward or away from the same outcome.

I turned to Hazel, nudging her forward. "You know, Ruby, Hazel used to drag me to readings all the time. She *loves* them."

"Come sit." Ruby waved to the lounge chair behind us, then floated the cards into her travel-sized cauldron. Hazel beamed, waiting for the coveness's crystal to stop swinging above the bubbling brew, then reached into the black goo inside. Just watching her reminded me of the slippery animal entrails sliding around the scattered deck.

"Have your intention, dear?" Ruby asked her.

Hazel nodded and drew three cards that floated up between them, the black ichor dripping back into the pot.

"The first—"

"Is about me, second is my life, and third is my love," Hazel cut in eagerly.

"I see you are no stranger to the cards." Ruby smiled like a cat that'd gotten the cream, then her gaze narrowed. "But no, you can't opt out of seeing the third."

Hazel jolted. "How?"

"She can apparently read your thoughts while you hold her cards," I whispered to her. "High witch magic."

Hazel raised her brows up in surprise, then turned back to the coveness. Reaching up for the first card facing Ruby, she pulled it down and flipped it over.

The Devil.

She held it in her hand, looking over the image of the dark prince, shallow carvings covering his skin like all of those in the Morningstar line. Ruby said nothing at all, which was perhaps the strangest thing. Just watched Hazel as she grabbed the second, twirling it in her palms with a frown. A set of mismatched wings with a heart in their center spanned the card.

The Lovers.

Still, Ruby was silent. She even gave me a look as if to remind me to hold back any commentary, like the two were in some strange unspoken conversation that I wasn't part of.

"Wicked, ready to get out of here? I think our little wildling wants to hibernate."

My eyes darted toward the gated corner to Lynx bouncing along with Aspen, who was beginning to fuss. Pressure swelled in my chest, and I knew it was time to get him fed and settled into bed.

"Yeah," I replied. *"Besides, we need to get things together for Atlas."*

"Can you not talk about me like I'm not here?" Atlas hissed through the line.

Saros came up from behind me, wrapping his arms around my waist and kissing me on the shoulder. *"Well, you aren't technically* here, *Thorne."*

"I can still hear you all." He sighed, his tone more impatient than usual. *"I do own this little frequency we all use."*

"Someone sounds hangry," I teased, heading over with Saros toward Lynx and Aspen.

My witchling reached for me, and Lynx settled him into my arms, patting his back a few times as I took him. "Make that two someones."

"We're on our way," I told Atlas before heading with the guys back to the corner of the room where Hazel and Ruby

were. The cards had already been shuffled and spread out again on the table.

"Hey, Haze, are you good to close up here? Aspen needs to get back and we do too." I paused a moment for quiet emphasis so she'd understand my meaning.

"No problem. I've got it covered." She stood, giving me a hug and Aspen a quick kiss. "I'll round up everyone to get them out of here."

"Thanks." Relief washed through me, ready to be home and put Aspen to bed, feeling the waning effects of my magic needing replenishment under the full moon tonight. It was going to be a long one—something that had me both wanting to yawn and salivate in equal measure. "What was the last card? I never got to see it."

"Don't worry about it," Hazel said nonchalantly, ushering us toward the door. "I'll lock up. Have a blessed full moon, sis."

"You too, Haze."

((((●))))

AN HOUR LATER, I'D GOTTEN ASPEN FED AND ASLEEP IN HIS CRIB after watching his eyelids flutter, staring at the gossamer wings on the wall while Atlas read The Little Hearse That Could. Luckily, he'd been sleeping for longer stretches recently, so we had at least three hours to recharge before he needed us. Now that we'd officially moved into 5 Blessed Crescent, the place that made the most sense for the five of us, we had a backyard that received plenty of moonlight and still gave us privacy. We could have all gone in shifts, but all my husbands were excited to recharge together for our first newly vowed full moon.

I shrugged on the chunky-knit cardigan over my lace

bralette and matching briefs before descending the stairs, clasping the smooth opalescent crystal glowing between my breasts, nerves and Desire fluttering low in my belly.

When I opened the door to the backyard, fairy lights twinkled in the air, framing the moonlit picnic spread. Most of the treats were the usual stuff Atlas and I would put together, with a few very perfect new additions: pumpkin cream cheese muffins and cups of dirt on trays set on a small table next to the large blanket. As the guys noticed me watching them finish setting up, they turned, drinking me in with their collective gaze.

"We're glad you liked your gift," Atlas said, glowing red irises aimed at the stone. It'd been an offering the night of our vow ceremony, a question—a *hope*—from the three of them.

Moonstones were believed to have hormonal balancing properties, making them ideal for dealing with menstrual symptoms, but they also helped boost fertility, at least with the right enchantments attached. While having another witchling seemed terrifying, impossible to even wrap my head around, if we'd been taught anything from our time together the last few months, it was that life was short. We didn't want to waste a single minute of it.

I walked over to my husbands, getting down on my knees and crawling between them to give each a lingering kiss. Hands drifted along my spine and sides. I had no clue who they belonged to, but I didn't really care.

"I'm ready to savor my witch," Atlas said as soon as my lips left his. He sat back and dragged me into his lap, brushing my auburn tresses away from my neck and running his nose up the column of my throat. I sucked in a breath, waiting. Then he pulled down the sweater so my shoulders were exposed.

"Help our wife relax before I sink my teeth into her," he

instructed Lynx and Saros.

Both shirtless, I admired the muscled panes of their chests bathed in moonlight as they moved closer to me. Nudging my legs apart, they slipped between them, peeling off my panties. I rested my legs on their shoulders while they took turns licking up my slit, swirling their tongues along my clit. Every so often they would kiss, sharing my taste before the other would dive back in.

Melting into Atlas behind me, he pressed his lips to the sensitive skin where my neck and shoulder met. I held my breath, eagerly anticipating the sting of his fangs sinking into my flesh. The momentary pain quickly subsided, though, replaced by intense pleasure that rushed through my bloodstream like molten lava, consuming me in its fiery haze.

Vampire venom.

The full moon affected all supernaturals, and for vampires, the subtle fang-fever we felt when we were fed upon amplified. It was part of how Atlas would recharge tonight, our vitality as his tethers strengthening him.

"She tastes incredible, doesn't she?" Atlas asked through our connection, cutting through the whimper slipping past my lips.

"So. Fucking. Good," Lynx agreed, continuing to devour me.

Saros shifted onto his heels and then removed his pants. My eyes locked on the bead of precum leaking from his tip.

"She better be drenched," he called over to Lynx, stroking himself.

Goddess, he was so perfectly thick. I often had to remind myself I'd taken moonlit rides on him before.

I moaned aloud, unsure where to look, who to touch, still getting used to experiencing so many sensations at once. Rough grips and gentle grazes. Kisses peppering my skin, a tongue snaking up my thigh, teeth and sucking pulses at my throat. Muscles pressed into me along with long, hard body parts that had me salivating.

"Holy shit." My Desire danced through me, eager to replenish under the golden moon.

"Oh, there's nothing holy about what we are doing with you tonight." Atlas chuckled darkly, then retracted his fangs, lapping up where he'd been draining me above my collarbone.

Desire chased after Atlas's fang-fever flooding my veins. My body shook, hips bucking wildly as stars exploded in my vision. I cried out, and pink and magenta swirls painted the air, love and lust surrounding us while Lynx's Empathy flowed into me.

My magic tingled along my skin as it began to recharge from the Moon Goddess's luminous blessings.

Atlas nudged my torso forward, and I ripped off my sweater before folding onto all fours, unhooking my bra and letting it fall to the ground. Then I swished my hips in taunt until he gripped them tightly. However, instead of lining himself up with my entrance, his tongue dove into my folds. It moved in delicious patterns, swirling around my clit.

"Goddess above, you taste like Heaven and Hell all rolled into one," he said through the link. *"I could spend eternity between these thighs."*

I arched for him in response, and when the tip of his fang hit the sensitive bud I hissed in surprise—until his venom swelled within it, rushing to my center. My hips jerked against Atlas's face as I erupted, screaming through another orgasm.

"Oh, that's *interesting.*" Saros chuckled darkly, hand gripping his shaft.

The fog of pink and magenta disappeared around me,

Lynx's gift replaced by Atlas's Illusion.

"That's our good witch," Lynx praised, undoing his belt and pulling down his jeans until he was beautifully skyclad along with Saros and me. The two of them stood next to each other, grinning like a pair of hungry wolves. "Show us some of your tricks, Wicked. Maybe we'll give you a treat."

"Maybe?" I asked, playing coy before flicking my finger to send some Desire at them. They doubled over, glittering beads dripping from their tips, making me salivate. "I think you meant definitely."

Saros shook his head. "Goddess, Midnight, warn a witch, would you?"

I shrugged as Atlas finished undressing behind me, the crisp breeze hitting my body that was desperate to be filled. A firm hand held my waist before the length of him rubbed up and down my slit. I pushed on my hands, baring myself more to him, ready for this—for us all to be together for the first time under the full moon.

Atlas wrapped my hair around his fist, tugging my head back, edging himself into me a few inches. "I'm taking you first. Then you'll take them together."

I nodded eagerly, pressing into him. He groaned, filling me to the hilt, pausing to let my body adjust around his length. I swirled my hips, our bodies doing an intoxicating tango. He led, setting the pace, one hand pulling my hair, the other clutching my waist.

Saros reached out, dragging Lynx to him, crashing their mouths together. More Desire sifted out from my fingers toward them. Lynx's hand trailed down Saros's chest, taking his thick shaft roughly in his palm and moving in brutal, possessive strokes, matching Atlas's thrusts in and out of me. Saros groaned, leaning into the touch.

My gaze shot skyward, wondering if the Goddess was

looking down on us right now. It felt as if she must be, for me to be so lucky.

"What do you want?" Atlas whispered from behind me. Picturing it in my mind, I released his magic, and he hummed approvingly. "Come here and give our greedy witch something to taste while I fill her up."

"Happy to oblige." Lynx strode forward, the thick crimson crown of his cock slick with want. "Ready to use that wicked mouth?"

My lips parted, savoring as he slipped between them. Taking a hand, I encircled his length sucking in time with the thrusts filling me from both sides. A zing of Lynx's lust hit my tongue, and I sent more Desire through my hand wrapped around him, lapping up every drop.

"So fucking sexy with the two of us," Atlas heaved out between each deep drive of his hips.

"I bet Midnight looks even sexier with all three," Saros said, his baritone carrying over from my side. He wrapped his hand around mine, taking it off of Lynx and guiding it to his cock. Rubbing the slippery tip, I used his precum to coat it.

The feel of them all around me, the moon beaming on us, recharging our gifts as we writhed together... It was almost too much to handle, but I wanted nothing more.

My entire body clenched, enveloped in delicious, messy pleasure. Warmth shot into my center, Atlas growling out curses, unleashing inside of me. He pumped with relentless fervor until he went slack against my back, hand trailing up and down the outside of my thigh.

"Goddess, you're perfect, Oakley," he said, kissing my shoulder.

I was trembling, another orgasm was cresting. Stroking Lynx with my hand, I slipped him from my lips, catching my breath. "I-I need more."

Pushing back, I rubbed against Atlas, seeking friction. Release. "Greedy witch, as much as I'd love to fuck you again, I'm trying to learn how to be better about sharing."

Lynx ran his palm gently along my cheek, sienna irises drenched with lust. "Ride me, Wicked?"

He stretched out on the blanket, the moonlight caressing every inch of his muscular body. The outline of his length cast in lunar light reminded me of the first time I'd seen him, silhouetted in the windowsill. And now, there were no walls or cul-de-sac between us. He was mine.

I crawled over, straddling him, enjoying the sensation of Atlas's cum leaking down my thighs. Then I sank onto Lynx in a smooth motion, so wet from the pooled pleasure within me. I lifted myself up until he was nearly out of me, then lowered until nothing separated us, swirling my hips. He groaned, his hands gripping my hips, supporting my waist with each rise and fall of my body.

He traced large circles on my back before pulling me flush with his chest.

"Ready, Midnight?" Saros's whisper licked up my spine in salacious invitation. I nodded, unsure if I was really ready thinking about his size. He slipped a hand along my ass, lubing the tight ring of muscle there.

My breath hitched.

"We've got you," Lynx reassured me, reminding me that he had the inside look at every excited and nervous emotion flitting within me. "May I use my gift... to help?"

I nodded, and he crushed me against him, warmth flooding from his chest into mine. Calm washed through me like water lapping at the shore. Then, his lust rippled across my skin, my Desire eager to continue recharging my magic. Saros's cock notched at my back entrance, and as soon as he breached the tight ring, my body felt overwhelmingly full.

"Oh Goddess," I whimpered, clenching around them.

"Midnight, if you stay this tight, I'm not even going to make it halfway into you before I come," Saros gritted out.

"Relax and swallow their cocks like a good witch," Atlas demanded, kneeling next to me. He kissed along my shoulder, up my neck, and then tangled his tongue with mine in a deep, bruising kiss that left my lips swollen and wanting.

"Goddess above..." Lynx's eyes were glued to the three of us, his lust now crashing through me in molten waves.

The two witches moved slowly in and out of me, my body adjusting to the give and take as we rocked together. I was so full, it didn't take much to make the sensations intense, my skin tingling in the moonlight, continuing to recharge my magic.

Lynx lifted his hand up to Atlas, who grabbed his wrist, thumbing over the vow mark there before sinking his fangs into it. The witches inside me increased their rhythm, the fang-fever overtaking Lynx and spurring Saros on.

Atlas continued drinking from Lynx a few minutes before moving to Saros. The newblood's length was steel, and I licked my lips, opening my mouth until he repositioned himself, his velvety skin smooth against my tongue. His fingers threaded through my hair, pelvis hitching forward while the other two continued to rock into me in perfectly timed thrusts.

Tears rimmed my eyes, pressure coiling deep below my belly.

"Look how good you take us," Atlas said. In a flash, he'd Illusioned me above them, watching the three of them fuck me into oblivion. It heightened every sensation. My body hummed. It was desperate for somewhere for this intoxicating energy to go.

"I'm gonna come," I warned them, not that I needed to, but it was a hard habit to break.

"Then come for us, Midnight," Saros gritted out, his words caressing my ear. "Show us that beautiful Desire and we'll fill you for eternity."

The sight of this moment, of me with all my witches, sent stars bursting in my vision.

Lynx and Saros were next, almost simultaneously exploding inside of me. My body went limp between them, but Atlas's hands threaded through my hair kept me upright. He came with a roar, and I swallowed his pleasure, my gaze locked with his. He released my strands, hand running along my jaw, looking at me with the devotion of a worshiper at the altar of a goddess.

Then they cleaned me up and held me tight. Atlas's Illusion gift had floated away, replaced by Recollection. Images flooded my mind, dueling for attention:

Saros making me my first midnight mocha.

Lynx chasing me around the counter, pudding smeared across his face.

Apple ciders at Phil's Pumpkin Patch.

Lynx's tongue tracing his constellation down my body.

A floating porch swing swaying with two bodies entwined in the moonlight.

Atlas holding a newborn Aspen, twin aqua pools shimmering at me sleeping in my hospital bed, full of awe and devotion.

I choked over my words, tears springing to my eyes at the beauty of the life we'd created already before we'd even accepted this love—this family—between us. I'd never tire of making memories together until our bodies crackled and became shimmering dust on the wind.

Saros thumbed away my tears, kissing my cheek.

I cleared my throat, starting to stand up, body still rippling with pleasure. I didn't know if it was the emotions of having them all together finally or the leftover effects of Atlas's vamp venom, but I swayed my hips, picking up the bowl of raspberries and popping a few in my mouth.

"Who's next?" I asked, surveying my husbands.

Atlas's arms were bent behind his head, staring up at the moon with a grin spanning his jaw, his fangs were still out, no reason to hide them here in our perfect little corner. "Already ready for another round?"

"I signed up for eternity, and I'm pretty sure that included infinite orgasms." I walked backward, enjoying a few more berries. "Now, which one of you will give me my next?"

Saros was already on his feet, prowling toward me, his smile in the buttery moonlight nearly blinding me.

Setting the bowl down, I scurried backward, smacking into a firm chest. Lynx captured me in his arms, helping Saros pick me up until I was straddled around his waist and sending some of my Desire out. Saros lined up with my center, and Lynx lifted me before impaling me on our husband's cock. They worked together, Lynx's hand slithering between the two of us to toy with my clit. More stars swam into my vision, mapping out a constellation of pleasure.

"You going to join in?" Lynx asked playfully toward the blanket across from us.

I glanced over at Atlas watching us and stroking himself languidly. "I think I'd rather savor you savoring our witch this time."

And as the clouds danced toward daybreak, I felt both recharged and worshiped, savoring that this was the best kind of magic a witch could ever desire.

EXCLUSIVE BONUS EPILOGUE

ATLAS

Hazy red light spilled through the restaurant. Black leather cushions lined the booths on either side of Saros and I as we strode toward the burly guard hovering in front of the otherwise unassuming door. We'd come here right after getting Aspen down for the night, a late-night meeting that no one could know about. I glanced over my shoulder, spotting the maître d' flipping the sign to **Closed**.

Opening the door for us, the large vampire stepped to the side. "He's waiting for you."

Nodding in thanks, we moved over the threshold.

Dante Vivaldi sat at the single table in the room, a few more of his goons posed ominously in the corners.

"This is his usual MO," Saros reminded me through our link. He'd prepped me for what to expect on our way over.

We pulled out the chairs opposite the Vampire King, taking a seat. There was a small tray of desserts and a decanter full of something more viscous than red wine.

Blood.

The server hurried over with a glass of actual red wine,

setting it in front of Saros before picking up the decanter and filling Vivaldi's glass. When he moved to fill mine, I held up my hand. I didn't need to feed more than once a day, and I had three more than willing participants.

"What are we doing here?" I asked, arching a brow at Dante.

"Don't play coy, Archon Thorne," he said before taking a sip of his *drink*, flicking his tongue out to clean his lips. "We both knew this was coming."

He grabbed a cannoli and sank his teeth into it. While we didn't need to eat food to live anymore, it still was enjoyable to savor the flavors. I had to admit, the cannolis looked good, but I would rather get home to our family and be out of this meeting.

"True." I clasped my hands together, leaning forward. "But why now?"

"Don't you head to the Archon Summit in a few days?"

Ah. "I do."

"Wonderful." He leaned back, resting an elbow on one of the arms of his chair, his chin perching atop his hand. His attention remained on me. "And how has your transition been going?"

"It has its challenges, but overall, it's going well." My attention darted to Saros, who nodded in agreement.

"Any concerns about keeping up appearances at the Summit?"

"No. Between my amplified abilities and having Agents Holt and Carver with me, we are confident everything will go smoothly."

"Perfect." Vivaldi grabbed the partially eaten cannoli and took another bite, groaning. "I want to be kept apprised of any important goings-on at the Summit."

"And why would I tell you anything?" I asked, gaze

narrowing.

"I don't believe in blind obedience, Archon Thorne. But I do believe in loyalty." He flicked a few cannoli crumbs off of his suit jacket. "Regardless what you may have been told about me, I am your king now."

"You may be king of the vampires, but don't expect to find me kneeling at your feet anytime soon." I chuckled darkly. "I only do that for one witch, and she makes the experience much more enjoyable."

I sent an illusion to Saros of our wife and what we'd do to her as soon as we got home from this stupid meeting. He uncrossed and recrossed his legs, his brows lifting a moment at me.

"Now that is something I wouldn't mind seeing for myself," Vivaldi agreed, flashing us both a sharpened salacious smirk. It would never happen, but I couldn't blame him. Our wife was extraordinary.

"However, let's not forget, you are alive because of me," he added, his tone steeled in warning.

My blood boiled. I'd been waiting to see what would come from him reviving me, changing me so that I had a future with my family. "That may be so, but I also was born into a legacy set to ensure the well-being of all supernaturals. I won't turn my back on that, even with what you've given me."

I clenched my fists under the table.

"I wouldn't dream of it," Vivaldi said, waving off my concern with a flick of his hand. "Our methods may be differ-ent, but I believe our goals are aligned." Finishing up the last bit of cannoli, he sucked each finger clean, then licked off the tips of his fangs before resting against the arm of his chair. "Work with me from the inside and we can really create that legacy your grandfather was aiming for when he created the

Council of Magical Welfare. Before all the bullshit and politics stained it."

I looked over at Saros.

"Do it. We will need any ally we can get to fight the corruption. There's only so much we can do from the inside."

Turning my attention back to Vivaldi, I kept my tone firm, wanting to stand my ground even if I were to work with this vamp. "I can agree to aligning with you under those terms, but I won't cross any lines on your behalf."

"Leave the line crossing to me. We both know that's where I belong." He chuckled, his words bleeding with mirth. "I'll skulk in the shadows, you stick to the light."

Nodding over to his guards, they stepped up behind him. "Should you need any assistance, Saros knows how to get in touch."

"Is that all?" I asked, looking up at him as he stood from the table, chugging down the rest of the blood in his wine glass.

"Yes." He started heading toward the door, Saros and I getting up to follow behind him. "I look forward to your update after the Summit, Archon Thorne."

((((●))))

While Saros and I had no problem living in silence together, neither of us a hugely talkative sort like Lynx, on the road home, a question that'd been nagging at me won out over the quiet.

"What is your deal with Dante?" Saros's gaze darted quickly to me from the driver's side before returning to the road. We'd taken his car since it was less conspicuous than my Archon-crested government-issued vehicle. "Were you two...together?"

"Not anything significant, if that's what you're getting at." The ball at his throat worked, a vein thick and ripe next to it, pulse beating a bit quicker than its usual steady rhythm. "I just helped him with something when I was undercover and working for him."

"Is that something I should be concerned about as your Archon or your vowed partner?" I arched a brow at him.

"I promise, it's not what you think." He shook his head. "And no, it's not anything that would be related to any case. But it's a secret best kept for Vivaldi, unless he decides otherwise someday."

"As long as our family is safe."

"It is." His tone was clipped. "You know I would never do anything to jeopardize that."

I did. It was one of the things I was always certain of when it came to Saros. Besides, we'd committed to as much in our vows, and there was no breaking those without a lot of pain involved.

We pulled into the long drive, then parked and headed into the house. Laughter spilled through the staircase while we ascended it. Such a beautiful sound.

Oakley and Lynx were smiling at each other, chocolate icing smeared on each other's faces. Lynx held Oakley close, swiping his thumb across her lips and dragging her in for a dessert-filled kiss. Giggling at him, she left his grasp before walking over to kiss me, a smudge of icing marking her nose. Saros went and put his arm around Lynx, kissing his forehead.

"How'd the meeting go?" Oakley asked, standing across from her husbands who'd perched themselves on the stools on the other side of the kitchen island.

"Pretty good," Saros answered. "Seems like he just wants to be kept informed of what happens at the Summit."

Lynx turned toward him, placing a hand on his shoulder. "Think Vivaldi can be trusted?"

"I trust him enough to keep him on my side," I said, getting a nod in agreement from Saros. "That'll have to be enough of a foundation for now."

His evergreen attention dropped to the tray of little cups filled with layers of chocolate. "What are you guys eating?"

"Devil's food cake parfaits." Lynx swiped some up with his finger and held it up to Saros in offering. "You want some?"

"I'll have a bite." He chuckled, then lapped up the mixture.

I grabbed one of the cups and a small spoon, scooping up a heap. "Same."

Chocolate burst across my tongue in crumbly yet smooth perfection. It was nice to break up drinking every meal to sustain myself with actual food, even though I didn't eat nearly as much as I had during my pre-immortal existence.

"Looks like you might need a bite of something else pretty soon." Oakley cupped my chin, lips pressing into a firm line. "The rings are returning."

She brushed her hair behind her ear, tilting her head in offering. Her spicy sweet smell, like apples and honey with cinnamon, and the beautiful purple veins running down to her clavicle beckoned me to taste her. And, Goddess, I wanted to.

"Mmm..." I said, setting down the parfait. Her breath hitched in response, still bared to me. "You're definitely much more appetizing than this." Running my nose along her throat, I kissed her fluttering pulse. "Unfortunately, I have to decline."

Her eyes dropped in confusion.

Nuzzling my cheek to hers, I set down the dessert,

splaying my hand across her pelvis and waving the other into the air above us. Two heartbeats pitter-pattered loudly from beneath my fingers, projected out through my amplified Illusion to the room.

Oakley gasped against my cheek. "How long have you known?"

"Since the last time I tasted your pulse and felt the faint beats." I pressed a kiss to her temple, then turned my attention to the other two. "Looks like you're going to be fathers. Again."

Lynx's eyes shone in awe, glittering with a hundred stars scattered across their caramel backdrop. "Oh, you've made me the happiest witch, Wicked."

Saros's gaze was still pinned to the beats and their rhythmic dance. Twin blessings for our family.

I released Oakley from my hold so she could go over to him, Lynx picking her up along her trek and peppering kisses across her rosy cheeks. When she made it to Saros, she wrapped her arms around him, and his attention finally drew back to our wife.

"You okay?" she asked, nerves fluttering with her erratic pulse and crackled words.

"Never been better." His voice was a rasp, a tear streaking his cheek that Oakley quickly kissed away. He captured her mouth with his, celebrating our witch with his lips and tongue. "This is everything, Midnight."

"Yes, it is," she sighed reverently.

Lynx slipped his hand into hers, leading the way toward the bedroom.

Scanning over our family, both present and future, I had to agree wholeheartedly. This was everything I could ever envision...

And *more*.

THANK YOU FOR READING

I hope you enjoyed the conclusion of Oakley's story with her magical crew.

You may be wondering a few things right now...

Will we ever see more of our foursome?

Yes!

Each romance within the Celestial Haven series will be told in a duet or standalone that are all interconnected and take place within the same supernatural suburban neighborhood.

So what's next?

If you were curious what was on Hazel's final tarot card, you will find out in Book 3 of the Celestial Haven series. I'm so excited to dive more into her character and what she's been going through post-kidnapping.

Make sure to sign up for my newsletter and join my reader group on Facebook at Books & Brews with L.R. Friedman to stay up to date on when that will be releasing.

And pretty pretty please, take some time to leave a review and some stars for this duet. They truly make a huge difference in indie authors getting our books into the hands of readers.

ALSO BY L.R. FRIEDMAN

<u>The Blaze Legacy</u>

Adult Dark Portal Romantasy

Descend

Scale

Pitch: Origin Story Novella

Ascend

AFTERWORD

Well, here you go. My first complete project.

While there are definitely a few open-ended threads that will be touched on in the upcoming Celestial Haven duets and standalones, I truly enjoyed being able to release a complete duet for your enjoyment.

It was so different not writing a long series with this one and getting to share Oakley's happily ever after with you all. I hope you enjoyed the wild and spicy ride.

Escaping to Celestial Haven with these characters brought me so much joy during the writing process. As you saw, *Wicked in the Pines* focused on Oakley's personal journey of finding herself within the messy, chaotic, and beautiful world of new motherhood. For *Midnight with the Hexed*, we got much more of her relationship dynamics and really owning her newly rediscovered confidence.

It was important to me to focus on what happens when life doesn't look anything like you've planned for this part their story. It's rare we get everything we anticipate having in life, but my wish is that the words within these pages give you hope that there's always something out there that's more beautiful than anything you could imagine.

For me, it reflected back the times in my life when I felt like things were out of my control, didn't go my way—and how they actually ended up better for it. Because of that, I know this duet will always hold a special place in my heart. So much personal healing was experienced while I wrote both books.

Thank you again for spending time in Celestial Haven. I cannot wait to visit with this world again and share Hazel's story with you next.

Acknowledgments

Thank you for reading this book. For all of my readers who take the time to tag me in posts, send messages and reactions, have supported me whether it's in this series or another—you are amazing and keep me going.

Sam - Words cannot express how much your friendship and hard work means to me. You stepped in and took things off my plate so that I could manage the insane workload to meet my deadlines. You cheered me on when I needed it most. I am so grateful for all you do and I could not ask for a better PA.

Thea - Thank you for talking me through those nights where I wanted to give up and throw in the towel. Your encouragement helped me get through these last few months. And thank you for bringing Oakley and Hazel to life through your beautiful cosplays. You're stunning inside and out. Pyewacket and I can't wait to hang out with you in person.

Vanessa - Thank you for all your friendship and support over the last year. It means the world to me how much you rooted for Oakley and her guys and I cannot wait to celebrate these books with you in person.

Jourdan - Thank you for helping me navigate how to juggle working with two series. Your knowledge and social media savvy truly were a lifesaver when overwhelm was taking over prior to releasing these books back to back.

Angelique - Your messages to me after finishing this beta

about this duet meant EVERYTHING to me. It was the first moment I truly felt like these books might be ready to go out in the world and I will forever be grateful for that.

Chinah, Sarah, & Emmerson - Thank you all for pushing me on this book. I was so exhausted with my writing schedule. When I didn't think I could give any more to this one, you dug in and managed to wring it out of me. Thank you all for your friendship, your honesty, and for always being there to lift me up. Love you all so much.

Aubrey - Thank you for these covers that so beautifully capture Oakley's arcs and the vibes of this duet. The details you included are swoon-worthy and I cannot wait for everyone to catch onto them now that they've read. You are so freaking talented.

Ashton & Brittani - Thank you for believing in this project before I did. I was so nervous about this series and you both always bolstered me when I needed it. Having you both in my corner is something I will always be grateful for.

To my Initiates - Thank you for always being there. For believing in me and these characters and their stories. For tagging me and posting about the books when I didn't have the energy to. You have no idea how many times your messages, graphics, and reels have perked me up to get back to the keyboard and keep writing. I would not have been able to tackle this crazy writing schedule this year without you.

Mom - Thank you for reading everything I write, even when it makes you blush. Not a day goes by that I'm not in awe of how your magnificent mind works and the great insight you have into everything. Thank you for instilling the love of reading in me, no doubt the catalyst that got me into writing. I wouldn't be here (on earth or at the end of this book) without you. Love you!

About the Author

Author L.R. Friedman loves curling up with a cup of coffee while diving into fantasy and paranormal romance worlds. A Virginia native, she currently lives in Texas with her husband and three children.

When she's not writing, you'll find her enjoying tacos, dark chocolate, and the occasional glass of whiskey.

As the girl that grew up trying to find a magical realm hidden in her closet, she hopes to transport readers to beautiful, sexy, dark, and enchanted places through her stories.

For updates about upcoming releases, please visit http://www.lrfriedman.com, sign up for her newsletter, or join her group on Facebook at Books & Brews with L.R. Friedman.

CONTENT & TRIGGER WARNINGS

In the Celestial Haven duet you will find:

Explicit language, on page descriptions of sexual acts (solo play, MF, MM, MMF+), voyeurism, oral/vaginal/anal sex, use of sex toys, blood play (think vampires), public shenanigans, mild dubcon, completely fictionalized magical rituals, horny supernaturals on the full moon, consumption of elixirs and potions—including caffeinated and boozy brews.

There are themes relating to motherhood including: breastfeeding, body image struggles (not weight related), hormonal shifts, spit-up, and poopsplosions.

Kidnapping, mention of torture, murder, and death.